★ "In this near-apocalyptic adventure and spiritual contemplation, McWilliams provides readers with a believable world, **deeply drawn relationships, and an inspiring heroine.... An empowering narrative and trope-busting plotting** earns this book a place on almost every shelf." —*SLJ*, starred review

★ "The **ornate, complex text** takes readers through Agnes' and Beth's journeys of reconciling their faith and desires, imbuing the **well-rounded characters** with purpose.... **An excellent read.**" —*Kirkus Reviews*, starred review

★ "**Strong apocalyptic worldbuilding** alternates with dialogue-laden scenes, while minor characters, such as the Burn Squad captain charged with eradicating nests, move the plot forward in **absorbing and dynamic** ways." —*Publishers Weekly*, starred review

By Kelly McWilliams

Agnes at the End of the World
Your Plantation Prom Is Not Okay

MIЯROR
GIRLS

MIRROR GIRLS

KELLY MCWILLIAMS

LITTLE, BROWN AND COMPANY

New York Boston

Copyright © 2022 by Kelly McWilliams
Excerpt from *Your Plantation Prom Is Not Okay* copyright © 2023 by Kelly McWilliams
Discussion Guide copyright © 2023 by Little, Brown and Company

Family tree © 2022 by Tristan Elwell.
Interior art: misty forest swamp © by rangizzz/Shutterstock.com;
vintage gate vector © by Kashtal/Shutterstock.com; New York skyline vector © by
Canicula/Shutterstock.com; vintage frame vector © by Olesia Misty/Shutterstock.com;
vintage ornaments © by Sakemomo/Shutterstock.com.

Cover art © 2022 by Katt Phatt. Cover design by Jenny Kimura.
Cover copyright © 2022 by Hachette Book Group, Inc.

Little, Brown and Company
Hachette Book Group
1290 Avenue of the Americas, New York, NY 10104
Visit us at LBYR.com

Originally published in hardcover and ebook by Little, Brown and Company in February 2022
First Trade Paperback Edition: March 2023

Little, Brown and Company is a division of Hachette Book Group, Inc. The Little, Brown name and logo are trademarks of Hachette Book Group, Inc.

The publisher is not responsible for websites (or their content) that are not owned by the publisher.

The Library of Congress cataloged the hardcover as follows:

Names: McWilliams, Kelly, author.
Title: Mirror girls / Kelly McWilliams.
Description: First edition. | New York ; Boston : Little, Brown and Company, 2022. |
Audience: Ages 14 & up. | Summary: Biracial twin sisters—one who presents as black and the other as white—are determined to put the ghosts of the past to rest and to uncover the truth behind their parents' murders in the Jim Crow South.
Identifiers: LCCN 2021010529 | ISBN 9780759553873 (hardcover) |
ISBN 9780759553859 (ebook)
Subjects: CYAC: Racially mixed people—Fiction. | Twins—Fiction. | Sisters—Fiction. |
Race relations—Fiction. | Ghosts—Fiction. | African Americans—Fiction. |
Georgia—History—20th century—Fiction.
Classification: LCC PZ7.M47885 Mi 2022 | DDC [Fic]—dc23
LC record available at https://lccn.loc.gov/2021010529

ISBNs: 978-0-7595-5386-6 (pbk.), 978-0-7595-5385-9 (ebook)

Printed in the United States of America

LSC-C

Printing 1, 2023

For mirror girls of every color, everywhere:
The world may not always see you.
Be brave.

Magnolia Heathwood

Blanche Heathwood

Dean Heathwood

James Heathwood

Charlie Yates

Marie Yates

Jeannette Yates

Charles Freedom

PROLOGUE
Jeannette Yates
EUREKA, GEORGIA
1935

For colored girls, there's no such thing as happily ever after.

My daughter knew that—it was loving Dean Heathwood that made her forget. That boy was as white as they come, but he sure did love my Marie. He showered her with gifts: an obsidian mirror, a leather atlas, a diamond ring.

Of all Dean's fancy presents, though, the books were easily the most dangerous.

Beautiful books they were. Romances and love poems, sonnets and fairy tales, all leatherbound with bright illustrations. The kind of books colored children never get to touch, let alone own. Soon enough, my daughter'd fallen in love with those lily-white stories, with the kind of happy endings she'd never live to see.

Now I carry Marie's favorite book of all, *Love Sonnets*, under one arm, protecting it from the night air. My daughter's child is strapped to my back. I take the long route through the swamp, the very path the ancestors traveled, running from Heathwood Plantation's shackles. Like them, I push past creepers and marsh grass, following the thick, slow pulse of the water. Peat bog sucks at my ankles, but I can't afford to fall.

It's long past sundown. If white folk spot me, they might arrest me. Or kill me like they did my sweet, lovestruck girl.

I lean against a cypress tree, letting grief well up for one heartbeat—then, no more.

For my grandbaby's sake, I've got to keep moving. Struggle on.

On my back, Charlene lets out a wrenching wail. Ever since we left Freedom House, she's bunched tight with rage, like she knows she'll never see her twin sister again. Like she knows, too, that I'm to blame.

I reach over my shoulder, catching her tiny hand. "I'm gonna fix this, baby girl. You'll see."

The scent of woodsmoke leads me to the conjure man's hut. The grass-roofed shack perches on the water's edge, hidden beneath a veil of Spanish moss. Preacher says it's a mighty sin to visit with a conjure man, but it's a risk I have to take.

The night Marie birthed my grandbabies, I smelled the sizzle of a curse cooking itself up. One twin came into this world white as goat's milk; the other, pecan brown. Doctor called it a miracle, but I wondered. After Marie died—and poor Dean, too—the hex-stench grew stronger. I got to remembering what my daddy used to say: *Only thing stronger than white magic is our magic. Don't forget: Our love's stronger even than their hate.* And that got me to thinking of Old Roland, brewing up potions in the swamps over yonder.

Thunder cracks; my grandbaby whimpers.

"Hurry on in, Jeannette!" Old Roland calls. "Sky's fixin' to fall!"

Inside, I catch my breath.

"Didn't expect you'd come calling," Old Roland mutters—it's so dark, I can't see him.

I spin around.

"Last I heard, you'd been Saved."

Finally, I do see. He's the shadow crouched behind a soup pot, stirring swamp-grass-green liquid with a broom handle.

Careful now, Jeannette. You got to be careful.

My grandbaby grabs a fistful of my hair, holding tight.

Roland rises, knees popping. Squinting, I see the spirits swirling in circles around his head. Growing up in haunted Freedom House, I'm plenty familiar with spirits. Haunts can't scare me—but Heathwood's white evil does.

"I'm here to buy some of your power, Roland."

"What you need with my power?"

Grief drags me down. My lower back twitches like it might give out. I'm old—only forty-five, but all my life lived under Jim Crow, working for white folks from sunup to sundown. I'm too tired to be raising a baby again. I sure don't have time for this man's games.

"My grandbabies are in bad trouble. I'll pay what you want, do whatever it takes—"

"I know you've been through hell, Jeannie. And you know why, don't you?"

Something slithers across the wall. A snake. Silently, my grandbaby points.

Tears roll down my cheeks. "It's my fault. I broke the bond between twins. Cursed them, though I didn't mean to."

Old Roland nods. "Spirits say the white woman tricked the child outta you."

"Yes." My voice breaks, thinking of the baby that I'll never hold again: the sin that'll never wash clean. "The Heathwood woman came to me weeping. Made me think she cared—that she longed, as I did, for all that's left of our children. But her heart is ice. She's never loved. Not once in her life."

"Did her boy love your daughter? Love her true?"

In answer, I hand Roland the book of sonnets, marked at Marie's favorite page. Even now she's gone, I can still hear her chanting her favorite verse, just like she did all through her pregnancy: *I love thee with the breath, smiles, tears, of all my life* . . .

While Roland reads—smoky, shape-shifting spirits peering over his shoulder to spy the pretty pictures—my mind slips over a past slick as ice, remembering:

Dean and my daughter gazing down at their mixed-blood twins, the dark twin holding on to the light one like she was afraid of leaving her behind.

Marie in her wedding dress, waving goodbye to me on her way up North to be married.

The wicked shine of Marie's casket as gravediggers lowered it into the ground.

"Cursed, oh, yes, they are!" Before I can stop him, Old Roland chucks the book into the pot.

I leap up, hands trembling. It's too late; Dean's beautiful book is melting.

"Dean Heathwood gave that book to my daughter with a pure heart!"

"Dean forgot how much this world hates love between Black and white. Those young folks never should've met, Jeannette. Should've kept an ocean between them."

"Don't you think I know that, Roland? Don't you think I tried?"

Roland's eyes gleam. "Question is, what we gonna do now? And what are you willing to pay?"

I've got five hundred dollars in my pocket, thanks to the Heathwood woman. But Old Roland doesn't deal in money.

He deals, like the ancestors, in time.

"I've got two questions that need answering." I grip Charlene's hand, more to calm myself than her. "I'll pay whatever you want."

Quick as a flash, Old Roland snatches the snake off the wall. He holds it before him, letting it writhe.

"Snake'll answer you two questions. But I'm gonna need two years of whatever's left of your life."

I suck my teeth. "Take three."

Roland's eyebrows disappear into his hair. "Well, that's new. No one ever wants to pay me extra! You got a death wish or what?"

I speak through clenched teeth. "The third year's for Magnolia. The light-skinned child the Heathwood woman took. If she ever needs anything. If she ever visits you..."

Roland cocks his head. Again, I see the spirits swirling, whispering about me and the baby on my back.

God may smite me for coming here, but what choice did I have? When all else fails, our people look to the old ways. Roland lives on swampland, but he's as much a part of Colored Town as the soil, the cotton fields, even the star-studded river itself.

"Spirits say Magnolia'll come," Old Roland growls at last. "By then, Jeannie, I warn you—it'll be too late."

In one smooth motion, Roland pulls the machete from behind his back and slits the snake from head to tail. The dying thing thrashes, blood foaming. Chanting, Roland dips his finger into the snake's open belly. He marks my forehead with gore—then kisses me full on the lips.

I gasp, feeling years leave my body. Pulled from my lungs like air. Released, I double over, battling for breath.

"Come back in the morning. I'll forge you a silver cane outta this snake's soul. Make him a cobra, like his proud African ancestors! You ask your questions, then catch your train. I know you're not planning on staying, after what happened to your girl."

My lips feel bruised. "No. I'm not staying."

Roland stirs the green waters, concentrating. The spirits ring an ever-tighter circle around his head, soaking up the fumes.

I want to say goodbye to Roland—goodbye to all Georgia, and the only world I've ever known. But grief clogs my throat, silencing me.

Gutted, I stumble into the dark.

It's an effort to put one foot in front of the other. For Charlene's sake, I walk.

And I plan.

I won't make the same mistake with Charlene that I did with Marie. Letting her head be filled with nonsense and dreams.

"Remember now, Charlene Yates. For colored girls, there's no such thing as *happily ever after*. No use chasing it. You've got to fight to survive, but don't hope for too much."

The next night, the two of us board the train, headed for

New York, a new life. I step carefully—a cobra's silver head nestled inside my palm.

It's a long journey for a middle-aged woman and a baby.

I don't sleep. Every time I start to nod off, a sound wakes me.

The murdered snake, hissing.

1
Charlie
1953

All our earthly belongings in hand, Nana and I ride the rails as fast as they'll go, hoping we reach Eureka in time.

The train ride from New York to Georgia is a long one for a dying woman—but Nana wouldn't take no for an answer. Her dying wish, to be buried in the town where she was born. The town she fled after my parents' murders. The town I've never seen before, except on a map.

I'm a city girl through and through, but Nana never felt quite at home in Harlem. Always calling Georgia home, even after it took her daughter's life.

The train rumbles over an uneven track. Nana squeezes

her eyes shut, every jolt agony. Dr. Brown was against this journey, but Nana insisted: She'd be buried in Eureka soil. Nothing else would do.

"Eureka's a dangerous town, Charlene," Nana says. "Cursed long before your parents lost their lives."

"If it's so dangerous, why are we going back?"

"Can't choose home. It's time for you to face your past. Just wish I'd done more to prepare you."

"You made me a fighter, Nana."

And she did—though she always said I shouldn't hope for too much. That colored folk fight for survival, not happy endings. The day we left New York, I was papering the neighborhoods for a protest against slumlords. The posters reading: NO JUSTICE, NO PEACE.

"Eureka's not like New York. I never did tell you about the river."

"I've seen the river on the map. It cuts through town, sharp as a knife."

"Yes." Nana's hands curl around her cane. "And you, Miss Charlene, had best be on the colored side of that river before dark. Or you'll have the law to reckon with."

"I go by Charlie now, Nana. Not Charlene."

I took the name Charlie when I started working at the community center after school. Organizing is a tough job for a girl. I needed a tough name.

"Charlie, Charlene, whatever you want to call yourself: You'd best be in Colored Town before sunset."

"Nana, maybe things have changed since you've been gone."

"Nothing changes in Eureka. Nothing ever dies, either."

Nana's talking crazy. I shiver.

"Now. Where was I?"

"The river."

Nana stares hard at me, as if deciding something. Molten sunlight pours through the oval window. The train car smells of overheated metal and dust.

Nausea rolls through me, born of heat and fear.

My mother and white father were murdered on a southern road, on their way to be married in Pennsylvania. Under Jim Crow, it was illegal for mixed couples to marry in Georgia. So one day, not long after I was born, Mama asked Nana to babysit me while she and Daddy took a trip. Mama put on her wedding dress, and Daddy gassed up the car.

Somewhere along the highway, they were shot to death. Dragged out and dumped in the swamp on the colored side of town. Nana believes it wasn't just murder, but a lynching. She believes my parents died because the Deep South hates race mixing.

In my nightmares, I see it all play out: the highway, the flash of gunshots, the swamp dark.

Since my parents died seventeen years ago, scores of Negroes have lost their lives in the Deep South. Killed to keep colored people in their place. Thousands fled North to escape, flooding into the big cities. Now here I am, going the opposite way.

"The river's haunted," Nana says at last. "Don't go near it. Don't touch it. Not ever. Understand?"

A haunted river?

With a spike of fear, I wonder if Nana's mind is going.

The other passengers, all white, bury their faces in newspapers or gaze out the window. We're in farm country, flying past yellowed fields. I don't remember when the last colored passenger stepped off the train—Trenton? Philadelphia? Nana and I are the only ones left.

Next stop: Baltimore.

The train car is hot, but I'm cold as ice. Nana's mind *is* going, and for the first time I believe—truly believe—that she's going to die.

"Nana, I don't believe in ghosts."

"You don't have to believe in anything, baby. Plenty of ghosts already believe in you." Her voice rises, too loud. "The veil is thin down South, Charlene. Don't forget it!"

Afraid, my hands clench. I never should've agreed to take my grandmother on this last trip. It's too much for her. Too hard. I'm a young woman now—two weeks ago, I graduated high school—but still I let Nana boss me around.

In the aisle, the conductor stops short. "What's the problem here?"

"Nothing." I use my best talking-to-white-people voice, but forget to call him *sir*.

Nana closes her eyes, pained.

The conductor snarls, "Where're your tickets?"

I fumble with my purse. "Here. Right here, sir."

He barely glances at my tickets—*first class*. I sold our Singer sewing machine to buy these seats.

"No good in Maryland. Move to the colored car. Now."

I can't believe this. "*Move?* Mister, we can't *move*. My nana's sick, don't you see?"

He looks at me with such revulsion my blood runs cold. "Say that again, gal."

"I said, *we can't move*. I bought this ticket, same as everyone else—"

Nana's eyes snap open. "Never mind my granddaughter, sir. We're going. Thank you kindly."

"But, Nana—"

She shoots me a look that could boil water. I clamp my mouth shut.

Witnessing our humiliation, two white businessmen smile, smug. My cheeks flame. I might be colored but my money's green. How dare the conductor kick us out?

The train shrieks into the station.

"Baltimore, all aboard!"

Finally, it clicks into place.

On the train line, Baltimore separates North from South. Under Jim Crow, the conductor has every right to order us into the colored car.

All of a sudden, I feel very small and far from home.

Nana and I struggle into the colored car as new passengers wash in like a tide. Her cane, tap-tapping. But we can't find a seat, and Nana can't stay on her feet all the way to Georgia. If she dies on this train, she won't be a passenger anymore but cargo. I'll have to ship her body to Eureka, and I can't bear to lose her like that. *I can't.*

A young man about my age catches my eye. Like a movie star, he wears a white fedora. He must see how scared I am, because he nudges the boy beside him. They stand, giving up their seats. My relief is so powerful it leaves me dizzy.

The boy grips a leather strap, swaying with the train.

I tell him with my eyes: *Thank you.*

He tips his hat: *You're welcome.*

His skin is deep brown, but his eyes glitter gemstone blue.

I try not to stare. Either he's the handsomest young man I've ever seen, or I'm just that grateful.

Nana chuckles. "Southern gentlemen. Sure did miss them in New York."

I think of the conductor, that ugly look he gave me.

White folks've treated me poorly in New York—salesgirls making me wait too long in line, policemen giving me the eye. Before we found our place on 125th, a slumlord evicted us because we refused to pay a "poor hygiene fee." I've been abused for the color of my skin countless times, but the way that conductor looked at me was new. To him, Nana and I weren't worth hating. We weren't even human.

I cross my ankles, adjusting my dress to cover the run in my pantyhose. The train barrels through a corrugated tunnel, and my reflection flickers in the oval window—light and

14

dark, dark and light. Reflected, I am warm brown skin, long lashes, and wild curls. My hair's not kinky, but loose. The legacy of a white father murdered on a lonely southern road.

Trying to slow my pounding heart, I conjure my earliest memory, which I know must be of Mama: a nose pressed against mine, the smell of her breath, sweet but tangy. The memory's gauze-thin, but it's all I have of her.

"Sleep well, Marie," Nana whispers—confusing Mama's name with mine.

"Nana, it's me. Charlene."

"Oh, yes," she says, startled. "That's what I meant."

I hate thinking of life without Nana. Like life without air. I squeeze her hand, fighting back tears.

Across the aisle, two older men drum on leather trumpet cases, singing:

This train is bound for glory, this train.
This train is bound for glory, this train.
This train is bound for glory,
Ridin' with but the righteous, the righteous and the holy.
This train is bound for glory, this train . . .

Against my will, the song, the rhythmic clatter of the tracks, and the afternoon sun tumble me headlong into an uneasy sleep—a river churning with nightmares.

2

Magnolia

EUREKA, GEORGIA

agnolia. Wake up, child."

I bolt awake as the clock tolls midnight. Odessa, my maid of many years, hands me a glass of water.

"Mrs. Heathwood's asking for you."

"Me?"

"Hurry. She doesn't have long."

Odessa helps me into a gown—layers of black lace, waterfalls of mournful tulle—and a pair of black silk gloves. These will be my mourning clothes, for if Odessa has come to wake me in such a fashion, then my grandmother, the famous Blanche Heathwood, will not survive the night.

I pull the gloves up to my elbows, glancing swiftly into

my vanity's mirror. My skin, contrasted with my black gown, is white as chalk—becomingly pale, for I have made an effort to keep out of the sun. Only my hair is wild, tumbled with curls. Grandmother always insisted I straighten it, because *a southern lady is never unkempt.*

Tonight, I do not have time to fix my hair. *Grandmother* does not have time.

Odessa hurries me into the hall. At the oaken door, I balk like a frightened mare.

"You must go inside. Miss Blanche asked for you alone."

"Whatever does she have to say to me? Odessa, you *know* Grandmother's always hated me."

"Time to let bygones be bygones." She nudges me forward. "Be brave, Magnolia Heathwood."

"But I am not brave."

"Then pretend. You will never get another chance."

For decades, Grandmother has been the matriarch of the Heathwood family and the owner of the largest cotton plantation in the county. She has lived through both World Wars. She has watched our family's fortunes rise and fall. There is no denying her on her deathbed.

A southern lady does not want for courage.

Before I can think overmuch, I fling open the door and plunge into darkness.

Grandmother's bedroom has always lanced my heart with fear. Inside, dozens of priceless mirrors gleam. The surfaces of those mirrors are all black: forged from obsidian.

They lean against the walls and each other, making the room look sharp and deep. They remind me of the hall of mirrors at the county fair, tugging and warping the light.

Aunt Hilda claims there are tens of thousands of dollars in glass here—that if we only sold away our heirlooms, we would have wealth enough to plant cotton once more. But Grandmother is too proud of her obsidian treasures to ever part with them. Never mind that mold spots the wallpaper, or that the curtains have begun to rot.

In the sheets of obsidian glass, my face echoes too many times. So, too, does Grandmother's four-poster bed.

"Magnolia."

I approach the deathbed carefully, and perch in a stiff-backed chair. Long ago, Blanche Heathwood was a southern belle of great renown. Now, she is a tattered, decaying thing. Only her ice-blue eyes possess any life.

Those eyes flick to my unruly hair. *"You look like a savage."*

I wince. "Grandmother, it is midnight. I have not had time—"

She coughs, pressing her handkerchief to her lips. The lace is bloody red. More awful yet, I believe I see chunks of flesh: the insides of Blanche Heathwood's lungs.

Tears travel down my face, because however coldly she treated me, Grandmother raised me. Now she is dying—and not gently.

"Do you know why I have summoned you?"

I shake my head.

"You're livin' a lie, girl."

"What—"

"Your mother. She was a colored housekeeper. A *Negress*. Because of her sin, you are colored, too."

Shock seeps into me like a slow winter's freeze. Surely these are the ravings of a madwoman, addled by morphine. After all, I know exactly who my mother was.

"Why, bless your heart, of course I am white! Grandmother, don't you recognize me? I am Magnolia Heathwood, your granddaughter."

Grandmother watches me with glassy, death-soaked eyes.

I speak faster, louder. "My mother was a Spanish woman. An aristocrat. She died birthing me, don't you remember? Her portrait is just *there*."

Triumphantly, I point to the painting of my ravishing raven-haired mother. She occupies pride of place beside my father, also deceased, and my grandfather in Confederate gray.

"That woman never existed, you stupid thing." Her words whip out like a lash. I brace myself, though I do not know for what. "Your mother was a common housekeeper. You have her ripe face. Such dreadful features didn't come from *my* side of the family. How you can bear to look in the mirror, I simply cannot understand."

Grandmother's words spill from her cracked lips like poison. I press back against the chair, away.

"Your mother convinced your fool father that he was *in love*. Can you imagine? Sleep with the colored woman, what do I care, but love between the races ain't natural. Only your father didn't listen. Do you know what he did?" Spittle flies from her lips. "He planned to MARRY HER. The TRAITOR!"

Grandmother is addled, and yet—isn't my hair a frightful mess? And doesn't my skin tan too deeply? Grandmother has always strictly forbidden me from exposing myself to daylight come June.

No, no, no. "I don't believe you."

Grandmother's gaze burns a hole in my cheek. "Then I saw you. As pale a thing as ever came from a Negro woman. Though tainted, you would suffice."

All at once, decisively, my stomach plummets. A single drop of Black blood makes you colored. In Eureka, that is no small thing. We live according to a strict caste system that has not changed for centuries. If this is true, my life will never be the same.

"Why are you telling me this?"

Quick as a snake, Grandmother grasps my wrist, nails digging into flesh. She lifts her back from the bed, unleashing the putrid stench of bedsores.

My eyes widen, but I do not dare pull away.

"You must be ever vigilant, for the mere whisper of the truth will ruin you. Lord, anyone can see the Negro in your face if they know what they're lookin' for. Above all, you must not truck with Negroes. They will try to claim you for their own, but this family did not survive the Union invasion for nothin'. I *will* have an heir.

"Magnolia, *your place is here.* Do you understand me? You belong *right here.*"

Grandmother's grip weakens; her head drops to her chest. Her arm, a white branch, falls. Between one heartbeat and the next, death sneaks between Blanche Heathwood's lips, snuffing her out like a flame.

Now I am alone with the secret Grandmother whispered. Alone and dreadfully afraid.

Oh so gently, I lay what's left of Blanche Heathwood against the headboard. Even dead, Grandmother's eyes hate me. I cannot bring myself to kiss her sunken cheek.

Colored. Grandmother says I am colored.

Lord, I can't breathe. I stand, knocking over my chair. I struggle to open a window, needing fresh air.

"You gosh-dammed thing! Open, won't you, open!"

At last the window flies open, but the air is not fresh. The wind carries the reek of swamp gas over the peat bog—death itself. On the water, putrefying vegetation layers ten inches thick. Sinking into that quicksand, you can break an ankle. Drown.

One of Grandmother's obsidian mirrors captures my attention. An antique, Beaux-Arts frame rims the glass in gold. Its surface, like all the others, is black as tar.

I do not realize, at first, that I cast no reflection.

Your mother was a common housekeeper, Grandmother said. *You have her ripe face.*

I lean closer, searching for my image in the shining emptiness.

Such dreadful features didn't come from my side of the family.

The mirror reflects the open window, the fluttering curtain behind me—and nothing else.

How you can bear to look in the mirror, I simply cannot understand—

Heart racing, I fly from glass to glass, wild to find my reflection in this hall of mirrors. How is it possible that not a single mirror reflects me? Though I spin and dart and turn, every mirror is the same. In every glass, I am gone.

It is just as if a girl were never born with the name of Magnolia Heathwood.

As if I were already dead.

3
Charlie
EUREKA, GEORGIA

Nana, the blue-eyed stranger, and I are the only people to get off at Eureka Station. It's nothing but a platform and an empty ticket box in the middle of nowhere. The late afternoon sun drips over us, hot as boiled honey. And there's something wrong with the air. It's too thick to breathe.

Relax, I tell myself. *It's only the humidity.*

But I don't trust this empty, rural place.

After the long train ride, Nana's barely standing.

"Pills," she whispers.

I shake my head. It isn't time.

Beside a wooden bench, there's a scarlet vending machine.

Sugar might help Nana, and I could use a cold drink. I step forward, then stop short.

ICE-COLD COCA-COLA, the machine reads. THE SOFT DRINK FOR WHITES ONLY!

You've got to be kidding me.

Who'd know if I bought a "whites-only" drink from a machine?

I hesitate, remembering the cruel conductor. I don't know the rules in this place. Mosquitoes buzz ferociously, seeking our sweaty exposed skin. Holding Nana, I'm helpless to swat them. Fresh meat.

Homesickness crashes over me. I miss the noise and hum of New York streets. The city's far too busy to care what type of soda colored folks drink.

Trees shudder in a muggy breeze. Nana slips lower in my grip. Can't hold her much longer.

"Hey." The handsome blue-eyed boy from the train hurries to help. "Put her arm around me, that's it. The colored hospital's not far. I'll drive you."

"No hospital," Nana moans. "Home."

The stranger's eyes meet mine, a question in them.

"We came all this way so my grandmother could die where she was born."

"She's from Eureka? Why didn't you say so? Ma'am, where can I drop you?"

"*Freedom.*"

I draw a blank, but he doesn't miss a beat. "Freedom House has been abandoned so long, folks say it's haunted."

Nana snorts. "Folks are right."

"Wait. You *know* my grandmother?"

"Sure. The Yates family is famous."

Of course. My parents' murders. A horrible thing like that would be whispered about for generations. Now, it feels like all my guts have spilled out. I drop my eyes. Look away.

"You must be a Lucien," Nana says. "Your people always had those remarkable baby blues."

"Darius Lucien, that's me. My father's—"

"Preacher Lucien."

"Welcome back to Eureka."

"Thank you, child. I'm…" Nana's cane clatters to the platform.

She sags, fainting.

I panic. "You've got to help her. Please, she's sick—"

"Let's get her home, call the doctor from Freedom House. You got a line?"

"Don't know. We came in a rush."

Darius scoops Nana up like she weighs nothing.

He nods to a parking lot. "See that Cadillac? You ride with me, Charlene, and I'll make sure you and your grandmother get home safe."

Nana in his arms, I let Darius Lucien lead me to his car.

Only as I'm sliding across the leather seats do I realize

with a jolt that he knew my name. Even though I never told it.

He called me Charlene.

I don't like Eureka any better from the car.

We drive past nice white-people houses with emerald lawns, past playgrounds and shops on Main Street. Weirdly, there's nobody outside. Gives me the creeps, but maybe it's just the heat. Nana's beside me in the back seat, passed out. I hang on to her hand.

Darius's Cadillac rumbles across a small wooden bridge, and I read the graffiti scrawled on the side: NEGROES, NO CROSSING AFTER SUNSET! OR ELSE!

Only, the graffiti doesn't use the word *Negroes*.

Chilled, I scoot closer to Nana.

On the colored side of the river, the road isn't paved anymore, but plain dirt. Like Negroes don't deserve to have their roads paved.

"Welcome to Colored Town," Darius says.

We trundle past shotgun houses on concrete blocks, poorer than anything I've ever seen in my life. Here, people are out despite the heat. Women hang laundry and tend weedy gardens, while hungry-looking children play around them. The women's backs are stooped. Their faces tired.

I'm relieved when we turn off that road, heading into

dense woods. Pine trees stretch so tall I can't see the tops of them. Soon, thick vines trail across the Cadillac's windshield. A clearing appears in the wilderness, and a small cottage.

Darius parks on grass. "Here we are. Freedom House."

"Oh," I say.

Freedom House's front door is painted bright ocean blue. There's a wooden porch, two battered rocking chairs, and a drooping roof. Creeping plants kiss the porch stairs, like the house is just an extension of the wilderness—another branch, another vine.

My eyes fill, thinking of Nana weeping in our kitchen on 125th Street. Every year on the anniversary of my parents' deaths, she'd let herself remember. Clutching her elbows and sobbing into her arms. Next morning, she'd dry her eyes. Get back to her life.

She'd tell me: *Life's a battle, Charlene. Got to keep swinging.*

And: *There's no such thing as happily ever after. Not for colored girls.*

"Come on, now," Darius says. "Let's get your grand-mother inside."

Stepping out of the car, I'm hit with a wall of tumid river stench.

"God, what's that *smell*?"

Darius slams the car door shut. "The river—it's mostly swamp. Don't worry, you get used to it. Where're you from, anyhow?"

"New York City."

A bemused smile lights up his face. "Well, okay, Miss New York."

Darius carries Nana to the ocean-blue door. I worry it'll be locked, but it opens easily. Then I'm leading the young man through my mother's house. The only place she ever lived, before she died.

The kitchen's a woodstove and a pantry. The living room, a single rocking chair. The furniture's unpolished, but there's not a cobweb to be seen. The little country house gleams with lemon oil.

"The house—it's so clean."

"Bet you the Church Ladies threw a cleaning party. They'll have stocked the icebox, too. Your nana must've told them y'all were on your way. Look there."

An envelope reads: *To Jeannette & Charlene Yates, God Bless! Welcome Home!*

But that's wrong; 125th Street is my home.

I pick the envelope up anyway. Drop it in my purse.

Then I turn my attention to a long, dark stretch of hallway. My skin crawls. I'm afraid, but I can't say of what.

Even in midafternoon, it's too dark inside this house. Moving quickly down the hall, I switch on lamps, flooding the place with amber light.

My arms break out in goose bumps, opening the first of two bedroom doors. Inside, a twin bed's all made up. The only decoration is an embroidered hoop—the kind Nana used to make, before arthritis ruined her hands.

I swallow. "I think this was Nana's room. You know—before…"

The murders.

Darius lays my grandmother on top of a quilt. "There's a phone in the kitchen. I'll call the doctor, Miss New York."

When he's gone, I give up being grown-up and crawl into bed with Nana.

Her eyes flicker open. "Did we—?"

"We made it."

"You feel it now, don't you?"

"Feel what?"

"The veil. How much thinner it is here."

"Oh, Nana." I put my hand on her forehead, checking for fever.

She swats my hand away. "I'm not fevered. *You.* You're the one in danger. Northerners don't believe. But in Eureka…"

Truth is, I do feel something. My eyes scrape the dark, alert.

Nana's hands are too dry. Did she remember to pack her shea butter? Suddenly, it seems like the most important question in the world.

"When I die, the veil will be even thinner—nearly gone, so long as my spirit's hanging around. Find a mirror. Your mama will tell you all you need to know."

I want to block my ears. "Stop. You still have time."

She shakes her head. "Be careful here, Charlene. Freedom House is old. She doesn't take kindly to strangers. Remember: Nothing ever changes in Eureka. And nothing ever dies."

"You're not making sense."

"Keep on swinging," she murmurs.

Hearing our secret phrase, I smile through a haze of tears. I still remember the day Nana caught me swinging a baseball bat in the middle of our street, trying my best to keep up with the boys. When she shouted my name from our apartment window, I was sure I'd get a scolding.

Instead, she cheered. *That's it, Charlene! You keep on swinging!*

It became our phrase for everything: *Keep on swinging.*

It meant: *Keep fighting, even if you'll probably lose.* I never was any good at baseball.

In her country bedroom, Nana's eyelids flutter. I reach for her hand.

And then she slips, too easily, into sleep.

"Phone's out." Darius appears.

I jump out of bed.

"I'll call Dr. Colt from my house. He'll be here in a few hours, Miss New York."

"Actually, I go by Charlie."

Amber lamps flicker out. Across the swiftly clotting dark, Darius's eyes lock with mine.

I don't for one second believe in ghosts, but this house isn't right. Walls stink of unfinished wood; shadows coat the doorways, thick as paint. And the air crackles. Storm's coming.

"You don't think the house is really..." I trail off, feeling foolish.

Nana shifts. *"Marie, the man's white! It's not safe!"*

At the sound of my mother's name, a chill streaks down my spine. Nana's eyes roll under her lids like she's fighting a war inside.

My voice pitches high. "Darius, I think you'd better hurry."

He settles his white hat on his head. "I'll be back real soon, Miss New York."

Then he's gone—and I'm on my own.

I've lived in tenement housing all my life. In those small spaces, you're never alone. Can always hear a baby squalling, a couple arguing, children laughing. Here the silence is so thick, it feels malicious.

"Nana, what's wrong with this place? *What's happening?"*

She's sunk too deep to hear.

Outside the window, the sun slowly sets. Another lamp flickers, hisses, and burns its bulb out. I huddle close to my grandmother. My eyes battle shadows, the room's deepening layers.

Words cling to my lips—a question that makes no sense. *Mama?* I want to say, but don't. *Mama, is that you?*

4
Magnolia

Perched before my vanity's mirror, I hold as still as General Lee's statue in the town square, waiting for my reflection to come on home.

Minutes pass, but it is no use. My reflection has been gone five days. In its place I am left with a powerful, swelling dread.

Since Grandmother died, I have managed to keep to my rooms, convalescing in my mourning clothes. Black silk surrounds me, cool as water. When I drift to sleep, I dream of black taffeta clouds. There's not much difference, now, between wakefulness and dreaming.

I open my diary, where I have scribbled theories of my case:

Theory One: *I am a monster, neither colored nor white. That is why I do not appear in the looking glass.*

Theory Two: *I am a liar, and liars do not deserve a reflection.*

I pause, wet my pen, and add:

Theory Three: *I am imagining things. Grandmother's secret has driven me insane.*

As I write the last, an icy thumb presses against my sternum. Do the insane know they have taken leave of their senses? Would *I* know?

Truth be told, I have never liked my vanity. All along the mirror's porcelain siding, Negroes serve masters on a pastoral meadow, ferrying lemonade to picnic goers or fanning them with palm fronds. These are familiar vignettes: depictions of our southern hospitality and the languid, summertime leisure for which we Georgians are rightfully famous.

But sometimes, I rather think the colored people *move*. It is not always the same servant holding the fan or smiling broadly at his master's guest. Occasionally, the painted people do not seem to be smiling at all—they are grimacing, baring teeth.

My aunt Hilda knocks. "Magnolia? Might I come in?"

"No."

The door creaks open anyhow. "Sugarpie, don't tell me you're still in bed."

Reeking of bourbon even at this hour, Aunt Hilda bustles into my room.

"Now, you listen to an old woman. You cannot withdraw

from your life. Not when you are of marrying age. Is that Finch Waylon home yet? Why don't you call him, see a picture show? Excessive grief is murder for the complexion."

In one swift motion, Aunt Hilda throws my curtains wide.

"No, don't," I cry, shrinking from the strong plantation sunlight.

"It's enough, Magnolia. Lord, don't you think I'm hurting, too?"

Shame rolls over me in a black wave. Grandmother and Aunt Hilda were sisters, after all. Like me, she wears silk mourning clothes.

"Sugarpie, Annamae Waylon's waitin' downstairs."

I am incensed. "Auntie, I'm in no state to entertain callers."

"Your best friend won't hold it against you. I remember when y'all were knee-high babies, catching crawfish down by the river, comin' home filthy as mice. Now get up and show your good breedin'."

Grumbling, I obey. A southern lady never keeps a guest waiting.

Aunt Hilda looks me over. "Let's see a smile."

I stretch my lips into a grimace.

"You look better already. Pretty as a peach."

In the vanity's mirror, my aunt Hilda is clearly reflected—but I am not. Does she notice? Does she see?

"What's wrong, Sugarpie? You look like a goose walked over your grave."

"Can you see me? In the mirror, I mean?"

She glances back to the spot where I ought to be reflected.

"'Course I can! I am not so old I'm blind!"

Powerfully drawn, I take another long look at the mirror. Whenever I studied my reflection before, I always saw a pretty young white girl, the future Mrs. Finch Waylon, looking back.

Now...why, it is like I am already a ghost.

Only I reckon nobody knows it but me.

Annamae greets me in the parlor, wearing a yellow dress patterned with sunflowers. Standing beside the marble fireplace, she looks none too pleased.

"Magnolia, where in heaven have you *been?*"

"Sorry, Annamae. It's been plumb chaos since the funeral."

"But why haven't you answered the phone? Didn't you get my flowers?"

It was terribly rude of me not to send a thank-you note when Annamae's roses arrived, but I had a lost reflection on my mind.

A southern lady always offers refreshments.

"Can I fetch you a glass of mint tea?"

Annamae cocks her head. "Why, bless your heart, there's lipstick on your teeth."

Oh, foot. Every day of my life, I have carefully

consulted my reflection, because in the end, my looks are all I have. I did not complete my senior year of high school—Grandmother, always old-fashioned, never believed in schooling for girls.

Annamae and the rest of my friends graduated last week. I was looking forward to spending a carefree summer with them. To picnics and drive-in movies. Normal life.

"Here." Annamae reaches out, scrubbing the scarlet stain from my teeth with her index finger.

The gesture reminds me how close we used to be. Suddenly, I am dying to tell my oldest friend everything—the whole truth.

Annamae, I am colored. That is all I have to say. *My mother was colored and so am I.*

Never before have words so eluded me. I am so frustrated, I could shriek. But Grandmother taught me better. Like sucking down an oyster, I swallow my ugly feelings in a single gulp.

"Listen, I came because—" Annamae smiles, transforming into someone beautiful, though her face is too thin, like a weasel's. "I have the grandest news!"

Annamae hops from hobby to hobby, loving whatever it is—knitting, cooking, crafting—with her whole soul for precisely six months.

Lately, it is segregation. She wants more of it.

"We've done it! The Junior White Women's Auxiliary

helped pass a law. Real change is happenin' because of little ol' me!"

Oh, Lord. *The Cemetery Segregation petition.* My smile wilts.

"We got near on five hundred signatures, so my daddy arranged a meetin' for me and the state senator. 'Course, the senator agreed that it is absolutely shameful, *disgusting*, that Eureka's only cemetery is the final restin' place for both white and coloreds alike.

"So he brought legislation before the senate and—*we won!* Magnolia, I helped pass a gosh darn *law!*" Breathless, she clutches her pearls. "*The Segregated Interment Initiative.*"

"How do you segregate a cemetery, Annamae? Are y'all diggin' up bodies?"

"Not white ones, silly! Just coloreds. We got to move them somehow, ain't we?"

Chilled despite the heat, I cross my arms over my chest.

"I'm certain no one will mind. It'll be such a relief—not just to us, but to the Negroes—to have everyone buried in their own place."

Annamae beams expectantly. When she won a ribbon at the science fair, she looked at me the same exact way. Only this is no science project, and whatever happens next, I'll bear some of the blame. Like all of Annamae's friends, I let her pressure me into signing that petition with my full name: *Magnolia Rose Heathwood.*

'Course, I never imagined anything would come of it.

Now the truth slams into me: I cannot tell my best friend who I am—not *ever*. Over the years, we have shared hairbrushes, toothbrushes, even beds. Her disgust, if she learns I am colored, will kill me.

Then there's Finch, her brother, who's fixin' to propose as soon as he gets back from his first year at Georgia State. Our marriage wouldn't just be illegal. To Annamae and the rest, it'd be the gravest of sins. *I'm* the gravest of sins.

"Anyhow, I'm throwin' a supper party to celebrate—a Gravediggers' Potluck. Ain't that a cute little theme? Gravediggin'? Magnolia, will you come?"

You must be ever vigilant, Grandmother said on her deathbed. *Anyone can see the Negro in your face if they know what they're lookin' for.*

I slap my smile back into place. "'Course I'll come. If the creek don't rise."

Annamae's in a rush, preparing for her potluck. She hugs me and lets herself out.

At first, I am too stunned to feel a thing.

Then my face prickles like a thousand needles lie beneath my skin. I hurry toward the grand stair, wanting nothing more than to cry in my room alone.

Not long after, Odessa visits me. Exhausted, I am tucked miserably into bed.

Odessa strokes my hair like she did when I was small. I feel like weeping, spilling all my secrets. I have just opened my mouth to tell her that I am colored, and that in signing Annamae's god-awful petition I have made a terrible mistake—when she covers my pale hand with her brown one.

"Miss Magnolia, I see how you are suffering. You've got to make a choice. Do you understand what I mean?"

Odessa's knowing look shocks the air from my chest. I toss my covers aside, furious as a southern lady should never be.

"Why, you—you knew I was colored all along!"

Odessa smooths the pleats of her apron. "I knew."

"Why didn't you tell me? I had a right to know!"

"Try to understand. Mrs. Heathwood was a harsh mistress. If I ever said a word, she'd have fired me quicker than you can spit."

For years, I struggled to be demure enough, pretty enough, *obedient* enough for Grandmother. I fashioned myself into the perfect southern lady, but all in vain. Grandmother could never love me—not truly.

My vanity's mirror reflects my lacy curtains, the peony wallpaper, and Odessa in her solemn maid's uniform. But it does not, or will not, reflect Magnolia Heathwood.

Odessa touches my cheek. "I tried my best to teach you about us. Remember all my bedtime stories, about Black and white and how neither is better than the other? And when you were older, I tried to teach you about Jim Crow—the evil of it." Her eyes harden. "I suppose that lesson didn't quite sink in. I heard you talking with Annamae. You should know better than to attend that awful Gravediggers' Potluck."

Ashamed, I shrink back. "Grandmother said I must always keep up appearances. Mustn't I?"

She puts her nose up. "Well. That's for you to decide."

Suddenly, Odessa seems a life raft. "Girls like me. What becomes of them?"

"Some pass for white. Lie their whole lives long."

"Then it's possible."

"'Course it's possible," she grumbles. "But passing for white is a dreadful thing—and dangerous. What if you married your Finch Waylon?"

"Grandmother said our family needs his wealth to restore our good name."

"Miss Blanche was only looking out for Heathwood. She didn't have your best interests at heart. Ask yourself: What if you married this white boy and your child came dark? How would you explain that, Miss Magnolia?"

Eureka's hatred of miscegenation—race mixing—runs fathoms deep. Women have died for less. An eerie pressure builds inside my head: mortal fear. Raised sheltered as a hothouse flower, I do not believe I have ever felt it before.

"You can choose different, Miss Magnolia."

I shake my head. "You're wrong. I have no choice. Never did."

For a long time, Odessa is silent. "Marie Ann Yates," she says at last.

"*What?*"

"That was your mother's name. Visit her grave. That's how you start to heal." She scowls. "But first, you've got to quit this ugly pretending. If you keep on playing white, I'll wash my hands of you."

I gasp. "You *wouldn't*. Didn't you raise me? Don't we love each other?"

"I don't *love* anybody white. But I'd die for any woman or child in Colored Town. That's how our people have survived for so long—by watching out for our own."

"Odessa, what would you have me do?" I hate the childish whine in my voice. "Must I truly give up everything I've ever known? How is that fair?"

"You ought to know by now that nothing about this world is *fair*."

Hopelessness rushes in, seeking to drown me.

Odessa does not coddle me. Does not dote or dry my tears, as she always has in the past. On the contrary, she simply walks out—leaving me alone with an impossible choice.

I huddle against my pillow. In an hour, I will have to get up and dress for Annamae's party. After all, Grandmother's dying wish was for me to lie.

And yet, pretending will take me apart piece by piece. It will begin with Annamae's grisly Gravediggers' Potluck, where I'll eat hors d'oeuvres while my friends congratulate themselves on digging up colored bones.

Meanwhile, I shall be holding back my secret, trying not to scream.

5
Charlie

wake in bed with Nana. Sweat's gathered behind my knees. The heat, unbearable. I kick the quilt off my legs.

A mosquito whines, zinging too close to my ear.

Takes me a minute to remember that I'm not safe in our apartment on 125th Street. That I've been napping in the house that once was Mama's, before she was shot to death on a southern road.

I curl toward my grandmother. Her face is drawn. Eyes open. Tears have carved rivers down her frozen cheeks.

Oh, my God.

"Nana." I shake her. "Nana, wake up."

Terror crashes like a subway train through my chest, rattling blood and bones. I shake her harder. Pinching, begging.

"We've got to get out of here, Nana. Back to Harlem. We'll make sweet potato pie and listen to the radio. I know you like Chuck Berry's rock 'n' roll, even if you pretend you don't." Horror floods me, because Nana won't wake. "This place...it's not good for your blood pressure, that's all. The doctor said rest. *No stress.* So we're going home. You hear me?"

Nana doesn't answer.

I pry my grandmother's weathered hands apart, needing to make her understand that she can't die and leave me all alone.

A piece of paper flutters from her loosened grip.

A picture.

I pick it up. When she passed, Nana was holding a picture of us.

In the photo, I'm nine at the West Harlem Block Party. Nana, wearing her church hat, didn't want to come—always said the streets were too loud—but I begged her. Mr. Alfie was there, selling gelato. All our neighbors came, too—everyone I've ever loved.

Like it was yesterday, I can hear the crack and pop of the photographer's flashbulb. I'd never had my picture taken before. Nana, either. We look excited, nervous.

I drop the photo like it burns me, because Nana's gone.

"My fault," I whisper. "Never should've come."

The air crackles, electric. My teeth chatter—the room gone as cold as New York in midwinter.

Something whispers: "*Charlene.*"

The word flutters by me like a scrap of newsprint. For help, I look to Nana. But her face is shuttered.

"*Charlene, baby. Come here.*"

I grab Nana's cane, wielding it like a baseball bat. My legs carry me through the hall to my mother's bedroom.

It's a country-plain room, with a chair and a wooden dresser. Country plain, except for one thing: a great, glittering mirror standing on clawed feet.

My jaw drops.

Takes all my courage to look closer.

Incredibly, the mirror's reflective surface is pitch-black. Darker even than the Hudson River at night. Can a black mirror even make a reflection? *Yes.* In the murky depths, I see the rough old rocking chair behind me—its outline silver in the dark glass—and me, with my loose curls falling around my face.

What must such a mirror be worth?

Plunk, plunk.

A sound like someone wading through water.

When I die, the veil will be even thinner—nearly gone, so long as my spirit's hanging around, Nana said. *Find a mirror. Your mama will tell you all you need to know.*

My hands go slack, and Nana's cane falls to the floor. A smoky shape forms in the glass, and then slowly solidifies. In another heartbeat, *there's a woman in the mirror.*

She's clear now. As real as the reflection of the rocking chair behind me. Her hair swirls around her face like she's submerged. She's soaked, dripping—and undeniably dead. A hole craters her temple—the bloodless outline of a gunshot.

I recognize Mama's face—so much like mine, like Nana's. She wears a white dress, dripping water.

A wedding dress.

I stop breathing, because ghosts are real. At least here, in Eureka, where the veil is thin. Or maybe I've wandered into some terrible dream.

Nana, I want to go home.

"Charlene?" The woman's voice echoes like she's speaking underwater. Little black bubbles rise from her mouth to the mirror's golden rim.

"Stay away from me—just keep away!"

"It's me. Mama."

Knees weak, I collapse to the floor. My wrists take the impact. The woman kneels, reaching for me, but the glass stops her hand. She looks anguished. Young, too. When she died, Mama was only seventeen. The same age I am now.

"You're not real. You can't be."

"Charlene."

"You're *dead.*"

"I never stopped loving you."

Her words bring seventeen years of yearning to the

surface. I stare like I could drink my mother, taking in every detail. The bump in her nose that mirrors mine. The color of her skin, two shades darker.

I try to ignore the signs that she's dead: the gray around her mouth, the tangled mess of her hair. Her fingernails, yellowed and overgrown.

"Oh, Mama. What happened to you?"

Remembering, her eyes grow vague. "Two men stopped us at the state line. Said they were police, but they lied. They didn't like seeing your father and me together." A shiver wracks Mama's shoulders. "Don't want to think of all that now."

As if compelled by a magnetic force, Mama glances at the dark behind her.

A tear slips down my cheek. "I can't believe this."

"Can't stay long. And you've got to get moving. Find your sister. Y'all have to fix what's been broken."

My mouth dries up.

Sister? I don't have one. Is this ghost really Mama? Or is it something else, pretending?

Slowly, I stand. Mama mirrors me.

"But I don't have a sister."

She looks back at the dark. "Can't stay long."

"Mama!" I'm desperate to keep her attention. "I said, *I don't have a sister.*"

In the depths of Mama's eyes, I see headlights, a long

stretch of road. My hands clutch into claws, because this *is* Mama, dead and sunk deep in her death. But what she's saying doesn't make any sense.

"Your grandmother made a mistake. She broke the bond between twins. But it's not too late to fix things."

Twins?

"Fix what's been broken, Charlene. Promise me."

And then she's leaving me. Trudging back into the watery, pitch-black glass.

"Wait!" I slam my hands against the black mirror. It shudders, ringing hollow. "Mama, I don't know what you want me to do!"

She turns, opening and closing her mouth. But she can't make a sound. If there really is such a thing as a veil between worlds, it's thickened again. The living and the dead: We're segregated, too.

Mama raises her left hand, her expression determined. My skin creeps. With one long, overgrown fingernail, she slashes once, twice. The glass shrieks—earsplitting.

I slap my hands over my ears.

She slashes again—and again—and again—mauling the glass like it's ice.

The house tremors, and I feel a gust of the otherworldly, like I'm standing on top of a subway grate while the train rushes beneath.

"Stop it! Mama, please stop!"

She doesn't listen. She continues to slice with her fingernail, filling the room with glass screams.

Overwhelmed, I bury my face in my hands.

When I look up again, Mama's vanished.

In the glass, gashes long and deep spell out a single word: *HEATHWOOD.*

6
Magnolia

Annamae was not always a horror.

When we were children, we used to sneak off to skip stones with two Negro girls. There didn't seem to be much difference between us—and then, suddenly, there was all the difference in the world.

One day Annamae didn't feel like skipping stones. She wanted to throw them at our friends instead. I held back her arm. Lord, but she was strong.

After, she told me she'd had a talk with her mother.

Did I know coloreds weren't clean?

Did I know they were evil, since Cain?

Did I know if white and colored mixed, they'd birth monsters?

That night I ran into Odessa's arms, her mouth twisting as I recounted those lies. She rocked me, countering every poisoned arrow.

Colored folk are just the same as whites.

The story of Cain is a lie.

Whenever there's love, the world begins to heal.

Living in a small town, I had no choice but to remain friendly with Annamae Waylon. No choice, even, but to sign the petition for a segregated cemetery. After all, every other girl in town *did* sign it—wouldn't it have been strange if Magnolia Heathwood did not?

In Eureka, there's nothing worse than looking like an integrationist. Since the Confederacy lost the war, Eureka's been frozen in amber. In this town, you have to go along to get along.

Or perhaps I am simply a coward.

Outside Annamae's house, her younger siblings play flashlight tag by moonlight.

Annamae and I used to play flashlight tag, too, during her parents' parties. Sometimes we even spent the night in her yard, slapping mosquitoes and whispering dreams.

Jackson, Annamae's ten-year-old brother, waves to me. He already looks so much like Finch. I smile. Then a stray beam catches his profile, revealing garish yellow bruises ringing his right eye.

His father always did have a temper.

Jackson's bruises feel like a bad omen, but it's too late to turn back. I straighten my black skirt and ring the doorbell.

"You made it!" Annamae squeals. "Heavens to Betsy, y'all, Mag-*no*-li-a is here!"

The faces of my friends are so familiar it hurts. There's Lila and Susie Gimble, the town gossips, and birdlike Annie Flake. Everyone sports pink pins, showing their support for the Junior White Women's Auxiliary—or JWWA, for short.

Annamae hands me a dish: I'm meant to wear a pin, too.

Furtively, I pocket it.

I remind myself of Grandmother's last words: *Your place is here.*

I wish it were true. But these girls wouldn't want me if they knew the truth about my race. They have gathered to celebrate digging up bodies like mine.

As usual, Annamae's decorated the party room within an inch of its life. At each table she's constructed horribly whimsical centerpieces: miniature painted headstones tucked among barbed wire.

I take my assigned seat beside Nellie Waylon, Annamae's mother. Fresh from the salon, her bottle-blond hair shines like spun gold.

"Magnolia! Our Finch is comin' home tonight, did you hear? I'm sure the very first person he'll want to see is pretty little *you!*"

My mouth's dry as the creek in summer, recalling the

kisses I shared with Finch—back when I believed myself white. If an upstanding southern gentleman like Finch ever discovered the truth, he might could wish me dead.

The Waylon housekeeper, Sandra, ferries a tray of hors d'oeuvres to our table.

I push away from the appetizers, because they don't smell right. Could they possibly be *rotten?*

"Not hungry, sweetheart?"

My stomach twists—I am starving. Since Grandmother's funeral, I have struggled to eat. I reckon it must be grief.

Must be.

Annamae raps a gavel against her podium. "Welcome, everyone! Now, y'all know how important segregation is to our way of life, which is why I began the Segregated Interment Initiative...."

Annamae launches into a too-long speech. Forks clink. People mutter. Truth is, none of the girls really cares about the Segregated Interment Initiative. They just want to stay on the right side of Annamae. If you cross her, she's mean as a snake.

"My uncle, may he rest in peace, is buried next to some colored man. They're close enough their elbows could touch! He deserves better. *We* deserve better."

"Amen." Mrs. Waylon winks at me.

I'm nauseated. Not once in my life have I ever stood up to Eureka's ugly race talk. *Not once.*

"Magnolia, are you quite all right?"

"Excuse me, ma'am. I need the powder room."

Alone in the bathroom, I splash my face with water. I try not to look into the mirror over the sink, but it seems I cannot help myself. Where my reflection ought to be, I see an ugly Rockwell print hanging over the toilet, the potpourri, and nothing else.

"Oh, foot."

I'd hoped it was only the Heathwood mirrors playing tricks, but it seems I am not reflected in any mirrors anywhere. I feel punched. Strangely empty. Dangerous, too— like a girl with nothing to lose.

Back in the party room, Annamae props a map on a metal stand.

I squint at it. Then reel back.

Dear God, they're building the new colored cemetery on *swampland,* out where floods swallow the earth half the year. The worst possible place for a cemetery.

Why, Annamae has done some ugly things in her life, but this takes the cake. You can't bury bodies in a swamp—not if you expect them to stay buried! Does Odessa have people out there? Will my mother also be re-buried in that fly-infested wasteland?

"No," I blurt out. "You can't put a cemetery *there.*"

Heads turn.

"Why, bless your heart, it's as good as *done,*" Annamae coos. "They're exhumin' bodies Thursday."

"That's swampland. If it rains ... if there's a flood ..."

A scream builds behind my tongue, imagining caskets washed up on lawns, bodies spread over Colored Town like litter after a hurricane. For the first time since I have known my friend, I truly hate her.

"You have to stop this, Annamae. And I mean *now*."

Whispers sweep around the room.

"Magnolia, think of your grandmother. Can she truly rest in peace, surrounded by Negroes?"

"She always lived with Negroes. So does everyone. So do you!"

"You sound like an integrationist."

I answer without thinking. "I am not! Take it back!"

Then I remember, and slump. Who in creation am I? *What* am I?

Your place is here, Grandmother said. But what loyalty do I owe the woman who kept my mother's name from me?

"I can't be here," I mumble.

Ice creeps into Annamae's eyes. "Yes. I think you'd best go."

Annamae just kicked me out of her party, and the room is eerily quiet.

Behind me, the kitchen brims with cemetery-themed cupcakes. They're decorated with black-frosted letters, spelling *R.I.P.*

God, the food in this house *reeks*. It assaults me, that

55

scent of spoil and rot. Sickened, I run for the door, crashing through the screen and onto the front lawn. My heart beats recklessly.

"Jackson! Can I borrow a flashlight?"

He scratches his head, avoiding the nasty bruise. "You wanna play?"

Oh, but I do feel sorry for him. "No, thank you. I'm takin' a walk."

He tosses me a flashlight, then scampers back to his friends.

I hurry toward Cemetery Road. The sun sets over Eureka's four-hundred-year-old longleaf pines, bathing them in crimson as the streetlamps switch on. A colored man crosses to the other sidewalk to avoid me, just like always—though I didn't pay it much mind 'til now.

The truth is, I have been sleepwalking through life.

Coward. I am a coward.

I sob aloud but do not stop.

It is not too late. I can still return to my thick, forgiving sleep, soft as cotton and just as white. With a few apologies, I could easily re-enter my life. Then—what?

I have lost my reflection and my respect for my friends. I have even lost respect for myself. If I travel the road Grandmother wished me to take, I will keep on losing things 'til the day I die.

My mother's name is Marie Ann Yates.

She was a colored housekeeper, and my father planned to

marry her. She is buried in the cemetery Annamae hopes to desecrate.

Jackson's flashlight swinging at my side, I walk on.

I would crawl over broken glass through fire to get where I'm goin' now.

7
Charlie

Three days ago, I didn't believe in ghosts.

I lived on a tree-lined street in the greatest city in the world—a city that's transforming in the year 1953, turning slowly, like a sunflower, toward justice.

Back home, I took part in countless boycotts, union rallies, and civil rights demonstrations. After school, I dreamed of becoming like Ella Baker, the first woman president of the NAACP, fighting for the soul of the city.

In Harlem, I felt strong. Brave.

Not anymore.

Mama told me to *fix what's been broken*—but I don't know what that means. Don't know, even, if the woman I saw in the strange mirror was real.

The gold-rimmed mirror gleams before me now. Soaking up the dying light. It looks so out of place in this country cottage.

Not for one second do I trust that murky portal to another world.

I pick up Nana's cane.

A knock startles me. I jump.

"Hello?" Another knock. "Jeannette Yates? It's Dr. Colt."

I run to the door. Three men stand on the porch—a doctor, a minister, and Darius.

My eyes burn. "You're too late. Nana is—she's—"

The doctor strides into the kitchen with his black bag; the preacher, Darius's father, follows behind.

In Nana's room, Dr. Colt bends over my grandmother's body. "No pulse."

I cover my face with my hands, tears leaking through my fingers even though I already knew. Mr. Lucien—a taller, sterner version of his son—touches my shoulder.

"I'm sorry for your loss, Charlene Yates. Be peaceful at heart, for Jeannette stands at Heaven's Gate, even now."

But what if she doesn't? Nana said the veil would be thin so long as her spirit hangs around. Nana might still be close.

Please, let her be here with me. Just a little longer.

With a practiced hand, Dr. Colt closes my grandmother's eyes. "Would you like to say goodbye?"

I almost say, *no.* I don't ever want to say goodbye to the

woman who raised me. But everyone's waiting for me to do something. I bend to kiss Nana's cheek. She still smells of the train, of dust and heat.

My grandmother didn't believe in happily ever after, but she believed in strength. Even dying, she marched me to the train station, suffered two days of heat and pain, and kept going. By the skin of her teeth she made it to Eureka, not because it was her wish to die where she was born, but because, in dying, she could help me.

She thinned the veil so I could finally meet Mama.

Nana performed a monumental act of love, a feat they ought to write about in history books—but only I will ever know the true strength of Jeannette Adeline Yates.

Only me.

Dr. Colt hands me two pennies.

"What are these for?"

"Local tradition. Fare for the ghost train. Put them on your grandmother's eyes."

I lay the copper coins on Nana's eyelids. Then I tuck the quilt around her sides.

Preacher Lucien prays: *"Yea, though I walk through the valley of the shadow of death, I will fear no evil: for thou art with me..."*

I'm still hanging on to Nana's silver cane. Clutching it to my chest. I don't feel like a young woman of seventeen anymore—only like a little girl who needs her grandmother.

Darius makes a noise low in his throat and crosses the distance between us. His eyes ask if it's okay to come close. I nod, and he pulls me into an embrace. His arms, though I've only just met him, feel protective.

"Her favorite hymn was 'Swing Low, Sweet Chariot.'" I speak into Darius's shoulder. "She used to sing it in the kitchen. Always wore a hat and gloves to step outside, too. I could never talk her out of it. Wish I hadn't nagged her."

"It's all right, Charlie."

Dr. Colt lays a white lace handkerchief over Nana's face; the preacher bows his head to pray.

Grief presses down on my shoulders, my head—heavy spirit hands, dragging me into the ground. In the circle of Darius's arms, I let my sobs come, loud and hard.

"You're not alone here," Preacher Lucien says, consoling me at the kitchen table. "In Eureka, we look out for our own."

"But I'm not from Eureka. I'm from *New York*, and I want to go home."

Don't mean to raise my voice. I'm only wounded, hurt.

"You *are* from Eureka," Dr. Colt says. "I delivered you here. Saw you take your first breath. You're of the soil."

I can't help but think of Mama. Her wedding gown, soaked and dripping.

Fix what's been broken.

"Preacher Lucien, who killed my parents? Does anyone know?"

Silence hangs heavy as a shroud.

"A little boy discovered your parents' bodies in the river. Later, we found their car in a field. Nobody knows any more."

"My parents were going to get married."

"Yes. They never made it, but on your mother's death certificate, we listed her as wife. Inscribed it on her headstone, too."

I grip Nana's cane, cobra teeth scoring my palm.

"Lucien," Dr. Colt says sternly. "We've got to tell her."

I straighten. "Tell me what?"

Preacher and doctor exchange a glance, but Darius's eyes are on me. Watching me like I might break.

Preacher Lucien clears his throat, settling in for a story. "The summer before I went to seminary, I worked on the white side of town, roofing houses.

"A boy named Don Bell worked alongside me. He had skin the color of wheat and hair just as fair. At a distance you'd think, *That's a white man.* Of course, he wasn't, or he wouldn't've died the way he did."

"I don't see what this has to do with—"

"Hush." Dr. Colt tugs his ear. "Listen."

"Roofing's hard work." The preacher's voice ripples across Freedom House's walls like stones skipped over water. "Hot shingles burn the skin right off your hands. Once, we worked for a white woman who pretended, whenever Don was around, that she wasn't married. She called him down every hour for a drink of ice-cold lemonade. The woman believed him white. Called him my Boss Man: *Mr. Bell.* Being young and dumb and flattered, Don never corrected her."

Apprehension creeps into my belly. It's not right to interrupt a man of God, but I don't want to hear this.

"Skin the color of wheat, and hair to match," Dr. Colt murmurs. "That's how it was. And what happened to him, John?"

"I'm ashamed to say I looked at Don with hell's own envy. White woman never offered me lemonade—not so much as a glass of water."

"It was 1935," Dr. Colt intones. "White woman'd rather burn her finest china than touch a glass after you."

"And my throat parched and aching."

It's a familiar rhythm, this back and forth. Old men talk the same way on porch stoops in Harlem—endlessly repeating their horror stories.

"So there I was staring down at the two of them, brick cooking my knees like hog meat. Wished it were me with that skin like wheat. *Me.*"

"Careful what you wish for. Careful."

"I saw it all from the rooftop on a hot day in July: The white woman kissed Don full on the mouth. Shocked me so bad I slid off the roof—nearly broke my leg. Don lifted me into his arms, cradling me like a baby, telling me I was gonna be okay. Finally, the woman got it through her thick skull that Don wasn't white but *colored*. She turned green as pea soup. I saw it. Well, Don and I beat it out of there fast as rabbits. Didn't dare wait for our pay."

"But you can't outrun destiny," Dr. Colt murmurs. "Not in a small town."

"God's will. His plan. In all its mystery."

Beyond the kitchen window, the dark's rife with sound: frogs, crickets, wind whistling through the pines.

"This has nothing to do with me," I say.

"So, then, the phone calls begin. White woman told her husband a colored roofer attacked her. Said she couldn't go to church on Sunday, for shame. And her husband told the grocer, who told the butcher, who told the sheriff's deputy. And all those white men waited until nightfall to ride up on Colored Town—"

"Don't they always?"

"Yes, Doctor, they surely do. To this day I remember the smell of horseflesh and leather. And the sound of his mama's shouts, because Don Bell wasn't yet seventeen. Like a fool, I ran into the street."

Dr. Colt clucks his tongue. "Nearly got yourself killed."

"But for the grace of God, Doctor! One of the hooded men trained his rifle on me. I shut my eyes, but the rifle jammed. It wouldn't shoot.

"Don wasn't so lucky. They strung him up not a quarter mile from here, Charlene. The shock of it sent your mama into labor before her time. Dr. Colt was only a medical student, but he stepped up while your mama birthed the two of you."

It takes me a minute to catch up to the preacher's words.

The two of you.

And Mama's ghost said I had a sister.

Darius looks at me with pity now. He's heard this story before.

How does it make any kind of sense that Darius Lucien knows more about my family history than I do?

"While Don was dying, your mother birthed twins," Dr. Colt says. "I'd never delivered a child before, and my hands were just a-shaking and a-trembling, because Don was my friend, too."

"Fortunately, Jeannette Yates knew about birth," the preacher says.

"Sure did. She knew when to tell your mama to hold off, when to push. Your mama kept screaming for your daddy, just wailing for him. He'd gone away on business, but he was supposed to be home soon. Odessa ran to Heathwood Plantation, searching, but your daddy wasn't there. The woman who came, in the end, was your *other grandmother*, Charlene.

"Blanche Heathwood."

My nostrils flare at that word—*Heathwood*.

Find your sister, Mama said.

"She died," I say—horrified. "The other baby. She's dead, right?"

"No," Preacher Lucien says. "But she was milk white, that child."

"When your mother birthed y'all, it was like a miracle." Dr. Colt speaks wonderingly. "One child so light. The other, brown."

65

"Charlene, I witnessed the hunger in Blanche Heathwood's eyes—she coveted that baby. It was the mirror image of what God saw in my own eyes, when I begrudged Don Bell that ice-cold lemonade."

Outside, an owl hoots, ghostly. Freedom House's shadows have thickened around us. Like the walls are listening.

"So my daddy—he was rich?"

Dr. Colt nods. "The heir to Heathwood Plantation itself."

"How could he love my mother if he was—who you say he was?"

"Well, they were young. Their love was a force of nature. Couldn't nothing stop it: not rains nor hurricane."

"A force of nature, that it was," the preacher repeats.

"Blanche Heathwood offered Jeannette five hundred dollars for the light-skinned baby. Your mama was still shivering, delivering the afterbirth, but Mrs. Heathwood opened her alligator-skin wallet and flashed those crisp green bills. Like we were still in slave times, and a baby was something you could up and buy."

"Well, Jeannette told the white woman to get outta her house. Mrs. Heathwood spat in her face, called her names. We thought we'd seen the last of her. But a week after your mama and daddy both turned up dead—"

A headache grips my skull. *Mama and Daddy, dead.*

"One week later," Preacher Lucien goes on, "Blanche Heathwood walked through the door for the second and final time. Again she opened her alligator-skin purse. Again your nana shook her head, *no*. I was there, helping your grandmother through her grief. Politely, I asked Mrs. Heathwood to leave Jeannette Yates alone. Let her raise up her grandchildren in peace."

Oh, Nana. *What did you do?*

"I know Nana," I say. "Not in a million years would she have sold a child."

"At first, she held strong." Preacher Lucien's voice drops an octave. "But then Blanche Heathwood spoke the two words that finally broke her.

"Don Bell."

I jump out of my chair. "Stop! I don't want to hear any more!"

An amber globe lamp pops, shattering. Dread loops around my spine.

Freedom House doesn't take kindly to strangers, Nana said.

"Sit down, Charlene," the preacher booms. "Story's not told!"

Like a marionette on strings, I sit.

And I look to Darius. I want to ask him to stop all this—to help. But a tiny window in my throat slams shut. *Shame.* I can't breathe for shame, though I can't say what shames me exactly: Nana's sin? My own ignorance?

Or my lily-white sister?

Nana must've given her up because the light child was safer with a white family. Being light-skinned means you straddle the color line, and that can be dangerous. I know, in part, because I'm relatively light. A pecan color, Nana always said.

I know what the preacher's trying to tell me. Don Bell died because though his skin was light, his soul was colored.

What color is my sister's soul? Does she know who she is—or who she's supposed to be?

"Now, then," the preacher continues. "Blanche Heathwood paid Jeannette for passage north—and for her oath of secrecy. But no human oath binds *me*.

"Only a few colored folk in Eureka know who your sister is, and we never speak of her. She lives like a white heiress, ignorant, but we don't begrudge her ease."

"No," Dr. Colt intones. "We don't begrudge it."

Finally, I've had enough.

This town is filthy with secrets. Sick. Before I came here, my life made sense. Fit perfectly inside the grid of New York City streets.

This swampy mess? I don't want any part of it.

"Charlene." Dr. Colt leans forward. "Would you like to know your sister's name?"

I can't think of anything I want to know less, because that would make my sister real. Someone I'd have to live with for the rest of my life.

"Please, just leave me alone."

The three men share worried looks.

"She's family, Charlie," Darius says. "Don't you want a chance to know her?"

I wish I'd never come to Eureka. Wish all these horrible secrets had stayed right where they belong—buried.

I stand tall. "All of you, please go home now."

"Charlene—"

"I said, *get out!*"

My own voice, like glass shattering, shocks me.

"All right," soothes Dr. Colt. "Coroner will be here in the morning."

The preacher leaves, then the doctor, then Darius. He's frowning, disappointed, but I don't care. I came to Eureka for Nana's sake, but I never signed up for long-lost sisters or gothic mysteries. I don't want any part of this southern-fried evil.

Shaking, I slam the front door.

Mama said, *Fix what's been broken.*

But how can I, in a town as cursed as this?

Soon as the coroner claims Nana's body, I'm catching the next train north.

8

Magnolia

do not relish the cemetery at night.

Mossy oaks cast frightful shadows, while stone angels glare warningly. In the distance, a train whistles, jangling my nerves.

I ought to be home. If Aunt Hilda's not drunker than Cooter Brown—a big *if*—she'll worry. Southern ladies do *not* go traipsing around cemeteries after dark.

Yet here I am.

I switch on Jackson's flashlight. Hill after hill unfurls beneath the moon, a vast ocean of headstones. Mausoleums rise: carved angels with stone trumpets, outstretched wings, obelisks. The cemetery's beautiful—bright Confederate flags decorate the benches, the trees. The air smells of azalea, but I'm the only creature in this cemetery alive enough to breathe it.

A sign directs me downhill: COLOREDS.

A week ago, my life was running along its charted course. I knew exactly who I would someday be: Mrs. Finch Waylon, heiress to Heathwood Plantation. Like a cog in the cotton gin, I knew my place. The colored cemetery never factored into my life's plan, and neither did my mother: MARIE ANN YATES.

A headstone leaps out of the dark, tripping me. I pause with my hand on my collarbone, catching my breath.

On the colored side of the cemetery, there are no fancy stone angels. The headstones are small. But though the graves are poor, the offerings are richer. There are bouquets of fresh flowers, wine bottles, whole chicken dinners pecked by crows. The people in this cemetery are loved, looked after. They have not been abandoned to time and hired help, as so many white graves are.

What on earth is Annamae thinking, disturbing colored people's rest? What has happened to my old friend?

What happened to me, that I signed that evil petition so thoughtlessly?

The flashlight's beam shines on the headstone that tripped me: OTTO LUCIEN, BROTHER, UNCLE, WAR HERO. 1920–1945.

Soon I'll be face-to-face with my mother's grave. It's inevitable, coming at me like a train. In the night, a throaty bullfrog calls for its mate. I move methodically, reading off names, some of which are ancient. Some of these people lived and died as slaves.

Johnson. Walker. Heathwood. Bell.

Heathwood again, because many slaves were called by their owner's surname.

Clemons. Freeman. Brown.

And then, finally, my mother's last resting place.

MARIE ANN YATES, her headstone reads. BELOVED MOTHER, DAUGHTER, WIFE.

A low moan escapes me. The stars rearrange themselves above my head, shifting because nothing will ever be the same. Whose daughter was my mother? Did she have sisters, brothers, other children? *Who was she?*

Pressing my face into grave dirt, I inhale the earthy scent of loss. I feel empty as every mirror that refuses to see me.

A hand touches my shoulder. I cry out.

"Miss Magnolia, that's enough." Odessa kneels, still dressed in her work uniform.

I fold myself into her embrace.

"How'd you know I'd come?"

Tenderly, she wipes the dirt from my cheek. "You're a good girl, Magnolia. That's how I knew I'd find you here. Right where you belong."

I shiver at the near echo of Grandmother's words: *Your place is here.*

"What was my mother like? Where did she live and how did she—" My throat clenches. "Odessa, how did she die?"

"I can tell you those things, but not tonight. If you stay out here much longer, you'll catch cold. Or worse, a haunting."

I laugh drily, and after a beat, Odessa laughs, too.

We both know there's no place on earth more haunted than Heathwood. Not even the cemetery holds a candle to the place I call home.

"Come on. Or we'll miss the bus."

We hurry uphill, and it's only when the bus pulls up that I wonder where we'll sit, Odessa and I. Together, in the back seats reserved for coloreds? Or will we separate as we always have—practically family and yet oceans apart?

I cannot bring myself to sit in the back of the bus, in those cracked leather seats reserved for coloreds—years of Grandmother's conditioning have ruined me. *You must always comport yourself as a lady of quality*, she said.

So I ask Odessa to sit up front with me, in the space kept for whites. The driver could pitch a fit, but he recognizes me—calls me *Miss Heathwood*. In Eureka, the Heathwoods get away with more eccentricity than most. Grandmother said we could even get away with murder.

'Course, there's one secret Eureka would never accept.

Marie Ann Yates, Beloved Mother, Daughter, Wife.

Odessa and I whisper, careful to keep our voices low.

"I thought I was white," I say. "I have always looked white."

"Heathwood's spirits knew the truth. Didn't you feel it?"

My eyes widen. "What do you mean?"

"How many times did Miss Blanche or Miss Hilda lose something precious, or cut themselves slicing garnish, or take a bad fall down the stairs?"

"They were old women," I protest. "Forgetful and clumsy and..."

Odessa purses her lips.

Finally, I nod. Why, I may as well admit it: The house *does* treat me differently, though I'm still, quite sensibly, scared to death of it.

As with all plantations, restless ghosts wander Heathwood's grounds.

There's a spot in the stables, a foot of dirt where light never falls. If you stand on it, an icy draft will make your breath steam and curl. Aunt Hilda once joked that we should sell tickets for the thrill, but the truth is something dreadful probably happened in those stables. A happening the house itself has never been able to forget.

"I remember a haunt once called my name from the library. Beggin' me to come inside. I was afraid, but...I don't think it wanted to hurt me."

Odessa nods. "Be careful of them now, Magnolia. They may not take kindly to your passing for white, now that you know who you are. If you ever feel the air spark, like the moment before lightning strikes, stop what you're doing, drop what you're holding, and run." She pauses. "You can catch worse than a haunting at a place like Heathwood. If you're not careful, you'll catch a curse."

My mind latches on to that word: *curse*.

I should tell Odessa about the mirrors. Inexplicably, the words catch in my throat like glue.

When I first started menstruating, Odessa taught me how to stanch the flow. It seems I am more ashamed of losing my reflection than of staining a good white dress.

Nothing a little bleach won't fix, Odessa said then.

No cleaning solution can help me now.

"Please don't call me Miss Magnolia anymore," I say quietly. "You know I'm not really a *miss*."

"When we're alone, I'll call you plain Magnolia. But your aunt will expect me to address you respectfully. As will every other white person in town." Odessa taps my wrist. "Unless you make a choice. Do you understand?"

Yes. I could stop lying. Stop pretending, forever and for good.

I struggle now to picture that life—Magnolia no longer of Heathwood, but of Colored Town. How would I live? Where would I go? Who, besides Odessa, would ever love me?

"Plantation Hill," the driver barks.

Odessa walks me to my door; I needn't have worried about Aunt Hilda. She's nowhere to be seen. Like as not, she's already sleeping her whiskey-thick sleep.

"Odessa, won't you stay the night?"

"My husband will miss me. Got to get home."

My brow furrows. "It's after dark. And you're on the wrong side of the bridge."

Odessa pins me with a penetrating stare. "We're *both* on the wrong side of the bridge. No matter what choice you make, you've got to start thinking of yourself as colored. Especially now Mr. Finch is coming home. You won't survive otherwise."

That pressure builds inside my head again—the unfamiliar relentlessness of fear.

"I've got to break up with Finch. Don't I? But then—what will happen to me? I don't even have a high school degree."

Odessa sighs. "Good luck's coming your way yet. You'll see."

But I do not believe it.

I sigh. "Lemme call you a car at least."

Odessa hems and haws. Finally, she gives me the number of a driver she knows. I offer to pay, but she's too proud.

"We can't be friends, you and me. Not until you make your choice."

I nod, feeling wrung out—I still have not managed to eat. The peach I meant to have for breakfast tasted sour, which was strange indeed. Heathwood's peaches are famously sweet. And then there was Annamae's party, her appetizers stinking of rot—though, somehow, I was the only party guest who seemed to notice.

I head inside. Heathwood is stuffed full of memories, ghosts, and as many lies as we have lace.

Wearily, I climb the grand staircase.

I wake in the depths of night, my nightgown soaked through with sweat.

I cannot hear anything but the heavy *tick* of the grandfather clock. There's no reason I should be awake. I blink at the glass of water on my nightstand and find it does not look like water at all. It looks, instead, like swamp murk.

I pick up the glass, examining it. Silt settles in the tea-colored water. I hold my hand to my mouth, afraid.

No reflection. Can't eat. Can't drink.

What's happening to me?

In my bedroom, a small voice whispers: *"Someone's come. Someone's here. It's time."*

"Odessa?" I murmur, but of course, she's home with her family.

A ghostly slip of light—a boy?—beckons me.

I can tell he's a colored child, though he's but a smoky outline. A silver wisp.

Reckon I ought to stay in bed, but lately I'm lonesome as a cloud lost in the hills over yonder. It makes me plumb stupid, this aching pain.

So I follow the patch of flitting ghost through the hall, then down the staircase and into the moonlit night.

Against the night sky, the child shimmers in and out of view. His feet stamp the earth, leaving footprints for me to follow. Acres of fields stretch beyond Heathwood's portico, rolling all the way down to the longleaf forest, where a dozen shacks cluster—old slave cabins with rotting wooden walls.

The child leads me to the abandoned stable, fit to house a dozen horses at least. Today, the red-and-white building houses only darkness.

I unlatch the heavy door, then pull it open.

Inside, moonlight falls through the rafters, and the air smells of moldering hay. I step forward, and my teeth begin to chatter—it's the cold spot. The place where something horrible must've happened, though I don't know what.

"*Here,*" the little voice whispers.

Swiftly stamping footprints lead me deeper, past stall after empty stall. Finally, we arrive at a hatch in the floor. I kneel, brushing off the dust and hay. Funny, I have never noticed this hatch before.

The boy's spirit, gauzy as Spanish moss, flickers meaningfully beside me.

"You want me to open that hatch?"

He nods.

Sweat gathers behind my ears, but I have come this far. Groaning, I pull the hatch open, revealing a staircase below.

It feels like a secret. The spirit wants me to follow him, but I dread setting foot upon those stairs. I do so only because the ghost is a child. Not long ago, I was a lonely, love-starved child, too.

I force one step. Another. At the edge of my vision, something moves, rattling: *chains?*

Yes. Shackles are bolted to the wall. A terrible remnant of Heathwood's slaveholding past. Below them, a large, locked chest. The little boy drapes himself over it, ghostly cheek pressed to wood. He begins to cry, hopeless, each broken sound a coin dropped into the bottom of a well.

Oh, I do not like this.

Those shackles... that *chest*... it's too terrible.

"What *is* this place?" I whisper.

The ghost does not answer, and, honest to goodness, I do not want to know.

Get out. I have to get out.

When Eureka's deep-sown evils break the surface, it's best to shut your eyes. Look away.

I scramble back. "I'm sorry. Whatever this is... I can't help you."

The boy's head snaps up, and an electric heat leaps into the air. The spirit, so demure before, snarls.

If you ever feel the air spark, like the moment before lightning strikes, stop what you're doing, drop what you're holding, and run.

I tear up the stairs and slam the hatch behind me.

"It's a ghost, Magnolia," I remind myself, willing my hammering heart to slow. "Just a lonely ghost."

And it's true. Sad as he seemed, that little colored boy has nothing to do with me.

Neither does that venomous room.

Shivering, I make my way back to the house, the hall, my own safe bed. I sink back against my feather pillows, drawing the white lace duvet all the way up to my chin.

Alone, my pulse quiets. No need to think about the sorry spirit in those stables. Or the shackles on the wall, the locked chest.

Heathwood Plantation is a maze of misery, after all—everyone knows that. But the misery is ancient; it has nothing at all to do with me.

Someone's come, the child said. *Someone's here.*

But not for Magnolia Heathwood. The ghost was only remembering, replaying some painful drama from his life. I huddle under my covers, wishing for the void of sleep.

My loneliness is starker in the dark, as cold as it is sharp.

I might could live with such loneliness if there were any hope of change. As it is, I cannot help but feel that everyone who ever could have loved me is already dead: my father, my mother, even Grandmother.

I still have my aunt and Odessa. But I will lose one of them if I choose to be white, and I will lose the other if I choose to be colored.

Oh, that little spirit—he was just so broken and *sad*.

But I cannot help him. Heck, I can't even help myself.

"Magnolia Heathwood," I whisper, a lonesome dread building. "Southern ladies do *not* despair."

9
Charlie

At Eureka's train station, I slide some cash across the counter to the ticket master, a young redheaded boy gnawing on a toothpick.

"One way to Penn Station, please."

He holds my five-dollar bill up to the sun like it might be fake. "Train's due in two and a half hours."

That's a long time to wait. Especially with the sun beating down so hard concrete shimmers.

I hate Eureka with a raging passion. *Hate it. Hate it.*

Mama said I have to find my sister—and *fix what's been broken.* I wish I could tell her that in Harlem, I do fix things. Back home, I spend all my free time trying to make change. Trouble is, I'm not used to being brave alone. Always, I've had the community center, the YWCA, the church—not to mention the NAACP—fighting along with me.

Here, now Nana's gone, I've got no one.

And, no, I don't want to meet my sister, passing for white. I'd rather not think of her—or ugly Eureka—ever again.

I carry my leather trunk and Nana's cane. I thought about giving it to the coroner, so Nana could be buried with it. But the thought of never seeing it again twisted my insides into knots.

I settle on a bench near the "whites-only" Coke machine, dabbing sweat from my face with a kerchief.

"Hey!" the ticket master shouts. "That's a white bench."

Without thinking, I snap. "It's the *only* bench!"

"Colored folks mostly *stand*." The ticket master rubs the back of his neck. "Guess that's what you'd better do."

I raise my eyebrow, because he sounds deeply uncertain.

"Yeah. You'd just better stand over there by the Eureka Station sign. Or—" He smiles triumphantly, having finally figured out how to handle me. "Or I'm calling the police."

My body aches with fatigue, yet I have no choice but to do as I'm told.

When I was twelve, on my way home from school, I stumbled on my first demonstration—a rally protesting the lynching of Caleb Hill. A white mob shot him to death in rural Georgia. The rally leader called for us to write letters to President Truman, demanding justice.

I went straight home and took out my good paper. Wrote the president about Caleb, about my parents, and about how much Georgia scared me. Next morning, when I mailed it, a weight lifted from my shoulders. Caleb Hill never did get any justice, but from that day on, I was hooked on the fight for civil rights. It made me feel powerful.

Still, I can't forget that in most situations, I don't have any power at all. In this Black and white world, I'm as small and easily swatted as a fly.

At the platform's far end, dusty railroad tracks grin up at me. A rat scuttles along the iron siding. The ticket master never takes his eyes off me, like he thinks I'm going to steal the darn stakes.

Fix what's been broken, Mama said.

But who's Marie to make me stay here, in the scariest place on earth? She didn't raise me; she *died.*

Maybe if Mr. Lucien hadn't told me that shocking secret about my sister . . .

I shake my head, refusing to think about it. I'm doing the right thing, getting out of Georgia while I still can.

This *heat.*

I open my purse, looking for something to fan myself with. My hand finds the letter addressed to *Jeannette & Charlene Yates*—the one the Church Ladies left on Freedom House's kitchen table. I scooped it up before I left, then forgot all about it.

Shifting my weight from one foot to the other—I won't give the ticket master the satisfaction of seeing me sitting on the ground—I unseal the envelope.

Dear Jeannie,

> *I squealed like a girl when I heard you were coming home!*
> *I know you're real sick, but hold on if you can. There's someone I want you to meet—a young lady who turned out all right. I watched out for her, like I promised. If you can't hold out, rest knowing the child's fine.*
> *Hold a place for me at heaven's table, won't you?*

> *Yours in Christ,*
> *Odessa*

Grief shears up my spine.

This woman—Odessa—was clearly a dear friend of my grandmother's. They ought to have had a chance to say goodbye. And I think the young lady she writes about is my sister—the one passing for white.

The letter trembles; my hand's shaking. To calm myself, I conjure my first memory: a nose pressed against mine, and the smell of Mama's breath, tangy as fresh yogurt. I breathe in, out. Carefully, I fold up the letter.

What does it mean, that my plantation-living sister *turned out all right?* How does she live? What's she like?

I shut my thoughts down hard, because none of that matters now.

Then someone shouts, "Hang on a second! Wait!"

Darius jumps out of his mint-green Cadillac, tipping his hat to the slack-jawed ticket master as he runs.

"Charlie." He leans over his knees, out of breath. "Worried I'd missed you."

I can't contain my smile. "Train's not due for another two hours. You didn't have to sprint."

"Yes, I did." He clutches his crumpled fedora over his heart. "Because if you'd left without hearing what I've got to say, I'd never forgive myself."

"How'd you even know I'd be here?"

In the distance, a train whistles. But it's only a cattle car, headed deeper south—if you can imagine such a thing.

"Last night, you were pretty shook up. I just had a feeling you'd walk out."

Approaching the station, the cattle car never slows. It roars by in a gust of foul-smelling air. We're standing so close to the edge that Darius grabs my wrist, pulling me toward him.

"Why'd you come after me?" I raise my voice over the furious rattle of the train. "What's so important?"

"Miss New York, I came to tell you that *you're making a mistake.*"

I roll my eyes. "Nope. I'm making an extremely reasonable choice to get the heck out of the worst state in the Union."

He cocks an eyebrow. "Well, you do *sound* very reasonable."

"Thank you."

"Charlie, you can't leave before you meet your sister. She's family."

I turn away, pretending to watch for my train. "I don't want to meet any sister living up in some big mansion. I never asked for that. I don't *need* her."

"What if she needs you? Kin is our responsibility. When you get right down to it, family's all we have in this world."

"Colored folks need family, but she's been playing white. She has enough money and power to be fine on her own."

"She's your twin. That's no small bond. If it were you, Charlie, could *you* play white forever?"

I snort. "Of course not. I'd rather die."

He gives me a meaningful look. "Exactly."

Fix what's been broken, Mama said.

"Her name's Magnolia," he tells me. Though I didn't ask.

I tap my foot, irritated. "Why do you care so much, Darius Lucien? What's all this drama got to do with you?"

A warm breeze blows across the tracks, stirring the hem of my brown dress.

"I know what it's like to lose somebody important before you ever get the chance to know them," Darius says. "It's bad—the constant wondering, regretting. Thinking on what might have been."

My body softens. Darius Lucien, like every other Negro boy I know, is working through his own thorny tragedies.

"Who'd you lose?" I ask.

"My uncle Otto. My father's brother, who was also my godfather. People always say how much I look like him, but I hardly knew him. He enlisted in the air force—became a Tuskegee Airman, one of the first Negro fighter pilots in the country. Uncle Otto didn't forget about me, though. Wrote me a letter every week."

"He die in the war?"

"His plane was shot down over France. He left me everything in his will. That's how I got the Cadillac." Darius gestures toward his car. "But I never really got a chance to know him, and I think I was meant to. We're connected somehow."

"Your uncle's buried here?"

Darius grimaces. "He's got a marker in the cemetery, but there's no body beneath. Just an empty box. He died for his country, but the air force didn't bother sending him home."

Black veterans are never treated with the respect they deserve. "Think they would've sent him home if he'd been white?"

"They never even sent a flag." His jaw hardens. "Now I'm worried they might dig his casket up."

I frown. "What do you mean?"

"White folks are segregating the cemetery. Digging up graves."

I imagine shovels striking earth, caskets fumbled into the air.

Nana's going to be buried in that cemetery.

"What kind of town *is* this? In Harlem, we would never, ever allow—"

"I'm planning a protest, Charlie. Trust me. I won't let it happen."

I gaze up at this tall, handsome boy ready to fight the whole South. At the exact same time, we realize how close we're standing. It feels like my whole body's waking up, all because Darius Lucien's here.

In a flash I remember something Dr. Colt said last night, about Mama and Daddy: *Their love was a force of nature. Couldn't nothing stop it: not rains nor hurricane.*

The ticket master taps the kiosk, puffing himself up. "Hey, boy! You know the rules! You can't hang around here. Time to say 'bye to your little girlfriend."

A shadow crosses Darius's face so fast, I'm not sure I really even saw it. When he turns to the young ticket master, he's all courtesy. All polished preacher's son.

"I will do that, sir. In just a minute, I'll be outta your hair."

The redheaded boy spits tobacco into a tin can.

"You should meet your sister, Charlie. She'll always haunt you otherwise."

That shakes me. Sometimes, I used to find Nana sitting in our kitchen, staring at nothing. Haunted.

Was she thinking of my sister? The light-skinned girl she left behind?

Find your sister, Mama's ghost said.

In my mind, Nana's voice joins hers. *Find your sister. FIND YOUR SISTER.*

A train whistle shrieks, and I hear it again through iron: *SISTER. SISTER.*

I throw my hands up. "Fine! I've got two hours until the train comes. Guess I can pay a quick visit to that place—that Heathwood." Darius grins, and I wag my finger. "But don't get too excited. I won't be staying long. I've got to get home."

Then, like the southern gentleman he is, Darius Lucien offers me his arm. I hesitate only a second before taking it— my hand resting lightly on his starched white shirt.

The ticket master frowns as we pass by. "No refunds, gal."

"I'll be back in two hours," I promise. "I just need two hours, sir."

The white boy smirks like I've said something dirty.

I fight not to roll my eyes. Or worse, talk back.

Two hours, I tell myself. I'll get a good look at this sister of mine. Then I'll be aboard my train, speeding toward New York.

10
Magnolia

ome morning, I perch before my vanity, gazing into the empty mirror—that evil, awful thing. The glass reflects my four-poster bed; the peeling wallpaper; the black mold spotting the closet door; and nothing else. Certainly not me.

How many times have I sat before this mirror, rimmed with paintings of Negroes enacting their antebellum scenes?

I unstick a sun-faded picture of Annamae and me from the mirror's base. In the photo, we've linked arms. We both wear Miss Eureka sashes, and we're flashing bright, calculated smiles. To keep our friendship alive, I've always made sure Annamae wins that pageant—that I'm ever the runner-up.

Last year, Annamae won the ribbon for tapping in blackface; I purposefully botched a pirouette in my ballet routine.

Annamae Waylon simply *hates* to be shown up. After my outburst at the Gravediggers' Potluck, I'm certain she loathes me with the passion of Hades.

In a fit, I crumple the photo of the two of us.

Automatically, my hand reaches for a makeup brush, but I stop. Wearing makeup just does not make any sense. Who am I even gonna see?

Not Annamae. Not Lila or Susie Gimble, or even silly Annie Flake.

Downstairs, the clock strikes noon.

In seventeen years, I have never so much as prayed for my real mother. Never imagined her as anything but the fairy-tale creature Grandmother made up: the Spanish aristocrat who died birthing me.

As for my father, he died in a boating accident off Tybee Island, where we kept our summer home before the hurricanes claimed it—or so I was told. According to Grandmother, my daddy was a quail hunter and a lady-killer. She said he had the best tutors money could buy, and that if he were still living, our financial situation would have been resolved long ago.

Now I wonder if my father—*Dean Heathwood*—is a fairy-tale creature, too.

Marie Ann Yates, Beloved Mother, Daughter, Wife.

Did Marie die in childbirth? Did Daddy truly love her? If so, *how*? Raised here in Eureka, how did he see past color, race, and class? And what did Grandmother, with her fierce disdain for miscegenation, have to say about his choice?

"Sugarpie? May I come in?"

"No."

My aunt blows through the door smelling of her usual breakfast: Bloody Marys mixed with Dr. Whitkin's Miracle Powder.

"You'll never guess who's come to see you. But—" Aunt Hilda frowns. "You're not dressed?"

Wearily, I drop my makeup brush back into its case. "Who's come? Surely not Annamae?"

My aunt looks stricken—which means she's already heard the news. I ruined Annamae's party, and in this town that makes me lower than a snake's belly in a wagon rut.

Aunt Hilda settles herself beside me at the vanity, her hip pressing into mine. She examines her pouf of salmon-colored hair, her teardrop earrings. She doesn't notice that she's the only one of us reflected in the mirror—or that I'm staring at her, sick with envy.

"Finch Waylon's come to see you. He's dressed up fine, with flowers. I think he's here to propose."

I inhale sharply. "Auntie, none of my friends are thinkin' of engagements yet—"

"Why, none of your friends are Heathwoods! An old southern name like ours comes with responsibility."

I raise an eyebrow. "Like marrying Finch Waylon for his money?"

"Well." My aunt blushes. "If you *must* be so blunt."

Gnawing my lip, I wonder about my aunt. What does she know about my parentage? And what might she have chosen, in her drunken way, to forget?

I do not ask her. Honestly, I am not at all certain I can bear the answer.

"Oh, but I didn't have a thing to offer your beau, Magnolia—not so much as a glass of mint tea! Odessa's taken the day off. Someone took sick, she claims." Aunt Hilda wrinkles her nose. "Though who knows, with those people."

"Odessa *never* takes time off."

At my scolding tone, my aunt's hand flies to her red-speckled throat. "She does!"

"Name one other time," I challenge her.

When Aunt Hilda cocks her head, I can practically hear the alcohol sloshing around in her brain. "Well, Odessa's never here on Sundays, is she?"

I leap up, furious. "Odessa goes to *church* on Sundays!"

Aunt Hilda's face crumples. "Why are you so angry, Magnolia? Ever since Blanche died, it's like you've been replaced by another girl. An impostor!"

I realize, with deepest horror, that my aunt's gonna cry.

At first I feel nothing but scorn for her—a grown woman with skin as delicate as old lace. Then I remember how Grandmother treated her—never failing to put her in her place.

Shut your mouth, you old spinster, Grandmother would say.

And always, Aunt Hilda would shut up. Hurting my aunt is senseless—like kicking a three-legged dog.

I put my arm around her. "There, there, don't cry. I'm just—still grievin'."

"Why, bless your heart. Our Blanche was like a mother to you, wasn't she?"

At the word *mother*, my hand flies to my unruly curls. Even after they became fashionable, Grandmother hated them with a passion. Annamae used to beg me to leave my hair curly, but Grandmother wouldn't hear of it. I had to use the hair iron every day.

Only once did I refuse: before my first date with Finch Waylon.

When Grandmother came to plug the iron in, I said, "Can we skip tonight? Finch has never seen my curls."

Grandmother didn't even answer me. She grabbed me by the upper arm—bruising—and held me in place before the vanity while the metal heated up, filling the room with its stink.

"No," I protested. "You can't *make* me! I'm not a doll you can just—"

"Oh, yes, you are, little *Miss* Magnolia. You belong to Heathwood. You'll do what's best for Heathwood." She squeezed my arm harder, making me wince. "Always."

She separated a thick strand of curl with the comb, preparing to straighten it.

"What does my hair have to do with Heathwood? Why do you care—"

And then she scalded me, pressing the steaming iron against my scalp, letting the skin smoke and burn. A lock of my hair dropped to the floor. I screamed, but the smell was the worst. Human skin, burning, smells of all evil.

"Why, my apologies, Magnolia!"

But our eyes met in the mirror—and I knew. Grandmother had done it on purpose. The woman who supposedly loved me had hurt me. Burned me where a scar wouldn't much ruin my good looks.

And, holding my gaze in the mirror, she *knew that I knew*. Her expression emptied, growing impossibly cold, and in that moment, I saw nothing—literally, nothing—in her ice-blue eyes. Only a deep, eternal crevasse.

"You don't know what it's like, tryin' to keep this ship afloat," Grandmother muttered. "You don't know how I have struggled since our wealth was taken from us by Negro-lovin' northerners. You don't *know*, Magnolia."

Then, sickeningly quick, Grandmother snapped back to her old, smiling self.

"Now, which dress are you wearin'? It might could be the most important dress of your life! The teal, I think, or the pansy print..."

That night, Finch took me to a drive-in movie. When the credits rolled, he wove his hand with mine.

At Heathwood, Grandmother stayed up to congratulate me.

"Lucky girl." She pinched my cheek before heading upstairs. "What a lucky girl you are, Magnolia. And—" She turned slowly at the top of the grand staircase. "Ain't you just *so glad* we straightened your hair?"

Now, in my pink-and-white bedroom, I shiver.

"Magnolia?" Finch calls from the stair. "Can we talk?"

Aunt Hilda's mouth forms a perfect O. I pat my cheeks, aware that I'm bare faced and in my nightgown. And of course, Finch has never seen my natural curls.

I open the door, but only a crack.

Finch Waylon is admiring himself in the great hall's mirror. He is undeniably handsome. Every girl in Eureka appreciates his cornflower-blue eyes, fair skin, and that summer sunburn, straight as a runway down his nose. With one hand, he adjusts his tie. In the other, he carries a lily bouquet. He is every inch the southern gentleman.

"Finch, you shouldn't be up here."

He turns, holding out the lilies. "I just got back to town. My sincere condolences on your grandmother, Magnolia."

I pass the bouquet to Aunt Hilda, who flits about with them like a blind bird.

"Thank you. But I'm not dressed."

He flashes a devilish grin. "That's all right."

I blush. Last summer, Finch and I spent nearly every

evening going to drive-ins and picnics, kissing whenever we could steal a moment's quiet.

Now, knowing who I truly am, all our cavorting is cast in a sinister light.

He can never know. Not ever.

"I have so much to tell you, Magnolia," Finch says. "Let's take the rowboat out, just you and me."

Aunt Hilda smothers a gasp, because a rowboat is the ideal place for a southern gentleman to propose.

It's after noon—long after Grandmother ever allowed me to go outdoors in summertime. *You look like a rotten apple when you've got a tan,* she used to say. Like a good girl, I followed Grandmother's instructions to the letter.

Now, a rebellious spirit rises in me.

Blanche Heathwood is dead. I can row in the sun if I want to.

And I can break up with Finch Waylon, too. At least, I think I can.

But after that...well, I simply do not know what I shall do with my life. Already, despair tugs at the corners of my mind, revealing the gruesome lonesomeness that waits no matter what choice I make.

It is like some god-awful riddle: Neither colored nor white, what am I?

"All right, Finch. Give me a minute."

Finch Waylon smiles; I shut the door in his face.

On the water, Finch's strong forearms work the oars, navigating the channel that leads from Heathwood to Savannah and then, eventually, to the sea. I relax, letting my sun-deprived skin soak up the heat.

On Eureka's river, the living world pulses like a heart. Water moccasins live out here—also shy black bears, otters, and pretty anhinga. Most of the river flowing past Heathwood is cypress swamp. Trees stretch roots below brackish water, and perilous peat forms little islands for gators to sun themselves on. It is a devastatingly beautiful stretch of swamp, lush and green, but it is not trustworthy. Yellow flesh-eating flowers grow here, and poison sumac, too.

Finch banks the boat on a little island. A dead fish has washed up; it's swarming with biting flies. Finch unfolds his handkerchief, to wipe a slick of sweat from his brow.

Oh, foot. Here it comes. The proposal that every other girl in Eureka would accept faster than a hot knife cuts through butter. The proposal I was bred to receive—and now, must turn down cold.

I do not know exactly what I am gonna do about my being colored, but one thing's sure: I cannot lie to Finch Waylon my whole life long. Annamae's party showed me that right clearly.

Finch fidgets. "I made some promises to you before I went to college, Magnolia. Regarding our coming engagement."

My answer's locked and loaded—*no*.

"But the world's so much bigger than I knew, and so much more modern. In Eureka, times never seem to change—it's like we're trapped in some Confederate dream, you know?"

I blink, confused. If this is a proposal, it is not a very good one.

"Not that there's anything wrong with the Confederacy," Finch hurries to say. "But a new age is dawnin' in this country. And I'm not the boy you dated last summer."

He won't look at me. Fear wends through my blood, wondering if, just maybe, Finch *does* know about my race. What if he found out somehow and tricked me into joining him on the river, alone?

My pulse picks up speed. "Finch, why won't you look at me?"

His blue eyes meet mine, and I feel silly. It's just Finch, after all. The thoughtful boy I have known since we were knee-high babies.

"At Georgia State, I got involved with the protests. Mama says I fell in with radicals." He laughs nervously. "I'm afraid I have become an integrationist, Magnolia."

This is so unexpected that I forget we're in a rowboat—and try to stand.

"Careful!" He catches my arm.

I pull away, only just managing not to topple into the river.

"I know you can't have me now," he says. "I want you to know, *I understand*."

"But," I splutter, "Annamae's initiative. Aren't you support-ing it? And your daddy—isn't he some kind of dragon in the Klan?"

"Daddy's not happy with me, that's sure." Finch rubs his jaw. "But I'm a man now, and a man's got to stand up for what he believes."

'Course, I stood up to Annamae at her Gravediggers' Pot-luck, but I reckon Finch hasn't heard the whole truth about that. Probably, Mrs. Waylon told him I got hysterical over nothing. I could tell Finch what really happened—but I don't.

Never interrupt a man, Grandmother said. *And never argue with them, no matter how stupid they are.*

"As for Annamae's initiative, I'm fixin' to make a trip to Colored Town. A friend of mine's organizin' a protest." Finch smirks. "He has no experience, bein' a local boy, but I'm gonna help him. Together, we'll stop the disinterment in its tracks."

Gazing into the tangled vines, thinking of more import-ant matters, Finch seems to forget I am here. He takes a stick of beef jerky out of his pocket and chews it.

The smell shocks me—like the food at Annamae's party, it's rancid. I press myself back against the side of the boat. I'm light-headed—I have not eaten today.

Or yesterday.

Or the day before.

Dread churning, I lean over the side of the boat, checking

for my reflection in the tea-dark water. But I am nowhere to be seen.

And I think, with a hot flicker of terror: *Oh, Magnolia Rose Heathwood. You are crossed six ways to Sunday.*

Finch pockets his wrapper. "What's the matter, Magnolia? You don't look well."

I have spent my whole life never speaking my mind. Now, I reckon I've got nothing to lose.

"Finch, segregation *is* wrong. Annamae, too."

His jaw drops. Lickety-split, his astonishment gives way to cynicism. That sneer of his I have always despised.

"You're only sayin' that because we're s'posed to—well, we were always s'posed to marry, weren't we? The Heathwoods need money, and the Waylons need land."

Does he really think so little of me?

"It almost sounds like you don't *want* me to believe in integration."

He shrugs. "It's different for you. You're *Miss Eureka*. My southern belle."

"Miss Eureka runner-up, you mean. I never won that pageant."

He isn't listening.

"Magnolia, the civil rights movement is important to the future of our nation. But I surely don't want you mixed up in it. It's not suitable for a nice white girl. I'm sorry I can't marry you. I hope you're not—well, I hope you're not too heartbroken."

Heartbroken? Why, the nerve of him! He speaks as if I am a frivolous southern belle, with nothing on her mind but her suitor and her flower arrangements.

Then again, under Grandmother's direction, isn't that exactly what I have always pretended to be?

The sun has bronzed my upper arms, turning them a deep golden hue I have not seen since childhood. The color makes me reckless. Bold.

"I never said I loved you, Finch Waylon. Never said I'd marry you, either."

His head jerks. "*What?* But weren't we—didn't you—"

It feels good, this truth telling. "I assumed you brought me out here to propose, but I was gonna turn you down. Because, you see, I've changed, too."

"I don't understand. How could *you* change?"

Poor Finch simply cannot wrap his mind around the idea that I might not want him.

"You think you know me, but you don't," I say, loud enough to silence the marsh frogs. "You don't know me at all, Finch Waylon."

And the really frightening thing is: No one does. No one *can*.

On the treacherous swamp, my throat burns with the promise of tears.

Suddenly, a gator lurches out of the river, snapping three-foot jaws.

"Stay back!" Finch shouts. With the butt of his oar, he

punches the gator's snout. The leathery animal shuts its mouth. One ancient, alien eye rolls, considering me.

Strangely enough, I am not afraid now. Only searching for my reflection in the dark of that gator's eye.

I do not find it.

Finch strikes the gator again, harder. Tail first, it sinks back into the water.

Cursing, Finch rows us toward home. I sit up, minding the gator: a floating log with watchful eyes.

"I apologize for my language." Finch rounds the bend; Heathwood rises in the distance. "You all right?"

He doesn't wait for my answer, running a jittery hand through his hair. "Hell, Magnolia, that was the biggest gator I've ever seen. How old do you reckon it was?"

Now, like a good southern lady, I keep my mouth shut.

Finch barks a laugh. "Last night, my father called me a race traitor. Can you believe that?"

I start, recalling the yellow-green bruise around little Jackson's eye.

"Finch, why'd Jackson get beat?"

"Daddy says he's got to man up. Guess he caught him tryin' on a girl's dress. Why?"

Sorrow courses through me, because Eureka doesn't tolerate difference. It will force you into its molds: man, woman, white, colored.

Faint, I sway in my seat.

Finch catches me, wrapping an arm around my waist.

"Sweet girl. You must've been so afraid." He's finally looking at me like he used to: ardently, longingly. "You know, I've never seen your hair curly before. It's real pretty."

He lays me down in the boat gently, like I'm made of glass. He has always loved to play the white knight. All he needs is someone to play the damsel in distress. I reckon that's what he sees when he looks at me.

"You're full of surprises, Magnolia Heathwood. I never imagined you'd be so open-minded about this country's race problem. But—well, s'pose I take you out this summer." He flashes that familiar, devilish grin. "We'll stay off Main Street, so I don't ruin your reputation. What do you say?"

Looking up at the clear blue above, I feel my lonesomeness, vast as the sky.

Finch never loved the real me. Only the illusion Grandmother created—the white girl, the sweet girl. He came to break up with me, but somehow, my rejection has made him want me again.

Oh, Grandmother would be *so proud*. But I have never been so afraid in my life.

Almost, I wish the gator had taken me.

It'd be quick, anyhow.

11
Charlie

Oh, my God. I've gone back in time.

Heathwood mansion looks like the White House—or some other structure built in that time when Darius and I would've been slaves. Ivy climbs a toothy, columned portico, and ornate ironwork scrolls up the windows. Sprawling all around the house is land, acres of green. Fields as far as my eye can see.

Of course, I've seen pictures of plantations before—heck, there's a plantation on the back of the nickel—but seeing it for real is different.

"Wow." That's all I can say. "Just—wow."

"Yep."

"Feels like we're in another *century*, Darius."

"That's on purpose. Eureka loves its history—and hates change."

I swallow. "What did slaves plant here?"

"Cotton. And lots of it."

In Harlem, I knew an ex-sharecropper with scars on his hands, white and fine as ten thousand paper cuts.

Cotton hates to come out the boll, he told anyone who'd listen. *You get used to it, after a while. But cotton sure do* hate *to come out the boll.*

I hold tight to Nana's cane. "This is a mistake. What if my sister still thinks she's white? She could call the cops."

"Being colored's a tough secret to keep. Maybe she's been waiting for you. Looking for an escape."

"You ever see her?"

"Yeah." Darius parks beneath a waterfall of Spanish moss. "I've seen her around."

"And?"

"Well, our paths don't cross much. She lives like a white girl. You know."

I do. It's not safe for Darius to even *look* a white girl's way. Down South, one mistaken glance might mean death.

Staring at the imposing, white face of that mansion, I try to imagine a sister of mine living in this palace. But I can't.

"How does a Negro turn out, raised in a place like this?"

"Only one way to find out."

Nothing, and I mean nothing, in my New York life has prepared me to walk into this plantation house.

"Don't be scared, Charlie. Some crazy old white women live in there, but they're harmless old bats. Broke ass to boot—what folks call *the genteel poor*. I painted their porch last summer for spare change. Just remember to smile, and you'll do fine."

"I can't fake a smile."

Darius looks amused. "Really? Good to know."

I blush, though I'm not sure why. I need a break from Darius's handsome face. No girl can withstand him when he turns on the charm.

Probably he knows it, too.

Darius turns toward me. "Okay, New York, listen up. If you can't smile, look down at your shoes. If you're offended or angry, just look down and blank out. That's the secret to surviving Jim Crow."

Got to fight, Nana always said. *Keep on swinging. But don't expect too much.*

I push open the car door, inhaling raw heat. I straighten my plain brown dress, wishing it were finer. At the very least, free of sweat stains.

Silly as it must look, I bring Nana's cane with me.

"Go 'round to the servants' entrance." Darius leans across the seat to tell me. "White folks don't like Negroes showing up at their front door."

Up close, Heathwood's not as fine as it pretends to be.

The water the fountain churns is clogged with algae, foul. Around the back of the house, the paint mysteriously disappears from the porch: They only freshen up what people can see from the road. The weeds are the worst, overgrown and scratching at my calves. The whole place has fallen into disrepair.

Finally, I discover a back door marked: ENTRANCE FOR SERVANTS AND COLOREDS.

I knock twice.

No answer.

Knock again, this time with the cobra's two front teeth.

There's no bell, but there *are* horseflies the size of soda cans. I tap my foot, annoyed. Nana died to get me to Eureka, and according to Preacher Lucien and Dr. Colt, I've got family inside that house. And not just any family. A twin sister.

"She's awful, I bet." I march back to the front door. "A spoiled little rich girl with no mind of her own."

Despite Darius's warnings, I knock on the impressive front door. A petulant voice whines, "Go away, Finch! *Puh-lease!*"

The voice—stressed out, tearful, young—could belong to some random white girl.

Or, my sister.

Memories wash up like seashells at low tide. The press of a nose along the length of mine. The smell of someone's breath, both tangy and sweet. Always, I thought those were memories of my mother.

But what if they weren't?

Something at the core of me begins to tremble. Won't stop.

"Magnolia Heathwood?"

I sense her standing on the other side. "Who are you?"

"You alone?"

"No." Her voice gives her away—it quivers.

I roll my eyes. "You certain?"

"My aunt'll be home any minute."

"This won't take long." I steady myself. "My name's Charlie Yates. I'm wondering—if maybe, you know me."

Do you know you have a sister?

My cheeks burn, because I know how crazy I must sound. But the door slams open, and there she is: Magnolia Heathwood.

She's buffed and polished like an expensive vase. Her dark dress hemmed with real lace. But looking past her fine clothes, I realize she looks *like me*, down to the last loose curl. Even our eyes are the same exact shape. Yes, she's white as they come—with a yellow undertone, if you squint. She's also my mirror image, if the face I saw in the mirror each morning were white.

"What'd you say your name was, now?"

Her shoes catch the light, and shine. This girl would look right at home on Fifth Avenue. Next to her, I'm a street urchin.

I clear my throat. "Charlie Yates. *Charlene* Yates, that is."

Her eyes skitter. I get the feeling she's scared. That she's been scared for a long, long time.

"Come inside. Quick."

And then I'm standing in a foyer painted a lush turquoise—though the paint itself is curling away from the wall. I sneeze, because the dust's thick. The air, too cold.

And I'm thinking: *This is a very bad place.*

Nana's house is creepy, but Heathwood Plantation is on a whole other level. A velvet armchair bulges stuffing; mold creeps up the walls. My heels click against cold marble floors.

Halfway to the living room, a monstrous creation freezes me in place.

"Oh, that's just the grand staircase," she says. "It frightens some folks, because it's so black, but it's only regular marble."

Only reg-u-lah mah-boll.

The grand staircase spirals upward, a terrifying black helix. I don't like it, though it seems dumb to mistrust a staircase.

We stop in a parlor room that looks like it belongs in a museum. The girl gestures for me to sit, but I shake my head. In this room dressed with antique furnishings, I don't feel comfortable.

"Marie Ann Yates," she says. "Was that your mama's name?"

What do I call this girl? Miss? Ma'am? Nothing at all?

I opt for nothing. "Marie Ann Yates is—*was*—my mother."

She lights up. "Mine too! But I never thought—I never

knew..." Her southern drawl, a praline coating on every word. "Oh, foot, I'm just *so glad* you're here. Can you sit a spell? You've just *got* to tell me everythin'."

In this too-fancy room, I feel like a servant, not a sister. This whole adventure is starting to feel like a really bad idea.

"Miss Heathwood—"

"Magnolia, please!" She blushes, red blooming in light cheeks. "I am colored, that's the truth, so there's no need for *miss*. Honest to goodness, I have not decided what I ought to do, but I cannot lie forever. Already, I'm having trouble with the mirrors... and I can't eat a bite...."

I squint at this strange girl. Is she crazy? Has passing for white driven her mad?

Fix what's been broken, Mama said.

But how do I do that? Why am I even here, in this decrepit old mansion?

The slick black staircase winks at me, menacing.

"I made a mistake. I should go."

"No!" She jumps to her feet. "Oh, please don't go!"

I'm backing away when I see it: the mirror over the mantelpiece.

It reflects the sofa, myself, the grandfather clock—but not Magnolia.

Magnolia Heathwood casts no reflection.

I look back and forth between the girl with my face and the big empty mirror, feeling like the world has rolled upside down, revealing its dark underbelly.

Is she a haunt, a spirit? Or worse—a vampire?

"You see it," Magnolia whispers. "*You* see what I've lost."

I can't tear my eyes away from the mirror.

Magnolia makes a muffled sound. She's crying. Uncannily, she cries *exactly like Nana*, silently but profusely. Soon, the tears will drop from her chin.

"I don't know who I am anymore. Or what I am. If you leave now, I'll die—I'm sure of it. *Please don't go.*"

"I never asked for any of this."

"The mirrors. *They're trying to kill me.* I can't eat. Can't hardly drink. Can't—"

A low voice interrupts. "Charlene, oh my Lord, it's you."

A woman in a maid's apron steps into the parlor, shopping bags in hand.

"Do I know you?"

"Growing up, Jeannette and I were dear friends."

I remember the note in my purse: *Dear Jeannie, I squealed like a girl when I heard you were coming home!*

I gasp. "Odessa? Is that your name?"

She nods.

I point to Magnolia. "Is she really my sister?"

Odessa answers like a witness on the stand. "She is."

"What happened to us?" Magnolia asks. "Why were we separated? *What happened to our parents?*"

Odessa sets her shopping bags against the wall, bending slowly, like her back pains her. A yellow onion rolls across the floor, but nobody moves. Not me, and not pretty, bewildered Magnolia Heathwood.

"Your parents fell in love in this house," Odessa says. "Marie, a housekeeper. Dean, the heir. It was not a safe match, but it was love."

"How can you know that?" I demand.

Odessa's eyes fix on me. "Because when your mama fell pregnant, Dean decided to give up his life here—to marry her. Most white men get colored women pregnant, then throw them away. Not Dean."

I picture Mama in the mirror. The bullet in her head.

"It wasn't right for him to love her," I say. "He should've left her alone."

Odessa nods. "Maybe so."

Magnolia stumbles into an armchair, face bloodless. The grandfather clock ticks, marking every second.

"Because of Blanche Heathwood's wrath, Dean had to leave Heathwood Plantation. Until he could get his finances in order, he lived with Jeannette and Marie at Freedom House. In all my days, I've never seen a white man live so poor. I'll never forget it. Never forget, either, how he held y'all, one in each hand."

Her eyes flick to Magnolia. "Dean Heathwood made his choice, you understand. He wouldn't abandon his colored family for anything."

"How long were we all together?" Magnolia asks.

"Your mama and daddy only had y'all for a few weeks. I believe they were planning to go North, eventually. Raise their family somewhere safer.

"But Dean got the idea to marry Marie in Pennsylvania. Take a road trip, make their marriage official. I remember Marie's wedding dress, studded with real pearls—Jeannette poured her heart into sewing it."

My hands ball into fists, remembering what that wedding dress looked like drenched in river water.

"Jeannette stayed home with y'all. Waited up for your parents to come home. Only, they never did. They vanished.

"Week after that, a little boy found their bodies in the river."

Magnolia cries out, but I'm not thinking about her.

I grip my elbows, imagining Nana waiting for her daughter and son-in-law to return while the sun dipped low. Caring for twin babies with shaking hands. Knowing in her heart that something had gone terribly wrong.

"Grandmother said Daddy died in an accident on Tybee Island," Magnolia whispers.

Odessa speaks bluntly. "She lied."

"But who would kill them?"

"My guess is, some Klansmen stopped a mixed couple on the road—or any poor whites just as hateful as Klan. Your grandmother was saving face, telling that lie about Tybee."

Silence falls, leaving me shattered.

"It's awful," Magnolia breathes. "It's just so incredibly *awful!*"

My light-skinned colored sister is very dramatic—but she's not wrong.

My sister. I have a *sister.*

With a jolt, I realize that I'm not alone in my grief for Mama and Daddy. Magnolia Heathwood grieves with me. Has she, too, always felt an empty place in her heart—an endless lack?

I turn, and see her fresh. She's biting her lower lip just like I do.

If I hadn't come here...if I'd boarded the train...

Tears course down Magnolia's face, streaming like Nana's used to. She looks at me with tender misery; her skin even whiter, for shock.

As if unable to contain herself, my polished double stumbles forward, reaching for me with pale arms.

At first I think she's going to attack me. That's how white she looks.

But she embraces me instead. Stiffening at first, I let her. I'm not a hugger. New Yorkers usually aren't.

Unexpectedly, I melt.

Pressed cheek to cheek, I inhale my oldest memory, tangy and sweet—*her.*

Not Mama. *Magnolia.* In my sister's arms, whatever's been trembling at my center since I set foot inside Heathwood finally stills, and for the first time since I came to this godforsaken town, I feel safe.

Odessa puts a hand over her heart. "If Jeannette had only lived to see the day."

And that's when I know for certain: I'm not going to make my train.

Because I can't leave Eureka. Not yet.

12
Magnolia

The day has taken the very strangest of turns.

An hour ago, I was sunk in lonesomeness so deep, it seemed better to die. Then a girl appeared, a stranger with my likeness if not my skin, and now I'm speeding toward Colored Town in the back seat of a colored man's Cadillac, not an arm's length away from my long-lost twin sister.

I do not hold it against pretty Miss Yates that she is rude, northern, and colored. On the contrary, I rather like her insolent ways. In the car, she sits with her arms crossed over her chest, casting a judgmental eye over everything. She prefers to be called Charlie, never mind that it's a man's name. When she speaks, her accent reminds me of machine-gun fire in the movies, *rat-tat-tat.*

Try as I might, I cannot stop staring at her.

In the passenger seat, Odessa holds her purse in her lap. Beside her is Darius Lucien—the colored man driving us to my grandmother's house. My *Negro* grandmother, that is: a woman named Jeannette Yates, who I learned of and lost in the same instant.

She came home sick, Odessa explained as she hustled me into the stranger's car. *She died last night. A stroke.*

I wish Charlie and I were alone. There's so much I want to ask her, so very much I wish to say. I have the strongest impulse to touch her, but I do not want to deter her with my eagerness.

Charlie grips the neck of the strange cane she carries: some kind of snake, very exotic and African-looking.

"Was that your grandmother's?"

Charlie levels her cool gaze on me. "This was Nana's cane, yes."

I wince. My own grandmother would never have permitted a pet name like "Nana."

"It's weird, though. I don't remember Nana buying this old thing in New York. Odessa?" Charlie leans forward, and Odessa cups her ear. "Did Nana get this cane in Eureka?"

"I believe Old Roland crafted it. His people worked metal since slave times. Brought the trade across the water, like Charles Freedom's family brought their woodworking."

"Charles Freedom—that's my great-grandfather, right?" Charlie glances at me. "Our great-grandfather, I mean."

"Yes. On Emancipation Day, he took the surname Freedom. Built your house with his own two hands. Some say he put a secret in it, too—a hidden engraving."

"A *what?*"

"It's just a story," Darius says. "People tell lots of ghost stories about haunted old Freedom House."

"Some ghost stories are true, Darius Lucien," Odessa says sharply. "If you're not seeing ghosts in Eureka, you're not paying attention."

My mind drifts away from their conversation. It's hard to care about ancient history now, when I am sitting beside my sister.

I peek at the rearview mirror to see what we look like together, my twin and I—forgetting mirrors utterly reject me. In the glass, Charlie sits alone.

My stomach twists painfully. I find myself pressing my hand to my heart, as if I could stop some invisible bleeding.

Charlie digs determinedly into her purse, fishing for a drugstore clamshell, cheap and plain. She opens the little mirror, holding it experimentally, searching for me. I wish she wouldn't—I worry Odessa will notice. But she's too busy lecturing Darius to pay us any mind.

Almost angrily, Charlie snaps the clamshell shut. "Doesn't make sense."

Charlie Yates is the only person on earth who realizes I cast no reflection. Because she sees, I breathe more deeply. I am not going mad, after all—though I feel nearly so whenever

I think of my mother and father. The secrets Grandmother kept from me.

There was something Charlie said, too, about Daddy: *He should've left her alone.* Her words, accusing. But if it was true love, then surely Daddy could not have been wrong to love our mother?

Beyond the windowpane, trees whip by, tall sentinels in the dying, golden light. We cross the bridge, and the road beneath us is rocky and unpaved, the houses shanties with tin roofs. We drive deeper into Colored Town, heading toward the river bend. I smell salt and marshland.

I do not believe I have traveled so deep into Colored Town before. There is far more poverty here than I have ever seen on the white side of town—though we have our share-croppers and hand-to-mouth families, too. Out here, though, the poverty seems purposeful—like it's meant to humiliate.

Why, for instance, are some of these families still drinking from a well?

And why do the people look so wary, afraid?

Darius parks outside a rustic cabin. *Freedom House.* Every nerve in my body tingles, knowing I lived here—if only for a few short weeks. It is a world away from Heathwood, this cottage where I was once an infant in my mother's arms.

Odessa turns in her seat. "Charlene, the preacher and I decided to hold off on burying your grandmother. What with the trouble at the cemetery."

I wince, remembering Annamae's centerpieces: headstones amid barbed wire. And I very carefully do not think of the petition I signed to help bring this evil about. I won't be able to face my sister, if I do.

Charlie's riled up. "Well, when exactly are you planning on burying her?"

"We don't know."

"She came all this way to be buried where she was born."

"We'd like to hold a repast for her tomorrow night. We can do that much, at least."

"A what?"

Darius Lucien interjects. "A funeral feast."

"Okay. Where's this thing going to be?"

"At her home, of course," Odessa says. "At Freedom House."

Charlie's brows knit. "I'm sorry—my grandmother just died and I have to throw a—what? A party?"

"All Colored Town will show out. Folks will bring plenty of food, but it's best to have something on hand just in case. Need any flour? Sugar?"

I watch, fascinated, as Charlie grits her teeth. "I don't cook."

"I do," I say softly.

Odessa smiles. "You're in good hands, Charlene. I'll see y'all tomorrow."

Charlie gets out of the car, grumbling under her breath. My palms begin to sweat.

Darius opens my door, offering me his hand. I have never touched a colored boy. Not once.

He raises his eyebrows. "You ready for this, Miss Magnolia?"

He is asking: Am I ready to be colored? Or am I still hateful like Annamae, the sort of girl who wouldn't be caught dead taking the hand of a Negro boy?

Odessa said, *You've got to make a choice.*

Charlie stands on Freedom House's rickety front porch, squinting against the sun. Waiting for me.

"I think so, Mr. Lucien."

He laughs. "Nobody ever calls me mister."

"Then I reckon you best not call me *miss*."

He tips his hat. "Magnolia, then."

"Thank you," I say—but he only has eyes for Charlie. She looks achingly lovely in the blue light of evening.

She smiles tentatively at me, and my whole body warms.

I was lost at Heathwood, a southern belle raised for marriage but doomed, since birth, to fail at my white woman's role. Now my sister is here, opening the door to a whole new world. For the first time in ages, I feel hopeful instead of empty.

It's like winning the lottery, a second chance at life.

Do not mess this up, Magnolia, I scold myself. *A chance like this won't come again.*

My sister and I do not go inside, not at first.

We watch Darius and Odessa drive off. We wave to

them. Then sit in the wooden rocking chairs outside the blue-painted door.

It's dusk. The flies are biting, and the wooden porch beams look rickety, unstable. Marsh fern and wild daisies grow between wooden slats.

I am not sure what I am supposed to say to my sister. Neither is she. And so, we simply sit.

Charlie twirls something between her fingers—a photograph.

"What is that?"

"Me and Nana." She hands the picture to me, a touch reluctantly.

Looking at Charlie and her nana, my heart sinks. Never once did Grandmother smile so brightly when I was around. Never once did I feel the love that's plain to see between Charlie and the woman who raised her.

I sweep my thumb over their happy faces. "How lucky you are."

"Well, she's dead now," Charlie snaps. "And with those fools segregating the cemetery, I can't even bury her."

"I'm sorry."

Charlie shrugs, not looking at me.

My stomach growls, loudly and unpleasantly.

Charlie turns business-like. "You said you can't eat. Is that right?"

At Annamae's party, the food smelled of rot. Even Finch

Waylon's jerky turned my stomach. And at Heathwood, the water glass on my nightstand was filled with swamp murk. It's been ages since I have eaten a meal. I feel impossibly light, like I might float away. How long can a person live without eating? And what does this have to do with my lost reflection?

Charlie scans my face, and I'm touched by how worried she looks.

"Okay," Charlie says brusquely. "Let's get you inside."

13
Charlie

I riffle through the pantry, but out of the corner of my eye, I'm watching Magnolia Heathwood take in Nana's country-plain house.

Fix what's been broken, Mama said.

I still don't know what she meant—and this Magnolia. She's just so *white.*

Doesn't help that her hands look soft—has she ever worked a day in her life?—or that she's clearly been pampered like a priceless creature. Sure, she's colored now. But for years and years, she was the kind of white girl the world bends over backward to protect from colored folks like me. Can't pretend *that* doesn't sting.

And yet, I asked her to come home with me. Let Darius

and Odessa drop us off alone. I can't explain why I feel so drawn to her. Maybe it's just that I don't have anyone else... unless you count Mama's spirit. If she's still around.

"I like your cottage," Magnolia says quietly.

"It's not really mine. Sit down."

She frowns at the table.

"*What?* Is this place too poor for you?"

She blinks. "I was only thinking—you need fresh flowers here."

In her southern drawl, *here* comes out *he-ah.*

"You want to decorate this place?"

"Wouldn't hurt to pretty it up before the repast." She pauses. "Why do you go by Charlie, anyhow? Charlene is such a pretty name."

"Too frilly. In New York, I'm going to be an organizer. I don't have time for flowers, or long southern names, either."

"So, you're a—civil rights protester? Does that pay?"

"Not really. I only participated after school. Now that I've got my diploma, I need to find a day job. Maybe secretarial work."

"Or you could marry someone with money."

A plate of chicken in my arms, I freeze. "Magnolia. We're *way* too young to marry."

"'Til recently, I was gonna be engaged." She runs a finger over my kitchen table, like checking for grime. "I was s'posed to marry Finch Waylon. He's quite wealthy, but—well. I can't lie to him forever."

The word sounds like, *for-evah*.

"You never wanted a job?"

"Oh, Lord no!" She pauses. "College might be nice, but a job would be terribly tacky. Anyway, I never got my high school degree. I'm three credits short."

"You never graduated?"

Magnolia examines pristine fingernails. "Grandmother always said schoolin' ain't worth a young lady's time."

What planet is Magnolia Heathwood living on? Raising me, Nana made darn sure I graduated from high school—with honors.

I set the chicken down. "Let me get this straight. Your life plan was to marry money and sit around looking pretty?"

She's so light-skinned she blushes pink. "There's more to it than that. I'd also keep house, manage our finances, hire the help. And throw parties. A southern lady must be social. Perhaps one day there would be children." She frowns. "Well. All that is impossible now."

"Magnolia, I hate to say it, but those are boring dreams."

Her face falls. "I was never allowed to have any others."

Across the table, we stare at each other. Color aside, it's like looking in a mirror—though our lives couldn't be more different.

"You need to eat. Here."

Daintily, she lifts a chicken wing. Takes a bite. Then spits it into her hand.

"What's wrong?"

Her eyes are very round. "It takes like—dust. Ash."

I try it for myself. "Tastes fine to me. Let's try something else."

Though I put plate after plate of Church Lady food in front of my sister, she can't swallow any of it. Not the oyster rice, not the grits, not even the blackberry pie.

Finally, Magnolia looks at me, eyes pleading. "You see? The mirrors are trying to kill me."

A chill runs up my spine. "Your reflection disappeared—when?"

"As soon as Grandmother told me that I'm colored. Charlie, it felt like a curse."

She looks so scared, this light-skinned girl. And then, for the second time today, she starts to cry. Holding her hands up helplessly.

I blow out a breath, because I know what I have to do.

I have to get this girl to Mama.

"Come on." I grab her arm.

"Where're we goin'?"

I pull her into Mama's bedroom, then settle her in front of the black mirror, still slashed and broken. The scarred glass spelling HEATHWOOD.

"Heavens to Betsy. This is a *Heathwood mirror!*"

"Magnolia, *Mama's inside it.* When Nana died, she thinned the veil. Made it possible for me to meet Mama. Maybe you can, too."

I know how crazy I sound. Don't care.

Though Magnolia and I stand together, in the mirror it looks like I'm standing alone. I see my brown eyes, my chaotic curls, my brown skin—but not Magnolia at all.

A curse, Magnolia said—and I don't think she's wrong. If anyplace on earth were home to curses, wouldn't it be Eureka? And hasn't my colored sister been living all her life in a plantation house?

Abruptly, the air is chilled, like a breath out of a refrigerator. I forgot how scary this black mirror is. The lights flicker around us, and there's a buzzing inside my head that won't quit.

"Charlie—" Magnolia says, uncertain.

"Hang on. Just wait."

My breath, in the cage of my chest, comes hard and loud. I'm ready to see Mama again. I'm dying to see her.

Clouds gather in the black glass. Magnolia and I both stumble back—we wind up on top of each other, clutching elbows.

Mama's watery voice whispers, *"I'm sorry."*

No. Grief slams into me like a freight train, because Nana's magic is wearing off. Mama can't appear in the glass anymore.

But whatever spell Nana's dying cast is not all gone—not yet.

Mama's using the mirror in a new way. *Showing us something.*

A scene shivers into view, and my stomach drops like I missed a stair. Two people—*Mama and Daddy*—smile shyly in a big, fancy kitchen. Mama's wearing the same apron Odessa had on at Heathwood. Daddy, handsome, says something to make her laugh. They hold a leatherbound book between them. It's titled *Love Sonnets*. It's a shock to see them like this—just teenagers, playing at being grown. Our age—and already doomed.

"It's our parents," Magnolia breathes. "That's Dean and Marie."

Smoky clouds crowd the image, dense as thunderheads. But Mama's not done. The clouds shift once more, coming apart like cotton candy.

Now we see Dean, dressed expensively in a three-piece suit, standing *in this very room*. The image is so lifelike, I look behind me—like I might see my daddy standing by the rocking chair. But of course, it's just an image. Magic.

Goose bumps race across my skin as Daddy strides toward us. He looks like any other white man to me—only warmer. Happier. I've never seen such tenderness on a white man's face before. Not even in the movies.

Dean Heathwood bends, lifting something into his arms. Magnolia gasps, because it's *us*.

When your mother birthed y'all, it was like a miracle, Dr. Colt said. And it is.

Dean Heathwood holds two babies: one Black, one white. He's crying for pure wonder, tears dampening his cheeks. My throat aches watching this stranger—my father—holding me.

Daddy. That's my daddy.

The glass goes dark.

This time, the darkness feels final.

"I'm sorry," Mama says again—faintly.

And that's how I know it's over. My mother has done all she can with Nana's magic. She's stretched the veil between worlds as far as it will go. There's no more.

"No," Magnolia cries. "Make her come back!"

I, too, burn to see Mama. But the mirror's finished with us. The glass only glass.

Desperate, Magnolia grips the mirror's golden edges. "Come back, I said! I want to meet you! Like Charlie did!"

"Believe me, you don't want to see her dead."

She whirls. "You did! Why not me?"

"Nana said the magic wouldn't last."

"No!" Magnolia stamps her foot like a sullen child. "It's not fair!"

That word, *fair*, galls me. After everything I've seen in Harlem—illegal evictions, police brutality, white men spitting at protesters—I don't want to hear Magnolia Heathwood talking about what's *fair*.

"You're spoiled. Always used to getting your way."

"I'm spoiled? You had Nana. A grandmother who loved you. *You're* the lucky one."

"You've got some nerve, calling me lucky. You live in a *mansion*. Didn't your white folks give you everything?" My eyes rake her dress, her hair. "Fine clothes, and all the food you can eat?"

She laughs bitterly. "All the cottage cheese I can eat! Grandmother put me on a *reduction diet* in the third grade, and do you know, I've been reducin' ever since?"

"Still. You're like a princess or something. I used to dream of the things you have!"

"I would trade it all for people who loved me."

I snort. "Miss Magnolia, *life for me ain't been no crystal stair.* Why do white people always have to romanticize us?"

"I ain't white. You know that."

"Pretty darn close."

Magnolia stares like I've slapped her. She doesn't make a sound. But I can see the sorrow sucking at her insides.

Slowly, she backs away from the mirror that doesn't reflect her face.

"I'm not white or colored. That's the trouble. I don't fit anywhere."

I'm stricken. "Look, I didn't mean it. It's just—this is all so weird. And you don't know what it's like, wearing my skin."

Magnolia nods, carefully not looking at me.

I'm really afraid she'll start crying again.

Fix what's been broken.

Okay, okay. Magnolia Heathwood's ignorant and a little annoying, but she's also hurting. We were babies together. Infants in our father's hands. Born light and dark, but still sisters.

I take her hands in mine, pulling her down to the wooden floor. We sit cross-legged. I lean my forehead against hers, trying to tell her I'm sorry. That I'm happy to have met someone else in this world who cares about Mama and Daddy.

Our heartbeats fall into step.

In the mirror, I saw the look in Daddy's eyes. He was thinking, *A miracle.*

Magnolia and I were a miracle. Maybe still are.

"I remember your smell from when we were babies," I say. "And I remember a pressure on my nose, just like this. But I don't know what to think about you. You're like nobody I've ever met. This whole southern belle thing..."

"If Mama and Daddy could love each other despite their differences, then we can learn to love each other, too, Charlie. Don't you think?"

I smile, remembering our parents laughing in Heathwood's kitchen over a book called *Love Sonnets.*

Magnolia and I were ripped apart before we had a chance to be sisters. And for what? To keep the secret of Magnolia's birth from the white community? Did Blanche Heathwood really want a southern belle so badly as that?

I shudder, thinking: *It could have been me.*

If it weren't for my brown skin, I could've been raised white in this miserable backwater, where it seems like nothing's changed since slavery. I could've been stuffed into dresses like a doll and told my mind didn't matter. I would've lost out on Nana, always urging me to be strong. To fight, even if you can't expect happily ever after.

I could've been *Charlene Heathwood*.

I hold my sister close, breathing her in. Accepting her, too, for what Eureka's made her.

"I'll try to fix us," I say. "I promise you, I will."

14
Charlie

At full dark, Magnolia and I cover all the mirrors in the house. Maybe if we do—if she isn't constantly reminded of her lost reflection—she'll finally be able to eat.

We use blankets and moth-eaten hand towels for the regular mirrors, and a sheet for the obsidian one. The music of millions of insects fills the night, but I'd trade it in a finger-snap for the sirens, neighborly shouting, and car horns of New York.

Embarrassing as it is to admit, I'm glad Magnolia is here. Freedom House gives me a serious case of the creeps.

With the mirrors covered, Magnolia tries to eat again—a

peach. She sinks her teeth into it, then coughs, choking. She spits the fruit into her napkin.

"Tastes like dust?"

"Worse. Grave dirt."

That rocks me. "How can you tell grave dirt from regular?"

Magnolia shrugs. "Just can."

Yikes.

Before all this, the scariest thing that ever happened to me was a protest gone wrong. One night, we marched outside the mayor's office. It was always going to be a dangerous action. To protect city buildings, New York called its police.

They tear-gassed us on the steps. Felt like my face had burst into flames.

When I finally got home, Nana held me. Told me, "You expect so much, Charlene, but there's no happily ever after for colored girls. No use chasing it."

In our isolated shack on the stream, someone knocks.

Magnolia's still scrubbing her tongue of the peach. "You expectin' anyone?"

"No."

Mama and Daddy were killed in this town—they took a drive and never came back. Now, we're isolated. Anything could happen.

"Charlie? It's Darius. I brought some friends over—"

Relieved, I hurry to let him in.

He quirks a smile, white fedora in hand. Two other boys

stand beside him, looking awkward and sort of cute. Country boys are different from city boys. Better manners, less attitude. Though Darius Lucien's got enough attitude for all three. Not to mention nerve, coming here at night.

"Me, Nat, and Joe here are planning to protest the cemetery disinterment. Trouble is, my daddy's forbidden protesting of any kind, so we can't meet at my house or church. I was hoping...Charlie, could we use your place tonight? Just to get our act together?"

It's ridiculous how happy I am to see Darius again. "Sure."

Magnolia leaps into action, setting out plates and cutlery. "You might as well eat. We've got pie, sandwiches, roast chicken..."

"*I've* got those things. That's my food you're giving away."

"You may as well be a proper hostess," Magnolia sniffs—reminding me, painfully, of Nana. "Reckon you wish you had those fresh flowers right about now."

I scowl.

Darius raises a paper sack. "I brought catfish if you have a plate for it."

Annoyingly accommodating, Magnolia provides a platter. How did she learn her way around Nana's kitchen so fast?

"Catfish! Why, how lovely! Did you catch it yourself?"

A hush sweeps over the room that I can't begin to understand.

"River's haunted," says the boy named Joe. "Nobody fishes in it. Not ever."

"Nobody *colored*, anyhow," Nat mumbles. "She looks like a white girl. What's a white girl doing here?"

Magnolia blanches; I'm at a loss for words.

The river's haunted, Nana said. *Don't go near it. Don't touch it. Not ever.*

"Simmer down," Darius says. "This girl's as colored as you and me—right?"

I lean forward, eager for her answer.

"Yes." Magnolia darts a raw, scared glance at me. "I am colored."

"And you know which side you're on."

She tilts her chin up. "'Course. I'm on my sister's side."

I'm touched—and surprised. If I were Magnolia, would I be so eager to give up everything—all that money and luxury—for a brown girl I'd only just met? What happened to her at Heathwood Plantation?

"There you have it, folks," Darius says, like he's closing the book on the subject. "Magnolia's Charlie's sister, so she's colored. Frankly, I've got cousins lighter than she is."

I feel a rush of gratitude. Even Magnolia looks pleased at his comment about his cousins. Not having grown up colored, she doesn't know how very many shades we can be. It's sad, really. Like a bird never knowing it has wings.

Darius, Nat, and Joe tuck into their food—which is actually my food. And they sure have a lot to say about this protest they're planning.

"It's got to be all of us, if we want to stop this thing. Get the word out however you can. I'll take care of the flyers for One-Eyed Red's—"

"You've got to get your daddy on board. The weight of the congregation—"

"Forget the preacher. He won't go for it. Keeps saying Eureka'll never change."

Nat cracks his knuckles. "Then you've got to talk to him again. We can't win this without Preacher Lucien. We just can't."

They argue some more, and I lean back against the kitchen chair. I had no idea handsome Darius was such a serious activist.

Of course, he's wrong about his father. A successful protest requires community commitment. Around here, that means it needs its preacher.

Meanwhile, Magnolia's running around like a woman in a television ad for a cleaning solution: Pine-Sol, or maybe Ajax. The pretty white woman in those ads always wears an oh-golly-don't-mind-me smile, and always turns out to have dessert in the oven.

I can't believe she's for real.

"We still need to talk worst case. What if they start shooting? Or use the fire hose?"

"Fire hose is easy," I put in. "Drop onto your stomach. That way, your back takes the water pressure. And cup your mouth with your hands, like this." I demonstrate. "The hose will welt your back, but at least you can breathe."

The boys gape. Even Magnolia stops wiping up crumbs.

"You've been fire-hosed?" Darius asks.

I shrug. "Oh, sure."

"In New York?"

"NYPD doesn't mess around."

Darius crosses his arms, eyebrow raised. "Okay, then, Miss New York. Do *you* think I need my daddy to pull this protest off?"

With all eyes on me, my face is hot. "For an action this big, yes. You need a preacher."

"And how should I convince the old man? He doesn't like his congregation taking risks. Says we'll just get ourselves killed, for no good reason."

Darius's father reminds me of Nana. Sure, she supported civil rights in theory. But like many Black elders who lived through Jim Crow, she never truly believed this world would change.

"Do townspeople want to protest?"

"Yeah. This cemetery business... it's the last straw."

Inspiration electrifies me. "Tell your father it'll be different this time. Because now, you have a big name on your side." I look at Magnolia, silently asking if this is all right. She hesitates, but nods. "You have a Heathwood."

Everyone looks at Magnolia.

"I knew you looked familiar," says Nat.

"I didn't know I was colored." Magnolia's voice squeezes small. "Not for the longest time."

"Passing's a sin," Joe mutters—though he has the nerve to take another bite of the pie she served him.

Darius looks thoughtful. "My father's big on symbols, being a preaching man. It just might work. With your permission, of course, m—Magnolia."

Out of reflex, Darius was going to call her *Miss*.

I get it. Her fancy white-girl outfit throws me, too.

Magnolia busies herself with dishwashing. "If I can help in any way, I will."

She says the right thing, but with an undertone that makes me anxious.

Darius, Nat, and Joe keep talking, planning. But my scalp tingles with foreboding, because I still don't know the rules in Eureka. What exactly have I just volunteered Magnolia for? If the preacher makes a big deal of having a Heathwood on the side of Colored Town, will her white friends discover who she truly is? And could that get her hurt—murdered even, like Mama and Daddy were?

The mirrors are trying to kill me, she said.

Suddenly, I can't wait for Darius and his friends to be gone.

15
Magnolia

By the time the boys leave, I am worn slap out.

Wiping down the sink, my face stretches into a yawn.

"That's enough cleaning for you," Charlie says. "Time to get some rest."

She helps me down the hall—my legs shaky as a foal's—then tucks me into our mother's bed. The one that faces the cracked Heathwood mirror.

It stings that I didn't get to talk to Mama, but I must endeavor not to be selfish. *A southern lady always makes the best of a bad situation.*

Only when I'm tucked in do I think to ask: "But Charlie, where will you sleep?"

She hesitates. "Not in the bed where Nana died. Guess I'll take the floor."

I sit bolt upright. "Not in your own house, you won't!"

"You know what? We can share."

Then, to my astonishment, Charlie slips off her shoes, leans Nana's cane against the nightstand, and climbs into bed with me. She lies on her back, hands crossed over her belly. My body sings, made joyous by her closeness.

Outside, the full moon's light falls through the window, illuminating precisely half of Charlie's pretty face.

"You ever guess?" my sister asks, in that blunt way of hers.

"You mean, did I ever guess I had a twin?"

"A twin? Colored? Any of it?"

"No. I never guessed."

Charlie's silent for a minute, and I work my tongue around my mouth. Since eating that peach, I can't shake the taste of grave dirt.

"Those white people you lived with treated you really badly, didn't they?" Charlie sounds like she's finally solved a puzzle. "*That's* why you're in such a rush to be colored."

Out of instinct, I start to protest—*Of course not! Aunt Hilda and Grandmother loved me!* Heck, the whole town loved Magnolia Heathwood, heiress to what was once the grandest house in Georgia.

And yet, I cannot forget the sizzle of the hair iron against my scalp, forcing my smile at the Miss Eureka pageant, the reek of bourbon in the morning.

"It doesn't matter. Not now that I've found you."

Charlie says nothing. Immediately, I wish I could take the words back. I am too needy. Always have been.

When Charlie speaks again, she's urgent. "Magnolia, are you absolutely *sure* you're ready to cross over? You'll have to give up everything—not just your family, but your safety. You'll have to give up Heathwood, too."

"Heathwood looks pretty on the outside, but inside it's rotten. Trust me."

Charlie rolls onto her side, bringing her face close to mine. "I do."

Impulsively, I take her hand, twining our fingers. Even in the dark, my paleness makes a sharp contrast with Charlie's warm skin.

I frown. "Charlie, even if I want to be colored—*am* I? Was it true, what Darius said about his cousins?"

My sister flashes a smile. "Ever hear of Walter White?"

"No."

"He's the secretary of the NAACP—that's the National Association for the Advancement of Colored People—and, Magnolia, that Negro's got *blond hair and blue eyes!* Down South, he worked undercover, investigating lynchings and hate crimes."

A thrill works through me, imagining this light skin put to such daring use.

"Trust me, Magnolia. You're as colored as I am. You just couldn't see it before."

Charlie rolls onto her back. Her breathing slows. Soon, she is sleeping deeply.

But I am awake, mind racing.

I met my sister today.

And in the mirror, I saw my long-dead parents. I basked, if only for a moment, in the glow of their true love.

From far off, I hear the murmur of the river. The one colored folk never fish in.

Grandmother's rasping voice leaps into my head: *This family did not survive the Union invasion for nothin'. I will have an heir.*

Blanche Heathwood's ghost would surely kill me if she ever found me here—sleeping at Freedom House in the same bed as my colored sister. Oh, Grandmother must have been simply horrified when she found out that her son, her pure-bred heir, had fallen in with a colored woman. But surely she couldn't have hurt a son the way she hurt me—could she?

I hear her shrill insults.

Forcefully, I push her spirit away.

In the morning, I help Charlie cook breakfast.

In New York City, they do not have log stoves like we do down South. My poor sister didn't even know how to light one.

At Freedom House, the food does not smell of rot—I can even drink a glass of water. But I cannot eat. Like the peach, every bite tastes of grave dirt, and it feels like a punishment.

Nevertheless, happiness warms me from the inside out, because today, for the first time ever, I am sitting to breakfast with my sister.

"What's it like living in New York?" I ask, eager.

She speaks with her mouth full. "Oh, wonderful!"

"It's not segregated?"

"Sure it is, but at least our roads are paved. White folks don't spend all day long trying to keep us down." She cracks a smile. "Maybe only half the day."

I nod, pretending to understand.

"What's it like, being rich?"

I am so shocked I nearly spit. In the South, it is very poor manners to discuss money. "Haven't you heard? The Heathwoods are on the decline."

She rolls her eyes. "Compared to everyone I've ever known, you're filthy rich."

"For girls in this town, beauty matters ever so much more than plain old money. Speakin' of which." I push myself to take a liberty. "You and Darius Lucien would make a lovely couple."

Charlie's jaw drops. "How did you—"

"I see how he looks at you." I bat my eyelashes. "Like you're the only girl in the world, the princess in her tower..."

"Stop it," Charlie says, giggling. "You quit that, right now!"

"Around here we say, *hush your mouth*."

"It's like another language down south, I swear." Charlie takes my accent for a spin. "You *hush your mouth*, Magnolia Heathwood! Darius Lucien's nothing to me."

"Tall drink of water doesn't suit your fancy?"

"Please. He's not half as handsome as he thinks he is."

I love talking with Charlie this way—like we're normal sisters. I'm sure it's only a matter of time now, before my reflection returns.

I hold up a tin plate, checking for it.

Suddenly, I'm about to be sick.

I stumble to the sink and vomit. Hands shaking, I run the tap, hoping to wash the mess down before Charlie sees.

"Stop trying to clean up." Cane in hand, she presses me into the kitchen chair. "Whatever's happening to you is serious, Magnolia. You should tell Dr. Colt."

"Oh, Charlie, I can't."

"Why not? Someone must've heard of this—this *problem*—before. Someone could help."

"I'm ashamed. I don't know what it says about me that I've lost my reflection, but it can't be good."

"But aren't you scared?"

I gaze at Charlie, wondering how to explain what it means to have lived white for so long. I couldn't bear it, if she ever came to hate me. Then I recall the little spirit who led me to a secret room—the one below the abandoned stables.

"Around the time you came to town, I discovered something. A hidden room underneath Heathwood, with a locked chest inside." I pause. "Charlie, there were shackles on the wall."

Horrified, Charlie takes a step back. "Are you telling me—did the Heathwoods shackle slaves down there? *People?*"

147

"That's just it—I don't know. I never wanted to face the truth about Heathwood. Or Eureka, for that matter. I can see slave cabins from my window, but Charlie, I don't even look at them. I pretend they're not even there." I force myself to meet my sister's eyes. "I have been sleepwalkin' through life. Pretending everything's just fine, when I know it ain't."

Charlie's quiet. I wipe my mouth with a kitchen towel, hoping she is not disgusted with me.

"I almost left Eureka without meeting you." Abashed, Charlie directs her voice to the floor. "I almost made that decision for both of us."

I don't believe her. "Really?"

"If it weren't for Darius, I would be in New York right now, pretending I don't have a sister. I tried to run away, Magnolia. How cowardly is that?" Charlie shakes her head, disbelieving. "Maybe if I'd gone, I'd be as cursed as you."

I do not realize I am crying 'til Charlie wraps her arms around me. It's a wonderful, unexpected joy when she squeezes me more tightly than before.

"At Nana's repast, everyone in Colored Town will learn who you are. I don't know how curses work, but…do you think that coming out as colored might break it?"

My spirits lift. What Charlie's saying sounds logical— assuming curses follow any logic at all. "Lord, how wonderful it would be to eat a slice of Odessa's pecan pie."

Charlie grins, and I smile back. I reckon it's our blood that has brought us together so quickly. Or perhaps it's the eerie similarities of our faces, making us feel like two halves of a whole.

I remember sitting in that boat with Finch, when I didn't rightly care if I lived or died. How startlingly quick everything has changed.

A hard knock interrupts us. "Magnolia Rose Heathwood! You get out here this instant!"

"Oh, Lord. That's my aunt Hilda."

So far as I know, Aunt Hilda's never even been to Colored Town before. Charlie trails me all the way to the front door. I open it, squinting against the sun.

Aunt Hilda's on the porch, her car parked catawampus on the street.

"So this is her," Aunt Hilda snaps. "The other girl." She looks Charlie over, taking in her cheap dress and bare feet. "You're *filthy*."

"Auntie!"

"Nice to meet you, too," Charlie deadpans.

"How'd you know where to find me, Aunt Hilda?"

"The *lawyer* paid a visit this morning, and you weren't even in the house! Odessa gave me directions to this—this hovel!" She purses her lips.

"Stop. Don't speak to Charlie like that!"

"The *reading of the will* is today, Magnolia! What if this creature—what if your *relation* inherits—"

Then Aunt Hilda's tears come, predictable as rain. She sinks down on the porch, half fainting.

"I guess I'd better take my aunt on home."

Charlie's brow knits. "Nana's repast—I can barely light the log stove."

"Don't worry. If there's one thing I know how to do, it's host a party."

Aunt Hilda groans. "Oh, my nerves, my poor nerves—"

"Get on up now, Auntie. Stop whining this instant."

I pull my aunt up by her flabby arm and tug her away from Freedom's porch.

On the street, an inexplicable fear seizes my throat: What if I never see Charlie again?

I look back. My sister is waving at me. Our eyes lock—mirror images.

A southern lady never raises her voice, but I holler: "I'll be back directly, if the creek don't rise!"

Charlie stamps her foot on Freedom's porch. "I told you, I don't speak southern!"

"I'll be back soon. I swear!"

16
Charlie

With Magnolia gone, the house feels too quiet—
and that can only mean one thing: I *like* my
white-looking sister. Breathy voice, southern
drawl, and all. It's weird, because I don't usually like frilly
girls, and she's as frilly as they come.

I could do with a little less drama, though. Why can't
Magnolia ever just say what she means?

I'll be back directly, if the creek don't rise!

Ridiculous.

But I hope she does come back.

Alone, I wander to Mama's mirror, still covered in a white
sheet. My fingers itch to uncover the obsidian surface and

call Mama's name. But I don't. It'll be too sad, when she doesn't appear, if all that's true about the thinning of the veil.

I open my mouth to ask Nana about it, forgetting she's dead. Truth is, I forget all the time. Seems like she ought to still be here, telling me what to do.

We didn't always agree, Nana and me. She always thought I expected too much from protest work. She understood, though, that I didn't have any choice but to take up with it. That it would hurt me not to fight, when I can feel civil rights roiling beneath the earth like the foreshocks of a great earthquake.

I remember when eleven-year-old Errol Lewis was shot walking into a bodega. The white man behind the counter said he looked menacing, but he was just a kid trying to buy bubble gum. After, the Baptist Church leaders took to the streets. I joined them, and it became my first march. I'll never forget the pins-and-needles feeling that lit up my skin, or how achingly good it felt to shout Errol Lewis's name. Nana said it was fine that we made our voices heard, but that we shouldn't expect too much. No happily ever after.

And yet...I can't stop hoping. Maybe it's the city in me. New York, with all its troubles, will always be the land of dreams.

I wander into the bathroom, splash water on my face. The bathroom mirror is cheap, closer to tin than glass. I see how tired I look. Wrung out.

And I see something else, too: The mirror is *loose.*

I grip its sides, gently pulling it away from the wall. There's a dark pocket behind the bathroom mirror. A cubbyhole.

I think of my great-grandfather, Charles Freedom.

On Emancipation Day, he took the surname Freedom, Odessa said. *Built your house with his own two hands. Some say he put a secret in it, too—a hidden engraving.*

Scalp tingling, I peer to get a better look at this secret place.

Around me, Freedom House groans. Impossibly, the floor beneath my feet tilts. I fall, hard, onto my hands.

Freedom House doesn't take kindly to strangers, Nana said.

Face-to-face with a haunting, I break out into a cold sweat.

"I'm sorry!" I gasp.

Whispers, all around. I can't see Freedom's ghosts—but they're discussing me.

Deciding.

Inside my head, an inhuman chorus barks: *"MIND YOUR MANNERS DOWN SOUTH!"*

Then, quiet.

A fine tremor works its way from my head to my toes. Freedom House's spirits don't want me prying into their secrets today. And, because the veil is thinner here than in New York, they have no problem telling me to my face.

I need to get out of here. Need to feel the sun on my skin. I run, full-tilt, for the porch.

Outside, I sit on the rocker, listening to the wind singing through pine trees. Wondering how anyone could live in a town so haunted as this.

Wondering, too, what on earth is behind that mirror.

A mint-green Cadillac pulls up. Scared as I am, I pat my hair, smooth my dress.

Darius Lucien cranks down the window. "Hey, Miss New York! You call for a cab?"

"Yeah." I shake off Freedom House's ghosts. They've got no place between Darius and me. "Can you take me to One Hundred Twenty-Fifth and Broadway?"

"Main Street, Eureka's as far as I go. But I know a place that makes a mean cream soda. What do you say?"

I really should be preparing for Nana's repast, but Magnolia did say she'd help. And tall-drink-of-water Darius wants to take me out.

How could I possibly say anything but *yes?*

17

Magnolia

W hy in Sam Hill did you treat Charlie like that, calling her filthy, calling her names?" I demand of my aunt Hilda, speeding away from Colored Town. "She's not some peasant; she's my sister!"

Aunt Hilda grips the wheel like she means to strangle it. "Heavens to Betsy, there's a colored sister in every house in the Confederacy! Why you have to go on and *stay* with yours is simply beyond me!"

"Did you know all this time that I am colored? Answer me, now."

The set of her jaw tells me everything: Of course my aunt knew.

Disgusted, I scoff.

"You are *not* colored, Magnolia. Not truly. You are not some common Negro, but a Heathwood—why, your breedin', your looks..." Aunt Hilda swerves, hard, to the right. "Blanche and I decided when we took you in that we would *not* think of you as a Negro. We banished the very thought from our minds."

"Maybe that trick worked for you, but Grandmother never saw me as full white and you know it."

"Whatever our failings, Magnolia, we did try. And we didn't raise you to go traipsin' around Colored Town, doing who knows what all. We raised you to be *white!*"

Like she's trying to kill us, my aunt leans on the gas. We're speeding so quickly up Plantation Hill we might just fly clear off it.

"Let me get this straight. You thought you could breed the Negro out of me; is that it? And then, once I married Finch Waylon, you thought you'd water my blood down even more. All along, you were only protecting the Heathwood line!"

The car nearly leaps from the hill. I grip my seat belt, praying we get home in one piece.

"I was protecting *you*, Sugarpie. I still am. Didn't we raise you to be a person of quality? A woman of *substance?*"

I glare at my aunt's profile. "Charlie has more substance than you ever will."

"Why, I oughta slap you from here to Atlanta!"

At last, the sedan screeches to a halt. Without waiting for

my aunt, I slam the car door and hurry inside, moving quickly past the mirrors that refuse to see me.

Though Aunt Hilda was kind to me, she, too, is part of Heathwood's deep rot, like the mold creeping up its walls. I will never forgive her. Not as long as I live.

"The library, Magnolia!" Aunt Hilda hollers. "The lawyer's been waitin' an hour already! Don't you walk away from your responsibilities, now."

I turn on my heel at the word *lawyer*.

I am ready to get this over with—whatever it is.

I follow red-faced Aunt Hilda into the library, where a fleshy older man sits behind Grandmother's desk, directly beneath her portrait.

In the painting, Blanche Heathwood poses on the lawn. But she does not look to be enjoying herself. She glowers down at me, stern and disapproving. And her eyes...they are frightfully lifelike.

I shut my eyes, telling myself: *She is dead. Grandmother is dead.* When I open them again, she's still staring, reproving.

I suppress a shiver.

"Magnolia, meet Mr. Cellars, come all the way from Atlanta."

Mr. Cellars wears black suspenders and a pinstriped suit. Red capillaries sprout over his cheeks, his nose. Like Aunt Hilda, he's a drinker. He raps the mahogany desk with stubby fingers.

"Now, young lady, my task is to make you understand the

choice set before you according to the terms of your grandmother's will."

Aunt Hilda sinks into a chair, crying like I shot her dog.

"My dear Miss Heathwood, might I offer you a clean handkerchief?"

"My niece has no compassion for my nerves!"

The lawyer nods sympathetically, but from the corner of his eye, he's assessing me. "It's a rather unique document, this will. In that it presents you, Miss Heathwood, with a choice."

Dread creeps up my spine, because Grandmother never gave me choices if she could help it. I glance again at her portrait, and this time, there's no denying it: There's malevolence in her gaze. A knowing, hateful smirk.

The air's begun to crackle, like just before a lightning storm.

Everyone's looking at me. I can't fall apart now. "What choice, Mr. Cellars?"

"Your grandmother's left you Heathwood Plantation in its entirety. In order to inherit, however, you must swear never to see your colored relations—your sister, or any kin of hers—ever again."

How on earth did Grandmother know Charlie and her nana would come back to Eureka?

The lawyer reads the thought in my face. "Blanche Heathwood believed in bein' prepared for any circumstance. She was not one to leave important matters to chance."

"Even in *death*, Grandmother seeks to bind me?"

"Hush your mouth, child," Aunt Hilda says sharply.

Mr. Cellars leans forward, curiosity lighting his face. I think that this must be, to him, an interesting assignment.

Above us, the electric chandelier flickers, throwing shadows like knives. In the portrait, Grandmother's face has hardened. She looks closer, too. Like she's inching forward on the painted lawn.

Convulsively, I swallow.

"It's a disgrace for Blanche even to doubt my niece," my aunt babbles. "Magnolia is a good girl, a sweet girl—"

"Miss Heathwood, I find myself parched. Can you ask the kitchen gal to fetch a julep?"

"Why, of course!"

Aunt Hilda leaves, but I do not think Mr. Cellars is really thirsty. When he works his girth around Grandmother's parquet table, my heart beats like a trapped bird.

What does this Atlanta lawyer see when looks at me? A white girl? Or a colored one? From someone like him, a white girl at least has some protection. Colored girls have none.

Oh, I wish I had never left Charlie.

"Listen, gal." Mr. Cellars flips his wallet open. "Your grandmother had some notion that these things can be kept secret. And they can, so long as you keep your two lives *separate*. These are my daughters. *Look.*"

He flattens a sepia-tinged photograph before me.

His daughters are colored.

The three girls stand outside a sharecropper's shack, alongside an ebony woman—their mother. She looks miserable.

"That isn't your wife."

"'Course not. It's illegal in the state of Georgia to marry a colored woman. Yet I do so enjoy my time with Mabel. Broke my heart when it came time to remove the girls from the city, set them up on a farm deeper South. It had to be done, for the sake of my professional reputation. So you see, I understand your predicament."

He smiles, revealing two gold-capped canines.

My skin crawls. "My father *loved* my mother, sir."

"No doubt." The words pour from his mouth like molasses. "But there's a limit to how much the races can love each other. God separated us for a reason."

Now I hold his eyes, willing them not to roam over the rest of me.

When they do, I quell my fear by pretending I'm Charlie. *She* wouldn't let this slimy man cow her. She'd stare him down, then spit in his eye.

"Perhaps God's made an exception in you," Mr. Cellars drawls. "You are the whitest colored creature I've ever seen. Cut ties with your colored family, marry well, and protect the Heathwoods from scandal. It's the right thing to do."

He is so close that I can smell his sour breath. "If I refuse, will my aunt inherit the house?"

"Unfortunately, no. In thirty days, the house and all its accoutrements would become the property of one Finch Waylon."

I gasp. "Why should Aunt Hilda lose her home? How could Grandmother—"

"Your aunt Hilda cannot bear children, or afford to keep the house for long, taxes being what they are. If she were to inherit, that would spell the end of the Heathwood line."

Poor Aunt Hilda.

She appears with a tea tray, biscuits, and drinks. But the refreshments reek. My nostrils flare.

"Now, sweetheart, all you must do is sign on this dotted line, swearin' on this good land that you'll cut your Negro family cleanly from your life. Soon as you do, Heathwood is yours."

Words leap to my lips: *I do not want Heathwood Plantation. I want Charlie. I want to be free!*

But Grandmother's painted eyes blaze. There's a warning in them: *Don't you dare.*

Oh, but I do hate her.

Because of Grandmother, I have never, ever looked into a mirror and seen my true self: a colored girl, not a white one. Because of Grandmother, I am cursed. Maybe dying.

Rebellious, I open my mouth—

And two cold, invisible hands wrap around my throat, thumbs pressing deep. An unearthly static leaps into the air, scorching it. I clutch my collar, looking to Aunt Hilda—she's still fussing with the tea tray, while the lawyer uncaps his gold fountain pen.

Nobody notices that I am choking to death.

Nobody, except Grandmother, picnicking on Heathwood's lawn.

My heart is beating terribly fast, and stars explode at the corners of my vision. Clawing, I find the contours of those ghost hands—*Grandmother's own papery, slender hands*—and pry them, finger by finger, from my throat.

Freed, I pull in a deep, hungry breath.

Mr. Cellars glances up. "I assume you find the terms acceptable?"

"'Course she does," Aunt Hilda scolds. "What girl in her right mind—"

"I have my answer." Voice hoarse, I look straight at Grandmother's evil portrait. "I refuse the terms of the will. I renounce my claim on Heathwood Plantation."

Aunt Hilda drops a plate. Glass shatters; biscuits roll across the scarlet rug.

Mr. Cellars bellows a great, belly laugh. "Well, seems I'm wrong! You got a colored gal on your hands after all. No, Miss Heathwood, don't waste your breath tryin' to change her mind. They're stubborn as mules. Matter of fact, that's what *mulatto* means. *A mule.*"

With thick, beringed fingers, the lawyer pushes Grandmother's will toward me.

"Wait, Magnolia, please think—"

Scribbling viciously, I sign on the dotted line, rejecting my claim on the plantation forever: *Magnolia Rose Heathwood.*

Mr. Cellars whisks the papers into his briefcase. "Well,

ladies, thank you both for a *fascinating* morning—but I've got a train to catch."

"Whatever will we live on?" Aunt Hilda cries. "Wherever will we *go*?"

Mr. Cellars is halfway out the door. "If the Waylons are a charitable sort, they might let you stay 'til you get on your feet."

"When will they be informed? When will you tell them that Magnolia—that she's—"

"Legally, I can't tell a soul what she is. However, the truth has a way of making itself known. My advice? Your gal should get out of town as fast as she can." His eyes roam over me again. "Atlanta's a fine place for a creature like her. Or so I hear."

It takes a moment, but Aunt Hilda finally catches his meaning. Mr. Cellars implies that I could become a prostitute in the city. There, my best and only hope would be to meet a man like him, who'd put me up in a shack somewhere—like his Mabel.

Aunt Hilda's face turns sheet white, then purple. "Get out! Get out, get out, you filthy man! How dare you make such insinuations in this house!"

Mr. Cellars closes the door behind him, leaving us alone with the library books, Grandmother's portrait, and a half-empty decanter of bourbon.

All of which will soon belong to Finch Waylon.

The Heathwoods are more than a family, Grandmother once

said. *We are torchbearers of the South's noble legacy, standing for white moral values. We are a symbol of southern greatness.*

To Blanche Heathwood, it did not matter that my insides were colored, so long as the face I presented to the world was white. The truth of my birth does not matter to Aunt Hilda or the lawyer, either, as long as I uphold the lie of white superiority. Passing, I played straight into the fantasy that protects their southern way of life. 'Course, no one cares that living that white lie will surely kill me.

I take one last look at Grandmother's grotesque portrait, and hurry from the library.

"Sugarpie! Wait!"

In the parlor, I turn.

"I don't understand what you've done." My aunt is shaking. "I don't understand how you could choose—*that girl*—over family."

"What family? Grandmother's dead, and anyway, she always hated me. You claim to love me, but you lied to me."

"Sugarpie—"

I raise my voice. "Would you truly ask me to give up my only chance at happiness, just to keep the Heathwood line alive?"

Aunt Hilda wrings her hands. "You love this sister of yours."

"Yes. I do."

Confusion flickers over her face. "But—is she not savage? *Vile?*"

"*Please.* Quit bein' ugly."

"Sugarpie, I only mean—is this what you truly want?"

I touch my throat, recalling ghostly hands. "It is."

Aunt Hilda dabs her eyes. "Well, if you're going to be colored, you cannot stay here. I simply cannot bear to look at you."

That stings, but I expected as much.

On my way to pack, I climb the grand stair.

In the parlor, my aunt weeps hysterically. I am sorry, so awfully sorry, for her pain.

But for Heathwood, for Grandmother, all I can think is: *Good riddance.*

18
Charlie

On the white side of town, Darius is a totally different kind of driver. Careful, slow. At a stop sign, he lets a Pontiac pull ahead of him even though he had the right-of-way.

"Why'd you do that? Let that man go?"

"You saw. He's white. Got to be careful driving this Cadillac. Now. Are you ready to see the sights?"

I snort. "Please. In Eureka, there are none."

"Miss New York, you'd be surprised."

Darius pulls up to a sign reading COLORED PARKING. Then he sprints around the car, all to open my door and help me out of it. I can't help laughing.

Southern gentlemen, Nana said. *Sure did miss them in New York.*

Together, we walk to the town square. But I'm still not used to this heat—the sun hot as a torch against my skin. By the time we reach the square, I'm dripping sweat.

"Can we sit?"

Darius nods. "Here, this is a colored bench."

"That's plain to see. They've put a sign up—misspelled it, to boot."

"Now, now, Miss New York, you save that attitude for city folk. Around here, whites and *colerreds*"—he leans hard into the poor spelling—"got to follow the law."

Before us is an imposing statue of General Robert E. Lee, vines crawling up the stone. Looking at his saber hilt, I feel sick. A statue like this exists to remind colored people of the bad past—the Civil War fought to keep us enslaved.

I don't like Main Street. Not one bit.

In Eureka, whites walk casually down the sidewalk, while colored folks duck and weave. Colored men keep to the road, well clear of white women. It makes sense. After all, it only takes one white scream to unleash hell.

"Did you talk to your daddy about the disinterment protest?"

Darius lights up. "The preacher's come around! And you know what did it? *You and Magnolia.* My daddy finally understands that Eureka's bound to change. We can have a better future, if we fight. And of course, there's my uncle Otto."

"Your uncle—who died in the war?"

"They're planning to dig up his casket on Cemetery Night. That bothers my daddy, too. Uncle Otto's body is still overseas, but we gave him a grave marker. Visit every week. Now white folks want to disturb his rest."

"I'm sorry."

"Don't be. I think we have a chance to beat this thing. We even have a white boy on our side—a Mr. Finch Waylon."

My ears prick up. "Finch Waylon—I think that's who Magnolia was supposed to marry. Back when she was playing white."

"Shoot, really?"

A wave of fear breaks over me once again. Have I gotten Magnolia in too deep?

"You have to keep them apart, Darius. Finch doesn't know the truth."

He touches my hand lightly. "I promise, I will."

After that we're quiet, looking up at General Lee. A kind of poison seeps into me, and then drips into my blood. The man memorialized in that statue hated colored folk so much, he was willing to *die* to keep us in chains.

Nana always used to say, *The world will tell you, over and over again, that you don't matter. But it's a trick, Charlene. You only stop mattering if you start to believe the world's lies.*

Definitely time to get away from this statue.

"Where can a girl get a cold drink around here?"

He offers me his arm. "Come with me, New York, and I'll show you the best cream soda in town."

North of the square, the ice cream parlor looks cool as

a breeze in July: all glass windows and metal fixtures. I'm smiling, feeling fine—*New York City fine*—right up until the moment I realize that we're not walking in the front door of Dale's Ice Cream and Sandwiches.

Because a sign on the front door says NO NEGROES OR DOGS ALLOWED.

Like Negroes and dogs just might be the same thing.

Darius is leading me into the alley between the ice cream parlor and the pharmacy. There's a little window in the brick for takeout. The alley smells musty, like a dumpster.

I'd rather jump off the Brooklyn Bridge than buy a cream soda from this place.

But Darius doesn't seem to mind. He knocks on the window until a beefy white man opens it. The smell of powdered sugar wafts into the alley, taunting me.

"New girl, D?"

I shoot a hard look at Darius—*new girl?*—but he doesn't see.

"What's your flavor, gal?" The white man's friendly, but I can't force my face to smile.

I try to mimic Magnolia: She'd smile brightly, tell him *Cherry Pepsi*, and call it a day. But I'm not her. I won't be responsible for giving this racist business a single cent.

"Actually, I don't like cream soda."

Simultaneously, Darius and the beefy man turn to me, astonished.

"In fact, I think I'll be heading home now. *Alone.*"

"What about a hot dog? Chicken wing?" the man calls after me. "Boy, you got your work cut out with that one!"

I feel better outside the alley, breathing the pine-scented air.

Darius catches up. "Hey now, what happened?"

"I'm not one of your 'new girls,' Darius. And I *don't* eat racist ice cream with a dumpster on my right and a player on my left!"

"We weren't gonna eat it there! I thought we'd take a walk to the city park—sit under one of those oak trees—"

I cross my arms. "I'm tired of this southern nonsense."

Blue eyes flash. "You think I'm not?"

"You put up with it, don't you?"

"That's where you're wrong. I just know how to pick my battles. The protest tomorrow—that's a fight that matters. Buying cream soda from a colored window? Who the heck cares when it tastes just as sweet?"

"*I* care."

A white couple's crossing the street—headed for the ice cream shop. Gently, Darius draws me out of their way.

His gaze intensifies. "Why, exactly?"

I answer in Nana's words. "Because every time I accept that I'm worth less—less than a man, or a white person, or a gosh-darn oil baron—it punches a hole in my spirit." I'm talking too fast, eyes stinging. "Punch enough holes and your spirit breaks."

I expect Darius to storm off, stranding me on Main Street. Instead, he looks at me in a way no boy has ever looked at me before.

For a second, I'm worried he'll kiss me here—now, in broad daylight. The air between us, magnetized.

"New York, I think you just cured my sweet tooth. Though there's always One-Eyed Red's in Colored Town. What do you say we buy ourselves some penny candy?"

My smile tickles my lips again. Darius Lucien will be the death of me. When he takes my hand, I let him. Feels good.

A shop window stops me in my tracks.

BRYCE'S ANTIQUES, the sign says.

There's an old book on display—the leather cover, oddly melted, and the pages swollen. Looks like the book was boiled before it wound up here.

Its title: *Love Sonnets*.

I lurch, because that's the book Mama was holding in the black mirror, standing in Heathwood's kitchen with Daddy.

"Something special about that book, Charlie?"

"Mama owned a book called *Love Sonnets*. Daddy gave it to her before they died."

I don't tell him that the only way I know this is because I saw it in a magic mirror. I'm too worried this preacher's son won't believe me.

"Could be lots of books called *Love Sonnets*. You sure this is the right one?"

"No. But..."

Enthralled, I can't take my eyes off it.

Darius nods decisively. "Girl doesn't like cream soda. Guess I'll buy her a book instead."

I straighten. "Stop it."

"I mean it. You're right about those holes. I got too many of them myself."

I roll my eyes—but my heart's not in it. I'm full of Mama and Daddy, smiling at each other in that kitchen, a book between them. Young and falling in love.

"It's whites only inside that store, too. But money talks. I'm gonna offer them double whatever they're charging. I want you to have it."

"Darius, no."

"I mean it. I want to."

Before I can stop him, a little bell rings as he opens the door to Bryce's Antiques.

I wait too long on the sidewalk, my shoulders bunching around my ears. Maybe it's just being alone on an unfamiliar street, but I'm scared. I never should've let Darius risk himself over some old book. Most of all, I regret turning down the darn soda. What's wrong with me that I can't accept what the world believes is my fair share?

A white girl approaches the store, steps slowing. I'm so lost in thought that I forget to step off the sidewalk.

"Gal, you're in my way."

"Sorry, miss."

Her eyes narrow. "Where have I seen you before?"

I blink. "Nowhere."

"Is that a Yankee accent? Where're you from, anyhow?"

I hold my tongue. The white girl's face is thin as a weasel's, her hair a limp brown. She's dressed fine like Magnolia, but she's nowhere near as pretty.

"I asked you a question! What's a Yankee gal doing 'round here?"

NO NEGROES OR DOGS ALLOWED, the sign said, and Darius had no choice but to buy me cola from an alley on a date. And I saw more of General Lee than I ever wanted to. I've had enough of Eureka's Dixie funhouse mirror.

"Trust me, I wish I'd never come to this backward town." I hesitate before adding: "*Miss.*"

The weasel-faced girl jabs a finger at me. "I'm callin' the sheriff on you. Yessiree. He'll see to it you *don't* stick around."

Then she yanks open the door to Bryce's Antiques.

No, no, no. Darius is in there, and that's just the type of white girl to—

Yep. She shrieks loud enough to wake the dead.

Belly braced, I run inside to find Darius, two white men, and the white girl, still shrieking her head off.

"Annamae," the younger white man says. "That's enough."

"That Negro can't be in here!" She whirls on me. "Neither can she! Whatever is this world comin' to? I'm surrounded by integrationists, I swear I am!"

The shop owner clears his throat. "Your brother vouched for the boy. Says he's an employee of the family. Here on business."

"That's right, he is."

I realize with a jolt that I'm looking at Finch Waylon, Magnolia's intended. He's lying to keep Darius safe. I guess that makes him an ally, but I don't like the look of him. He holds himself like the prince of the world—entitled. He's handsome, I guess, but in an icy, unpleasant way.

I worry he'll notice that my face is the mirror image of Magnolia's—but his eyes slide right off me, like water off a duck's back. Racism's blinded him. He never sees past my brown skin.

"Thank you kindly, Mr. Finch," Darius mumbles.

Then he takes my arm, steering me swiftly toward the door.

I glance back, once, at the white girl.

She glares. "Don't you come back here, you little tramp. I don't like your face. Next time I see it, I'm gettin' my daddy. He's got a pack of dogs trained to hunt the likes of you!"

I shudder as we hustle out the door, because the little viper means it.

"I'm so sorry," I say to Darius, safe again on Freedom's porch. "I didn't mean to put you in danger. I was foolish. *Citified.*"

In dusk's failing light, Darius's blue eyes are stormy. "No. I played it up, how brave I was being. I happen to know Mr. Bryce is friendly to our cause. And Mr. Finch helped organize for integration at Georgia State. His sister, on the other hand…"

"The girl who screamed."

Darius pinches the bridge of his nose. "That racket could've gotten me killed."

A cold wind blows through me, because it's true.

"But we're safe now, Charlie. Mr. Finch'll handle his sister. And you've got yourself a fine book of poetry. Can't account for what happened to it, though. The cover's melted or something."

He holds out a cardboard box, tied with a green ribbon. Gingerly, I open it, revealing *Love Sonnets*. Though the leather's warped, the cover looks sculptural. The eerie, beaten beauty of this book must be why Mr. Bryce displayed it in the window.

An uncomfortable heat gathers in my chest, because Darius put himself on the line for this book—for me.

"Darius, why are you even here?"

He quirks a smile. "Because I can't resist a pretty face?"

I blush. "No, I mean in Eureka. In Harlem, colored folks got a world of their own, newspapers of their own. It makes sense to organize there, where things are bound to change. You can feel it in the air."

"Daddy wants me to carry on his legacy. When we met

on the train, I'd just visited a seminary in Baltimore. I'm supposed to start next fall."

I can't imagine Darius hunched over a Bible. "Do you want to be a preacher?"

He shrugs. "We've got three generations of preachers in our family. I plan to be a protest preacher, at least."

"Seems like Nat and Joe would follow you to hell and back."

He smiles, but it fades too quickly.

"You're worried about the protest."

His jaw tightens. "There've been too many lynchings around here. Your parents were only one. The first time I got behind the wheel of my Cadillac, my daddy told me their story, you know."

I remember how carefully he drove near Main Street. "You ever have any trouble, driving a fancy car like that?"

"Sure. There's a reason I took the train to Baltimore." He stuffs his hands into his pockets. "Cop pulled me over at the state line once. Didn't believe the car was mine. I was just driving, trying to feel free. Nothing but fields out there, Charlie. Emptiness. The cop's eyes were empty, too, like he wouldn't be bothered by shooting me. Like he wouldn't think twice."

I shudder, picturing the conductor who ordered Nana and me into the colored car.

"What did he pull you over for?"

"Broken taillight. But actually, he was the one who broke it—after the fact. Beat all my lights in with a tire iron. Then he made me take off all my clothes—every stitch—and marched me into the field."

"Oh, my God," I breathe.

"I knew then I was gonna die. What I couldn't figure was *why*. How'd a white cop learn to hate so hard he'd kill a Negro just for driving a car? And why me, if it could've been anyone? Was my luck really so bad?"

"What happened?"

"He got a call, some problem more urgent than me. Tossed my keys into the field and left me there, stark naked. Took me an hour to find those keys.

"Charlie, that cop didn't see a person when he looked at me. I stay up nights, wondering what he saw instead: A criminal? An animal? *What?*"

I know to wait, because I've seen colored people talk about such things before. Darius needs to feel what happened to him all over again. Let it run through his body. Then he'll come back to the present. To me.

I see the moment his soul returns—boyish, carefree, strong.

And I think: *Darius Lucien is something else.*

"So. Is this really your mama's book?"

I open the damaged front cover to the title page and suck in my breath.

The inscription reads: *To my dearest Marie, who rescued me. I will love you forever and a day.*

Darius reads over my shoulder. "Well, doesn't that beat all."

Marveling, we leaf through the volume. Must be a hundred poems inside this big old book.

I can't tell if I'm sweating because of the humidity, or because Darius is leaning over me, close enough to touch. He smells like his Cadillac, like smoky leather and motor oil.

Darius's finger stops on a well-thumbed page.

In the deep, resonant voice of a preacher, he reads: "*I love thee with the breath, / Smiles, tears, of all my life; and, if God choose, / I shall but love thee better after death.*"

For a moment, the words shimmer in the air.

"Come back to New York with me," I say impulsively. "After the protest."

Darius leans back, taking me in.

My cheeks warm. "I just mean, you could be anything you want to be, there."

"Are you inviting me home, Miss New York?"

I try to play it cool. "Harlem's the best place in the world."

"If it's as pretty as you, I'd never leave."

I frown, thinking how many girls he must've courted—the preacher's son with the gemstone eyes. "You're feeding me a line."

"I'm sorry. You're right. I just want to get close. That okay by you?"

"What do you mean, get close?"

He pulls me to standing, then places one hand on my hip. "You know what I mean."

My body hums at his touch.

Yes. I've wanted to get close to Darius since he first gave up his seat for Nana on the train. It's new to me, this sweet, aching feeling.

Is this how Mama felt around my father? Did she ache and burn, as I do now?

Darius bows his head toward me, and my senses flame alive. I'm so ready to fall into him. But to my surprise, his lips avoid mine.

"Sorry." He looks pained.

"What's wrong?"

"Not one of my girls, you said. Guess that means we'd better take our time."

Church bells toll, scattering birds across the sky. It's late afternoon already. I really should be getting ready for Nana's repast.

"Will I see you tonight?"

"Wouldn't miss it."

"Thank you for the book."

On the porch stairs, he tips his hat. "It was nothing, Miss New York."

Only, we both know—it was everything.

19

Magnolia

With Odessa's help, I gather my last mementos of Heathwood.

Nothing expensive. I would not want Aunt Hilda to think me greedy or grasping. I am aware that everything I do now inevitably reflects on the character of colored people—and it is a strange, heavy burden to bear.

For Nana's repast, I collect some of our daily china, leaving the fine porcelain and silver behind. One cake stand, two serving platters (that do not reflect me), enough plates and forks to go around. I bundle the lace from my hope chest and remove the curtains from my bedroom window. I have no compunction about taking our lantern lights—they are not worth much. I leave my jewelry, but pack clean underwear.

Finally, with Odessa at my side, I linger on Heathwood's veranda. Aunt Hilda is in her bedroom. Her nerves too shattered to bid me a last goodbye.

Odessa shepherds me toward our car, but I stop, drawn toward the abandoned stables. I cannot help thinking of the room with shackles—or the little ghost who led me there.

"Odessa, did it ever bother you? Working in a house that once held slaves?"

She huffs. "All the time."

"I always managed to put it out of my mind." I pause. "I don't even know the names of most of the people who lived here. It's like they were erased."

The sun dims in the sky, casting a tangerine glow over fallow fields.

Odessa and I stand for a moment, taking in the breeze and Heathwood's familiar song—of insects, water, and susurrus of wind through moss. The girl I was before I met Charlie might have found the evening beautiful. But now, I see history peeking out from behind the moss, no less menacing for the passage of time.

Odessa pinches my forearm—all bone. "You're not eating enough."

It's true. I have not eaten. But I have a feeling that tonight, I will reclaim my reflection at last.

I have given up Heathwood, and all Colored Town will attend Nana's repast. Once I have officially entered colored society, the curse will break. I am sure of it.

I smile, feeling lighter. "I'll be fine, Odessa. You'll see. Everythin' will turn out right."

Charlie waits for me on Freedom House's porch. Odessa hugs us both, then runs home to fetch a pie.

I get straight to work. "What libations do we have?"

"Libations?"

"Food and drinks."

Charlie's face scrunches. "Water?"

"I'll whip up some lemonade." I hand her the stack of lace. "Cover every surface with these." On top of that, I dump the string of lantern lights. "To decorate the trees." I point to my luggage. "Of course, I also brought china. I do hope a yellow sparrow pattern is all right by you."

I do not realize at first that Charlie is on the verge of tears. I want to wrap her in my arms, but I know she will be skittish, like a cat.

"Don't worry, Charlie. We'll send your nana off right."

"Did you eat?"

It is sweet of her to think of me. "Not yet. But I am sure I will, tonight."

And then we get to work.

First off, I show Charlie how to sprinkle firewood with sweet fern, and then burn it beside the porch to keep mosquitoes away. I teach her, too, about which outdoor flowers are fit to bring indoors—the periwinkles, the sweet bay blooms—and which, like the poison sumac and stinging nettles, to leave well alone. We wipe down every surface with cleaning oil, and sweep the wooden floors.

Soon enough, the house smells of lemon, sugar, and fresh-cut flowers. The trees glitter with lantern light. Odessa stops by not only with the pecan pie but also with a radio, which she tunes.

Finally, I replace the plain cloth over the mirrors with black velvet. A southern lady knows: The little things make all the difference.

"Well, I have tried my best. I hope your nana enjoys her send-off."

In silent thanks, Charlie takes my hand.

At sunset, mourners arrive in their Sunday hats. Every family brings food for our lace-draped table: rice, red beans, fried tomatoes. No one acts surprised to see me. It seems that word has gotten around that a Heathwood's come to Colored Town, and if anyone holds my past against me, they politely do not say so.

"I remember your daddy," an older woman says. "What a shock it was when he came to live here at Freedom House. You have his cheekbones, Miss Magnolia."

"Just Magnolia, ma'am. Thank you kindly."

"And so polite!"

Darius Lucien arrives with his preacher father. He is drop-dead handsome in a suit.

I mouth to Charlie: *Oh, my Lord.*

She makes a face: *Oh, please!*

"It is truly a gift to have y'all with us, Charlene and Magnolia," the preacher says. "Come inside, won't you? In a minute, I'll address the mourners."

I expected to feel nervous among so many colored people. After all, I have spent my life with whites. Yet with nothing to pretend, no lie to uphold, my shoulders relax.

A couple dances in the kitchen, and a family laughs over a slice of pie. Children dart and weave around spare wooden furniture before they are scooped up by whichever grown person happens to be closest. They are not banished to the lawn while their parents swill expensive drinks, as Annamae and I were. They are loved by everyone, and I believe—*I hope*—that they will never be as lonesome as I have been.

I'd die for any woman or child in Colored Town, Odessa said to me. *That's how our people have survived for so long—by watching out for our own.*

One child, only eight or nine, stops before me. She is near as pale as I am.

While she studies my face, the world slows.

"You're yella," she says. "Like me."

A feeling of kinship nearly sweeps me off my feet. Then the child scampers off.

Sweet Charlie has never left my side. "What did I tell you about light-skinned folks? You're common as dimes."

"Thank you," I whisper.

"You're welcome."

"We threw a good party, didn't we?"

"Sure did."

Darius herds us deeper into the room: to the table arranged with flowers, white candles, and Charlie's photograph. Jeannette Yates has a face like mine, like Charlie's, but broader and scored with worry lines.

One by one, people lift the photo, kissing it.

"Rest in peace, Jeannie," someone says. "You rest, now."

"We sure did miss your casseroles at church, Jeannette!"

"All except the potato chip one. Even the children wouldn't touch that—remember?"

It's the word of the evening: *Remember? Remember?*

I think back to Grandmother's miserable wake. Aunt Hilda got drunk as a skunk. The few people who came all dressed in black, and there was nothing, really, to say.

When Charlie bends to kiss the photograph, the room quiets.

People sigh, murmuring, "Poor child, poor thing."

Then it is my turn. I lift the picture, looking closer. Jeannette and Charlie loved each other so. To my horror, resentment and bitter envy knot inside my belly.

Why did Charlie's nana leave me in Eureka? Surely she must've known how I would suffer, neither colored nor white. Why didn't she love me, too?

Oh, but I hate myself for feeling such anger toward an old woman—and a dead one, at that. Hastily, I kiss the picture, then set it down like it scalds me.

The preacher claps his hands for our attention. "We are gathered here today in honor of Jeannette Adeline Yates. Y'all remember her, though she was gone too long."

"Amen," someone says. "We did miss her."

Charlie presses her side into mine.

"Y'all know, too, that this is a strange time in Eureka's history. Jeannette's body will not be buried, not tonight and not tomorrow. She rests at Sugg's Funeral Home, awaiting the outcome of an ugly, segregationist plot to banish our dead to the swamp."

People grumble, stamp feet.

"Jeannette Yates deserves better than a marshland grave. We all do."

"Yes, sir! Amen!"

"Charlene and Magnolia Yates, please step up," the preacher commands.

Magnolia Yates. That is what he called me.

I wipe my damp palms on my dress. Then the preacher takes our hands in each of his: mine, white as milk; Charlie's, brown. Triumphantly, he raises our arms above his head. I flush, but the crowd cheers. As twin sisters, white and Black, we are a symbol of coming victory. A promise of change.

"These are Jeannette's grandchildren, our very own miracle babies. Their parents saw no justice, yet these brave children found their way back to each other. Though Magnolia lived in the Big House, she found her way home to Colored

Town. And Charlene, praise the Lord, came all the way from New York."

"Amen. Yes, Lord!"

The preacher nods once to Charlie and once to me. "Together, these girls are a symbol of our righteousness, our hope, and the justice that must finally come after long years of darkness. Gather with me now, on Cemetery Night, to join our historic protest in defense of our right to be buried with dignity.

"It will not be an easy march or a painless one. But remember that we are on the side of angels, and that Jeannette Adeline Yates, who suffered so much, depends on us now."

People applaud, and my own blood stirs. If this is what Charlie's protest work is like, then I think I like it. I feel galvanized. Ready to join Colored Town's march.

Then the air thickens, crackling.

In the midst of the cheering crowd, a little silver figure stands unmoving. Thin arms crossed over his small, bony chest. He's smoky, refracting the light trickily, like cobwebs do. He wears the plain sackcloth of a slave.

The little boy spirit from the abandoned stables. He's followed me here. No one seems to see him but me. I want to call out to Charlie, but my sister's already hurrying into Darius's arms. He spins her in a circle, and then they're dancing, unaware of the stone-faced child.

Though standing in a crowded room, I feel entirely alone.

The silvery specter's mouth opens and closes. I cannot make out his words, but they are condemnatory. I am certain of it.

I want to ask him, *What have I done?* But terror traps the question in my throat.

He points his finger at me, and the shadows in this room become suddenly wild.

Static sparks snap in the air—a sure sign of a wrathful haunting. And it is frightening the children.

"No, Lisa Bell, don't be scared." The light-skinned child clings to her mother's legs. "Go fetch another slice of pie."

Others have noticed the change in atmosphere; the crowd shifts, disturbed.

The little boy's gaze holds mine. The room narrows until it's just the two of us: the colored child who must once have been a slave, and me, the light-skinned Heathwood who casts no reflection in mirror glass.

"Charles Freedom built the place too close to the river, is the problem," someone mutters.

"Never knew how Jeannette managed to raise a child in this house—"

"Well, but you remember. She was a tornado, no ghost gonna stand in *her* way—"

The preacher claps once—and the little boy spirit vanishes.

Stunned, I blink.

"Enough talk of Jeannette's suffering," the preacher says. "We've come to celebrate her *life*. Sing with me, now, her favorite spiritual. 'Swing low'..."

Like an orchestra conductor, the preacher stirs the room into song, and soon every voice pours itself into the hymn. Chin lifted, Charlie sings, too.

I looked over Jordan and what did I see
Comin' for to carry me home!
A band of angels comin' after me.
Comin' for to carry me home.

The *amens* die away, and that frightened little girl, Lisa Bell, is once again smiling. There's no sign anymore of the Heathwood ghost.

Relieved, I sigh—and resolve not to think of that spirit tonight. After all, this is the night I become a colored girl—and, God willing, break my mirror curse.

The dancing starts up again, and music soon restores my mood. When Nat offers me his hand, I take it without reservation. Whirling in Nat's arms, I am at long last the person I was always meant to be: a colored girl among colored people, a sister, a twin.

Damp with sweat and deliriously happy, I feel in my bones that my curse has finally broken. When I look in the mirror now, I will see myself for who I truly am.

When the music slows, Charlie finds me. "Well? How do you feel? Do you think you could eat?"

"Oh, Charlie! I might could eat a horse."

She winds her arm through mine. "So, we broke the curse?"

"I think so. Truly, I do."

"Then let's get you a plate."

"And a mirror. Lord, I haven't seen my reflection in I don't know how long!"

Charlie nudges me, teasing. "But, Magnolia, color aside—all you have to do is look at me."

Tender feeling floods my veins, hearing Charlie say that. Because I found my sister, I will never again face a great, wide nothingness—that lonesomeness so vast, I wished to die.

From now on, wherever I look, my sister will always be there.

20
Charlie

'll never forget the giddy smile on Magnolia's face when, in Mama's room, she prepares to take a bite of Odessa's pecan pie. Sitting with her on the bed, I realize how much I missed her today. How wrong it felt to be in Freedom House alone. And when Preacher Lucien raised our arms to announce the Cemetery Night protest... well, I knew Magnolia was family for real.

As soon as she swallows her pie, I'm going to rip down the black velvet sheet that covers Mama's obsidian mirror, revealing Magnolia's reflection to her. I want her to see, for the first time, what she looks like as a colored girl, not a white one.

I'm so ready for this nightmarish adventure to finally be

over. After the protest, after Nana's finally buried, I'm going back to New York.

If I can convince her, maybe Magnolia will come with me.

I've got my arguments all lined up: There're no mosquitoes in New York (only roaches, but I won't mention those), and we won't die because we forgot to call a white person *sir* or *ma'am*. People may question our color and our relationship, but they won't care too much. In the city, everyone's too busy spinning their dreams to hassle a pair of mixed-blood twins.

In August, we'll turn eighteen. We'll be old enough to live on our own in my apartment on 125th Street, and I'm sure the landlord can turn a blind eye until then, so long as the rent's paid. I'll find secretarial work, and maybe Magnolia can take courses toward her diploma, because there's not much good work a woman can find without a high school degree. Anyway, it's what Nana would've wanted. *Any grandchild of mine's gonna be educated*, she used to say.

Magnolia loads her fork with a sugary bite of pecan pie. She closes her eyes in anticipation. She eats.

Swallows. Smiles.

Then she chokes.

I pat her back. "Did it go down the wrong pipe?"

She shakes her head, gesturing wildly.

"Oh, my God. What should I do?"

The lamps flicker off and on. Behind me, a gust sweeps the velvet cloth clear of the obsidian mirror. I am reflected in it, but Magnolia Heathwood, my twin sister, is not.

The mirrors are trying to kill me, she said.

"Magnolia." I take her by the shoulders. "Tell me what to do."

She points at the bedroom door, mouthing, *Odessa.* Her nails scrabble over her throat, the beds showing blue.

My sister's dying. Choking to death.

I've already lost Nana. I can't go through this again.

I dash into the party, already breaking up. In the kitchen, I grab Odessa's arm.

"Charlene?"

"It's Magnolia. She's—"

Odessa takes one look at my face and runs, hollering for Dr. Colt. Magnolia stumbles into the hall. The doctor, the preacher, and Odessa surround her. For a second I can't see my sister through the crowd, and I want to scream.

Dr. Colt has hold of Magnolia now—I hear a throaty *hack*. A chunk of pie lands at my feet, releasing a bad stench. It's foul like standing water. Like the swamp.

My stomach flips over.

"She's all right!" Dr. Colt wipes the sweat from his brow. "Everyone, give her some air."

As quickly as it arose, the foul reek is gone.

While people clear out of the hall, I settle Magnolia back into Mama's bed. Her eyes water. She gulps air.

I snap open my clamshell, hoping to find her reflection in my mirror, if not Mama's.

In the tiny glass, she's nowhere to be seen.

"I sure am sorry, Charlie," Magnolia drawls—just as if she guessed all my dreams of new family, of twin sisters living large in New York City. "For a while there, I thought everythin' would turn out right."

I grit my teeth, fighting heartbreak.

For colored girls, there's no such thing as happily ever after, Nana said. *No use chasing it.*

After the last mourners leave, Odessa stays behind.

Magnolia and I tell her everything. All about Magnolia's lost reflection and her lost appetite; my ghostly visit from Mama. We tell her, too, about our fear that Magnolia's cursed, or, as she puts it in her drawl, *crossed six ways to Sunday.*

By the time the story's through, it's past midnight. Odessa fingers the gold cross at her throat, eyes lingering on the hulking black mirror.

"You should have come to me the minute you lost your reflection, Magnolia. A person can die from a curse as wicked as that."

"But I did everythin' right." Sweat slicks Magnolia's hair to her face. "Why should my reflection still be gone? What have I done to deserve it?"

"I see your reflection, Magnolia. You're right there."

"But *I* can't see her," I say.

What will happen if Odessa doesn't believe us? Where will we turn?

She thinks a minute, and nods. "We need to see an expert."

"Like a doctor?"

"A conjure man. Charlie, be sure you bring your nana's cane."

Odessa leads us out of the house in a hurry. Outside, I can practically taste Magnolia's fear—a copper tang in the humid night air.

We walk straight toward the swamp, dense with devious green.

The way is hard, full of nettles that nip my ankles. Magnolia guides me, keeping me from tripping into a bed of poison sumac. I'm proud that my sister knows her way around a swamp. We hurry along the river, its sludgy, slow-moving water the color of tea, its current choked with cypress roots and lily pads. Strangely, the moon casts no reflection on the water's dark surface. The swamp swallows the light.

The river's haunted, Nana said on the train. *Don't go near it. Don't touch it. Not ever. Understand?*

Like a run-down windup toy, Magnolia suddenly stops walking.

"I can't go on, y'all. I'm too tired."

Odessa prods her. "Got to keep moving."

"Why?" Her voice pinches thin—petulant. "Don't you know I'm a lost cause?"

Under the moon, Magnolia's despair terrifies me.

"No! You've got to keep on swinging. Keep fighting."

"Easy for you to say, Charlie. You're not so worn down as me."

"I promised Jeannette I'd look out for you, and I will," Odessa says firmly. "But I made a mistake. I should've told you, long ago, who you are."

"So why didn't you?" I demand, wanting to blame someone, anyone, for the bad mess we're in.

Moonlight illuminates the silver in Odessa's hair. "Blanche Heathwood is dangerous."

The seriousness of her tone stuns us. I realize I'm afraid of that name—*Blanche Heathwood*. In French, I think *blanche* means "white."

"Roland's house is just over yonder." Odessa points. "See?"

A thin plume of smoke rises up from the green.

It's after midnight. If I were home in Harlem, I'd be leaning out my apartment window watching colored folk parade down my street: men in zoot suits and feathered hats, women in cocktail dresses with long silk gloves. It'd be noisy— people hollering, taxis blaring.

In the misty dark, I've never felt farther from home.

Following the smoke to the water's edge, a terrible sight freezes us in our tracks.

Graves.

In a clearing too near the water, there are rows upon rows of open graves, dug out of quicksand. The swamp's already lapping at the soil, ready to claim this ground for its own.

"Is *this* where they're putting the colored cemetery?" I ask.

"Lord have mercy," Odessa murmurs.

"Why, they'll wash up at the first big storm!"

Like the swamp water, those empty graves soak up the moonlight. It's the greatest evil I've ever seen with my own eyes—the true meaning of horror.

I think of Darius, forced to undress in a field.

Think of Mama and Daddy, shot on a lonely road.

Think of that sign: NO NEGROES OR DOGS ALLOWED.

A sickly fear works its way up my spine: a tiny under-skin monster, climbing my bones. If the Cemetery Night protest fails, I'll have to bury Nana in one of those sloppy graves.

"Old Roland lives just here," Odessa says.

The conjure man's hut shelters beneath a fall of Spanish moss. It's barely even a hut—just a few wooden planks nailed together.

The door opens before we have a chance to knock, but there's so much smoke, it's hard to see. I cough, hard.

"Magnolia. Charlene," a man's voice greets us. "Come in. I've been expecting you."

21
Magnolia

The conjure man settles behind a metal pot, stirring it and whistling low. Since inviting us inside, he has barely glanced our way.

I want to go back to Charlie's house. Want to drift into a gauzy, warm sleep. But if I do, I am afraid I might never wake up.

The floor is mud, slippery beneath my feet. Jars and vials crowd makeshift shelves, filled with odd liquids, bird wings, innards, bones. I startle at the jar nearest to me, which contains a round gator's eye. From a cage, something hisses.

Afraid, I take Charlie's hand in mine. I can feel her pulse beating in her palm. Odessa stands on my other side. She believes the conjure man can help me—I must try to believe it, too.

"I know why you've come," Old Roland says. "The light-skinned child's cursed. No reflection. No food. Dying soon."

I gasp. "How do you know that?"

Old Roland peers at me. "It's plain to see."

I shudder.

Charlie hangs tight to my hand. "But *why* is she cursed? She didn't do anything wrong."

He chuckles. "Is that true, Magnolia Heathwood? Have you done nothing wrong?"

I do not answer, thinking of the little ghost's accusing eyes.

"Ah, you brought that old cane. May I?"

Charlie hands it to him, stepping close to a cage full of snakes, who flick their tongues at her. Quickly, she darts back to me.

Roland sighs. "I remember when I forged this cane. Bound a snake's soul with silver for Jeannette Yates. Snake answered her two questions."

Charlie perks up at the sound of her grandmother's name. "What did she ask?"

"She wanted to know when her dying day would come. Said she needed to make it back to Eureka before then for her grandbabies. Snake told her the date and the hour."

"Nana knew when she was going to die?"

Roland swivels to face me. "As for her second question— that pertains to you, Magnolia. Are you ready to hear it?"

I hesitate.

"She's ready," Charlie answers for me.

"Jeannette wanted to know: What would happen to the light-skinned child, raised white?" Tenderly, Roland strokes the cane's head. "Snake answered, *She'd be lost in the veil. A wandering soul.*"

The words burrow into my bones.

"Well, Jeannette didn't like that one bit, specially not after the price she paid. Cost her three years of her life."

Odessa stiffens.

Charlie drops my hand. "You took my grandmother's life? *Three years?* Would she still be here today, if you hadn't—"

"The price of power, Charlene Yates," Roland snaps. "The spirits demand it."

"I don't believe you. I don't believe you're real."

"Don't challenge him, Charlene," Odessa warns.

But the conjure man's already straightening. "You don't believe, *Miss New York?*"

Old Roland snaps his fingers, and wraithlike spirits fill the air. They swirl around the conjure man's head, glimmering foxfire green. Thin as smoke.

"Don't see this much in Harlem, do you? There, the veil's solid as brick. But on the swamp, spirits will follow you from one side to the other, easy as passing through water. If you know the right words to speak, that is."

I can't tear my eyes from those swirling spirits. Terrifying, but beautiful, too. They're silver as the brocade on a fine, living tapestry.

"Okay." Charlie's rattled. "But what do you mean, Magnolia's lost in the veil? She's not lost. She's right here."

"I can ask the spirits why the light child's gone wandering. But that will require power."

In their cage, the snakes seethe and writhe.

"No," Odessa says. "Magnolia, you heard him. It cost Jeannette three years of her life. His price is too high."

Roland lets out a deep, belly laugh. "The price is high, indeed! But Magnolia Heathwood's paid in full. Paid *in advance*. Jeannette offered that third year up in her name—in case she ever came calling."

I recall the picture I struggled to kiss: the photo of Nana and Charlie, beaming love. I am sorry now for my resentment. Though she never met me, Nana still loved me better than Grandmother ever did. She gave up a sliver of her own life, trying to save mine.

"A whole year—for me?"

"That's my grandmother," Charlie says proudly.

"Well, Magnolia? Shall we ask the spirits what they think of you now?"

I have run out of choices. My heart patters—but weakly. That's lack of food. My head is light, packed full of wool—that's lack of proper water. Behind my eyes, my head aches, dully throbbing.

Oh, Lord—I do not have much time.

"Please help me, Mr. Roland. Please."

Quick as a flash, he grabs a snake from the cage—a cottonmouth known to kill with its bite. Charlie cries out when he reaches for a machete. He slits the snake right down the belly.

Roland rubs warm blood between his fingers, and then approaches me. I am certain I will faint dead away, but Odessa places steadying hands on my shoulders. I close my eyes as Roland decorates my forehead with blood and gore.

"River spirits, ancestors in the water. Tell me what you know of the cursed girl."

I open my eyes. Those thin shadows keep swirling, circling. Roland cocks his head, listening. Though I hear nothing, he listens for a long time.

"Spirits say you're caught *in between* ever since you learned your race. Neither white nor Black, your soul's lost in the veil. Got to land on one side or the other. Or you'll twist like a fly on honey paper."

Not fair. "Mr. Roland, I already chose a side. I gave up Heathwood—my whole life! What more can I do?"

"Your choice alone is not enough. *Your side must choose you, too.* You understand, don't you, *Miss Heathwood,* why the spirit world is not well pleased with you? Haven't you been sleepwalking through your life? Living in a white dream?"

Watching those spirits swirl, I ride a surge of guilt.

The disinterment is happening, in part, because I signed Annamae's petition, and never in my white life did I stand up to Eureka's bitter hate. Grandmother was frightful, but that does not absolve me. I should have tried harder. Done more.

"Well, can't you help her?" Charlie demands.

"I told Jeannette the light-skinned child would come too late. And she has."

Charlie taps her foot, growing angrier by the second. "So, what—she's just supposed to starve to death?"

Old Roland looks at the dead snake in his hand. To my horror, he grabs its jaw—and snaps one of its long, sharp teeth clean off. Then he puts the broken tooth in a jar. Part of his collection.

"There is another way."

Charlie and I speak together, voices twined: *"What?"*

"Go back to your life, Magnolia Heathwood. Pass for white. Choose the other side—and live."

Beside me, Charlie freezes; Odessa drops her head into her hands.

"But I don't want to be Magnolia Heathwood anymore. I want to be with my sister."

Roland waves my words away. "You can't, if you want to live. Go back to your white dream, Miss Magnolia. Your reflection and your appetite will return. A Negro's life is not for you, as much as you might wish otherwise. The spirits have made up their minds."

Numb, I say nothing.

"How can you say that to the child, Roland?" Odessa cries. "Shame on you."

The conjure man shrugs. "The curse is rooted deep."

"So, you're useless," Charlie says acidly. "You're not so powerful after all."

Old Roland's eyes narrow. "I'll prove to you how deep the curse goes, for all the good it'll do." Angrily, he picks a vial off a shelf. "This is grave dirt, twice blessed. When you're ready to know something true, blow it onto glass. It will show you the moment the curse took hold. Like a sapling, taking root."

Charlie doesn't budge, so I accept the grave dirt with trembling hands. Carefully, I tuck the vial into my dress pocket.

In the smoke-filled hut, I look at Charlie, just as she looks at me. Though the firelight flickers just right, I cannot see my reflection in her eyes. I am not really here. Never have been. This adventure we have shared together . . . it might as well have been a dream.

"I'm sorry," I tell her—and in my words, I hear another: *goodbye.*

"You can't give up. You can't leave me. Passing . . . for your whole life . . ."

Charlie told me that I didn't need a mirror—that all I had to do was look at her. She is my mirror image, after all. Now fear strikes my blood, wondering if Charlie's cursed, too.

"Mr. Roland, what about Charlie? Is she cursed?"

Grudgingly, he cocks his head, once again listening.

"Spirits say yes, but she won't lose so much as you. Only her blue-eyed African prince."

Darius.

Charlie flinches. "You're lying."

Oh, my poor, poor sister.

"The spirits never lie. And everyone knows that revolts in Eureka always end in blood. Just look behind your bathroom mirror, Charlene."

My sister's head snaps up—though I do not know what Roland's referring to.

"Give me back my nana's cane," she snaps.

Old Roland hands it over. "If it makes you feel any better, I was rooting for y'all. Twin girls...that's powerful blood. Might even have changed things around here." His eyes flick to me. "I am sorry your story doesn't end happily, Miss Heathwood."

Hearing my white name, my heels sink an inch deeper into mud.

Scowling, Odessa tugs my arm. "Come on, Magnolia. Don't listen to this old man. Every word he said...forget it. The swamp waters must have gone to his head, since I saw him last."

Old Roland laughs; Odessa shuts the door.

Outside, wind stirs the cypress trees, making them whisper.

Your choice alone is not enough. Your side must choose you, too.

The colored spirits of Eureka have rejected me—just like Nana did, long ago. Yes, she gave up a year of her life for me. But what I really needed was her love. I needed my Black grandmother, and, most of all—my sister.

Cold acceptance works through me. What's done is done. Can't change things.

Walking home, Charlie fumes. "Forget him. He's wrong. A charlatan."

But we both saw those foxfire green spirits swirling around his head. We both know, too, that every word he spoke is true.

22
Charlie

n the dark of night, I press close to Magnolia in Mama's bed. We whisper together, trying to figure a way out of this trap. But I can tell Magnolia's losing heart.

"It doesn't make any sense," I say. "Even if Old Roland's telling the truth...colored people don't reject other colored people for being *light*. It doesn't make any sense."

"Colored *people* did accept me. Joe, Darius, Preacher Lucien...but the spirits. I must have upset them."

"It wasn't your fault. Your grandmother was awful."

Magnolia's quiet a heartbeat too long. "Charlie, I signed the petition."

"What petition?"

"The one supporting the cemetery segregation. My friend needed signatures, and I signed my name."

It takes a minute for her words to sink in. "But—why would you do that?"

"I wasn't thinking. It's so easy, in Eureka, just to go along."

And I guess that's the most horrific thing I've ever heard—my sister telling me it's easier to be white and racist than white and good. Easy as sleepwalking.

If I'd been in Magnolia's place, would I have signed that ugly petition, too? I can't imagine it.

"See?" Magnolia wraps a curl around her fingers, then tugs too hard. "You hate me for what I've done."

I don't hate her, but all this is...confusing. Sometimes, I look at Magnolia and see a white girl—like the one who screamed in Bryce's Antiques. Then the light falls in another way, and I see my sister. It's like that optical illusion, the one where you can see a black vase—or, looking another way, two women's faces.

I reach out to touch her, reminding myself of what's real: this terrified girl who looks like me, whispering in Mama's bed.

"Your grandmother raised you to be that white girl whose name you signed. But she's not really you."

"What do you mean?"

I pause. "When I first met you, it was like you were wearing a costume. Playing a role. The southern belle."

She covers her face with her hands. "I betrayed Mama. Your nana."

There's no doubt about it—Magnolia made a huge mistake signing that petition. But surely, even living her whole life at Heathwood Plantation, Magnolia is the least of Eureka's evils. So why are Eureka's spirits—colored and white—trying so hard to tear our family apart?

"The spirits will see you at the disinterment protest. They'll understand, then, that we need you on our side. Preacher Lucien held both our arms up, remember, Magnolia? He called us a miracle. *And we are.*"

"Charlie, Old Roland said the protest will end in blood. If it does, we'll be responsible. Having a Heathwood involved is what got the preacher on board."

"No. The protest's happening because the disinterment is wrong. Digging up those bodies . . . it's just evil."

"But if the protest can't change anything, is it worth it? What about Darius? What if he dies?"

A lump lodges in my throat. "You've never been looked down on for the color of your skin. Never been turned away from a store. Colored Town's got to protest—and so does Darius. We've got no choice."

Magnolia sits up. "But Charlie, I know Eureka. Colored Town will *always* lose."

Irritated, I bite the inside of my cheek. "So what are you saying? We should just give up?"

My sister, animated now, climbs out of bed. "No. I'm gonna talk to Annamae Waylon. See if she can stop this disinterment from ever happening. That's what I should have done in the first place."

Annamae Waylon.

The name rings one big, nasty bell. "Is this Annamae a brown-haired girl, face like a weasel?"

"Yes, I reckon so—"

"I met her and she's *awful.* How's she going to help you stop the disinterment? *Why* would she help you?"

"You met her?"

"She yelled at me on Main Street. Threatened me with her daddy's dogs."

"She *didn't.*"

"Oh, yes, she did."

"Why didn't you tell me, Charlie? Somethin' like that..."

This, right here, is what Magnolia just doesn't seem to understand, even living in the belly of the South. Being abused for the color of your skin is normal. It happens every day. If you obsess over every little wrong done to you, it'll drive you nuts.

"White girls have threatened me before. That's not the issue. You can't talk to her about the disinterment, Magnolia. Why would she possibly help us?"

My sister winces. "Because she used to be my best friend?"

Now I wince, too.

"Charlie, something good can still come from all this. If I tell Annamae who I am . . . well, maybe she'll understand. She started this thing. She could find a way to stop it."

I stand, legs shaking—from fear or anger, I don't know. Mama's obsidian mirror glints in the corner of my eye, but it's dark now. It's been dark a long time. Magnolia and I—we're on our own.

"Are you really planning to out yourself to this white girl?"

Magnolia presses her lips together. "Reckon so."

Stupid. "She could get you killed!"

"What does that matter, when I'm already dyin'?"

I press my hands against my temples, because none of this is right. Mama said we could *fix what's been broken.* So how come it feels like this mess just keeps getting worse?

"You're stupid if you think this white town is going to listen to a couple schoolgirls. The disinterment's serious business."

"Charlie, people *do* listen to the Heathwoods, and the Waylons have so much wealth to throw around."

"You're playing the martyr, Magnolia, but your guilt won't help anything! I don't care how white you were before. I need you alive *now.*"

"But I am guilty, Charlie."

I reach for her hands. "The world doesn't need your guilt. It needs your *anger.* That's what makes change."

"But Darius, the other protesters . . ." Magnolia gasps

like someone drowning. "Annamae might still be able...she might could..."

And then she's breaking, tears streaming. "Please, Charlie. I have to try."

I swore to myself that I'd accept my sister for what Eureka's made her. Despite her privilege and self-importance, Magnolia's my twin. If she needs to try to stop the disinterment this way, I guess I have to let her.

Is that right, Nana? Do I let her try?

Magnolia thinks the protest is doomed—and maybe we can't win. The thing about civil action is, it doesn't matter if you win or lose. What matters is that you express the power of your convictions. That you keep swinging, even as you're going down. For Magnolia, confronting her old friend might be the same.

"You get back here as fast as you can, Magnolia, you hear me?" Ordering her around, I sound like Nana. "Don't linger on the white side of town. I want you back across the river before the protest starts. That's sunset. We clear?"

Magnolia smiles through her tears. "Of course I'll come back."

"Don't disappear on me, okay? I'm your *sister.*" My voice catches. "If you decide to go back to your white life, I deserve to know."

"I'd never leave without tellin' you," she says.

But she did not say: *I'd never leave.*

Finally, the truth lands in my stomach like a stone:

Magnolia and I might not be forever. To survive, she really might have to leave me. Become white again. We'll always be blood, but never together. Just like Mama and Daddy before us, love won't be enough.

Not here.

Maybe not anywhere.

I help my sister find her shoes; she helps me find my courage.

"We won't let anythin' happen to Darius, curse or not. Be brave, Charlie."

At the front door, my lip twitches. "I haven't felt brave since I left New York."

"Odessa always said, *Pretend.* Sometimes that's enough."

"Nana always said, *Keep on swinging.* But—" A dark thought stops me.

Magnolia furrows her brow. "What?"

"She also said, *For colored girls, there's no such thing as happily ever after.*"

Magnolia's pale throat constricts. "Don't think like that. Not yet."

"You're right. Just come back."

"If the creek don't rise."

And then, as the sun casts its first rays of light, Magnolia steps into the day—and leaves me behind.

23
Magnolia

Aunt Hilda is still asleep when I arrive at Heathwood. Still sleeping when I place a call to the Waylon house, asking Annamae over. Still sleeping even while I wait for my former friend in the parlor, below the mirror that cannot see me.

Charlie thinks I'm downright foolish for trying to stop the disinterment, but I have no choice. I should have been trying to put a stop to this evil since the moment Annamae first mentioned cemetery segregation—and I should never, ever have attended that Gravediggers' Potluck.

Though I have chosen to be colored, Eureka's colored spirits have not accepted me. Why should they, after the gutless way I have lived?

Waiting for my old friend, I drop onto a couch.

The air at Heathwood really is quite strange. Moldy, I think—intoxicating. The floral wallpaper seems to undulate, shapeshifting. In one instant, the flowers on the wall are fresh and plain—in another, wilted and dying. I drift to sleep, lulled by the ticking of the grandfather clock. My eyes close, then blink open. For a second, I think I see Mama, pregnant, in the chair across from me. Then she dissolves. A bit of dream.

But I hear a sound, and that much is real.

The *stamp, stamp* of little feet.

I sit up straight, facing my ghost.

He says, *"It's time."*

Last time this spirit visited me at Heathwood, he led me to the room below the abandoned stables. In terror, I fled.

This time, I'll try harder.

The boy flickers out of sight, vanishing like fog burned off by the sun. But his feet stamp compression footprints on the antique rug. Heart hammering, I follow him into the blue-bird morning.

The abandoned stables are not far. The spirit's footprints, swift, lead straight there.

Hurrying after him, a horrible stench sweeps over me like an unwelcome breeze—it's Grandmother's straightening iron, heating up.

An icy voice whispers: *"Don't take another step, you ungrateful wretch."*

I freeze.

Across the field, the little boy flickers back into view. His outline shimmers uncertainly. His eyes do not accuse me, as they did at Freedom House. He looks crestfallen. Disappointed.

I have just summoned my courage to follow him despite Grandmother's tricks, when the little ghost winks out like a star.

"*No.* Come back. Please, won't you come back?"

Like a madwoman, I holler in an empty cotton field.

Devastated, I drop to my knees, hanging on to the grass. Pulling it viciously from the root. That was my last chance to help Eureka's spirits. My very last.

Annamae's candy-pink car pulls up the driveway, and I stumble up. She parks it beside the cupid fountain and steps out, slamming the door. She sports a silk headscarf and a glower.

Spotting me, she yowls, "Why, Magnolia, what on earth was so important it couldn't wait for a reasonable hour? Haven't you ever heard of beauty sleep?"

I stride toward her. "It's important, Annamae, I swear."

Suspicious, she looks me up and down. "Why, bless your heart, you look like somethin' the cat dragged in."

I dust dry grass from my skirt. "I have not been feelin' my best, that's sure. Come on and sit a spell."

On the veranda, we take our customary seats in twin rocking chairs. An early morning dew clings to the sky, and Heathwood's vast, green fields roll all the way down to the longleaf forest. If you did not know any better, you would think it blessed.

What on *earth* did Grandmother keep in that chest below the stables? What did the boy spirit want me to see?

"I assume you invited me to apologize for what happened at my Gravediggers' Potluck, Magnolia Heathwood."

Anger flares. "No. I'm givin' you a chance to make things right. You've got to know the disinterment's wrong—"

Annamae fiddles with her scarf. "Oh, I'm over all that. I'm startin' a new club now, the Future Homemakers of America—"

"*Annamae.* If Colored Town protests tonight, people are gonna die."

Annamae startles like I've woken her from heavy sleep.

In a way, I reckon I have.

"*Puh-lease*, Magnolia. Protests only ever happen up North, everyone knows that! Anyhow, there're twenty men signed up to dig tonight, and Lord knows they're eager to start. No one can stop them now. Let alone little ol' me."

Twenty men, oh my Lord.

"It's *wrong*, Annamae. Can't you feel it?"

"Colored people don't care about their cemeteries. Why, they're practically children—they won't mind a bit. When'd you become such a Negro lover, anyhow? I swear, Magnolia, I don't understand what's happened to you!"

Go back to your life, Old Roland said. *Pass for white.*

But I heard Old Roland's prophecy. I cannot sit by and let the preacher's son die.

I square my shoulders. "Annamae, I'm colored. That's why I care."

It's a relief to say it out loud—a great unburdening. Pride swells in my chest, too, because Charlie's taught me that being colored is a powerful, wondrous thing. I have changed so much in such a short time. My words reflect no shame.

Annamae's face contorts. "Why, you—you're white, Magnolia—quit lyin'!"

"It's nothing but the truth, Annamae Waylon. My mother's buried in the colored cemetery. It's *her* body they'll be diggin' up tonight. If we were ever really friends, you'll call the senator. For me."

The silence thickens between us, growing teeth.

"I can't," Annamae says, at last. "The president of the *U*-nited States couldn't stop this thing now. The whole town's fit to be tied."

When it comes to Annamae, I could always tell truth from lies—and she's telling the God's honest truth now. Fear coils at the base of my spine.

"At my Gravediggers' Potluck. You knew you were colored then, didn't you? Ate our food, drank our sweet tea— *how could you?*"

I expect Annamae to whip at me like a snake. Instead, she thrusts her hand into her purse, digging for her wallet. She brandishes a picture of the two of us at the Miss Eureka pageant.

"Look." She shakes the photo in my face. "You are *not* colored. You're my best friend!"

"No, Annamae."

"Who else knows?"

"Why—all Colored Town."

Annamae presses her lips together. "No, I mean who else *white?*"

I lean away. Afraid, though I do not know of what. "Annamae, I think you'd best go on home."

She grips my wrist with red-painted nails, reminding me of Grandmother, clawing me on her deathbed. "Listen, Magnolia, it's not too late. We can still keep your little secret under wraps."

"Annamae, I can't. I have a sister—a twin. Her name's Charlie."

"A colored sister? Who cares? You can forget her, too!"

"What on earth are you *talking* about?"

Her weasel eyes darken. "At Dearing Hospital, they have machines. Electric ones. They can make you forget all about being colored. Then we can go back to what we were before—the best of friends."

The horror of it makes my skin crawl, but finally, I understand: Annamae needs me ever so much more than I need her. Without me as her faithful accessory, she'll have to invent a whole new life, and deep down, she knows she's nothing special. Her world has become so small: a bubble of parties and blue ribbons, all seasoned with a dash of fear and hate. After all, what are her achievements really worth, if she's no better than the people suffering around her, washing her clothes, making her meals, living in poverty?

"I have a better idea. Why don't *you* forget, Annamae? Quit clinging to the past. It doesn't suit you."

Evil slithers into Annamae's expression. "I gave you a chance to rise above your station, Magnolia Heathwood. No wonder you always played second fiddle in everything. The pageant, the spelling bee—"

Revolted, I rise.

Her hand comes out of nowhere, snatching a hank of my hair. "You can't walk away from me!"

"Quit bein' ugly, Annamae! Lemme *go!*"

The porch door slams open, and my aunt Hilda appears. She wears her rose-patterned nightdress, her hair disheveled.

"Annamae Waylon, you stop that this instant!"

"I'll do no such—"

Aunt Hilda's fast as a mongoose after a snake. She's still drunk, but when she reaches us, her aim's good. She slaps Annamae so hard her head snaps around.

Freed from Annamae's grip, I rub the sore spot on my scalp. And I gaze at Aunt Hilda in wonder, because she defended me. Even after I lost her the Heathwood house, even after I chose being colored over my family name, Aunt Hilda still loves me.

"So it's true." Annamae rubs her cheek. "You're nothing but an uppity half-breed *bitch*."

"Don't you speak to her like that," Aunt Hilda snaps. "Not on her own land."

"Oh, this land won't be hers for long! Once word gets out, they'll burn Heathwood to the ground. Just you wait!"

"You gonna tell them, Annamae? You want to watch them hang her from a tree?"

Confusion twists her face. "We're not *barbarians*—we wouldn't—"

"I've always thought you were a darn stupid little girl, Annamae Waylon, and this proves it. Eureka's men will kill her if you so much as breathe a *word*."

Annamae leans into her hip, sulking.

Slowly, she wipes the smeared mascara from her cheeks. "I won't tell Daddy, all right? But you'd better believe I'm telling my brother. He deserves to know, after what the two of you got up to last summer! Oh, you'll burn in hell for this, Magnolia Heathwood!"

My heart seizes. *Annamae's gonna tell Finch.*

What will he think of me? What will he do?

Annamae backs away from Aunt Hilda and me, watching us close. She stays watching us, even as she opens the door to her candy-pink car. Glaring, she slides across the leather seat and accelerates down the cobblestone drive.

"Good riddance," Aunt Hilda mutters.

"Auntie—" I am so grateful, my voice snaps clean in two.

"No, you listen to me, Magnolia Heathwood. I was wrong to chase you away. We're family, you hear?" She holds sagging arms out to me, and I rush into them. "You'll always be my Sugarpie. Even if we can't live together...even if you hole up in Colored Town...maybe I can't follow, but I do hope you can still feel me lovin' you."

Aunt Hilda's breath smells, like always, of bourbon.

"Come on, Auntie. Let's get you back to bed."

"When's Odessa comin' by? I could use a glass of her vinegar tonic and a boiled egg...."

"Odessa won't be around today. They're diggin' up the cemetery tonight. Colored Town's protesting."

"They're diggin' up *what*?"

Tenderly, I tuck my aunt into bed. "Don't worry your head. I'll fix you that egg and tonic myself."

Poor Aunt Hilda is only weeks away from losing her house, and I simply do not know what she's gonna do. Don't know what I'm gonna do, either.

Old Roland said, *Go back to your life. Pass for white.*

The crazy thing is, I still could. Eureka balances on a foundation of pure hypocrisy. If I apologized to Annamae before she had a chance to tell Finch...if I made her feel virtuous enough...why, I could still go back to my white dream, I think. Or, if Annamae's feeling vengeful, Aunt Hilda and I could start over in another town. Just two white women down on our luck.

Bile washes into my throat, thinking of living this lie for decades to come.

Go back to your life. Pass for white.

In the powder room, beneath a mirror that will not see me, I am violently, wrenchingly sick.

24
Charlie

All morning, I pace Freedom House like the caged leopard at the Central Park Zoo, trying to think my way free. Even here, in haunted Eureka, there has to be a way to protect the people I love. Magnolia, Darius. There's just got to be.

Old Roland told me to look behind the bathroom mirror again.

Told me, *Everyone knows that revolts in Eureka always end in blood.*

It's time to see what he means.

In the kitchen, still cluttered after last night's repast, I find a candle and matches. Daylight's streaming through the windows, but Freedom House's shadows sop it up. Dust hovers in the air, thick and strange.

My candle lit, I stub toes in the dark. I'm careful to cup my hand around the flame. In the long hall, shadows explode around me: Contorted shapes prowl the floor, the walls. For an instant, I think I see a snake uncoiling on the ceiling.

This house was built by my first free ancestor, Charles Freedom. It's a part of my family—I shouldn't be so afraid.

Only, Nana was a little afraid of this place—wasn't she?

By the light of a single candle, I observe my tired face in the bathroom mirror. I can't help but think of Magnolia.

It's not a fair choice, between passing for white and death. I want to yell at the colored spirits who won't accept her—but I remember last time, when I tried to look behind the mirror without asking. That ghastly, choral shout: *MIND YOUR MANNERS DOWN SOUTH!*

Like Magnolia with all her southern lady nonsense, I've got to play nice.

I clear my throat. "Spirits? Mr. Freedom? It's Charlie Yates. Can I see the secret behind the mirror?" I hesitate just a second before adding, "Please?"

At first, I feel nothing.

Then a cold wind blows past my face. Ghostly.

I think that was a *yes*.

Standing on tiptoe, I unhook the mirror from its hanging.

There's a wooden etching behind the mirror. It's incredibly

detailed—lifelike. I imagine Nana's father patiently carving the shore, a starry sky, and a long row of people in raw wood. It's beautiful.

So why's it hidden?

I lean forward, peering closer.

The etching paints a scene: Dozens of people—men, women, and children—hold hands at the river's edge. When I bring the candle near, the etched water seems to churn.

"Slaves."

Hot wax drips down my wrist. I look deeper.

Those people—their feet are chained. Shackled together. They stand beneath a full moon. In the distance, I make out Heathwood crowning its hill.

Why are people shackled at the riverside in the middle of the night?

A light-skinned woman turns. In the wood, she comes *alive*—and looks straight at me. My skin breaks out in a sick sweat. The woman nods, then raises her hand high.

On her mark, every one of the shackled people—Heathwood's slaves—leaps into the churning water. Even the children. Even women with babies in their arms.

"No, no, no!"

Feet shackled, they'll drown. The water thrashes like a beast, but not a single face breaks the surface again.

I sink to the floor, horrified.

Head in hands, I sift through my memories.

No colored person fishes in Eureka's river—to this day,

no one fishes the water because slaves died there. Hundreds of them. They took their own lives because that's all they had to take; their only means of rebellion against the men who claimed to own them.

Hopelessness fills my lungs, thick as swamp water. In my mind's eye, I see the open graves near Old Roland's hut, sucking up moonlight. See Mama in her white wedding dress, a bullet hole in her temple.

And I see Magnolia, trapped inside Heathwood Plantation's white coffin—screaming for help no one can give.

I want to lie down on the floor forever. Curl into a ball and never rise.

But I force myself to stand, taking one last look at the gruesome etching. The water's quieted. The people are gone.

As I lift the mirror, preparing to put it back in its place, motion startles me.

In the etching, a little boy peeks from behind a tree. His features look somehow familiar. His nose, like Magnolia's— and mine. Slowly, it dawns on me: This must be my great-grandfather. The man who lived to build this house and crowned himself with the majestic surname, Freedom.

"You didn't jump with the others," I whisper. "You hid."

The little boy nods his head up and down. He opens his mouth, speaking a word that looks like: *change*. Or maybe I only imagined it. Then he drops to the ground, soundlessly weeping.

Gently as I'm able, I cover him with the mirror.

Adrenaline rushes out of me. I can't stand the viciousness of this place. I just—can't. Seeing the slave revolt now, on the day of the protest, feels like a bad sign. Especially for Darius, who the conjure man said I'd lose.

Would Eureka really kill him for standing up for what's right?

Of course it would. Wouldn't even bat an eye.

A gust blows my candle out, and the pipes behind the walls groan. In the dark, my head spins, trying to figure a way out of this maze for me and Darius and Magnolia.

But I just can't see it.

In my mind, I sound just like Magnolia—thinking, *Not fair. Not fair.*

25
Magnolia

Cemetery Night has come at last.

By the time I make my way back to Freedom House, Colored Town has already begun its march. I can hear them from far off. They sound like an ocean wave, gathering strength. With every footstep, I pray for their safety.

The sun is setting. The sky, heavy with rain. I am worn down, too terribly tired to be out tonight. But I promised my sister I'd come back, if the creek don't rise.

Charlie opens Freedom House's blue door before I have a chance to knock. Her face twists, anguished.

"What took so long!" she cries. "I thought something happened to you!"

"Charlie, I couldn't stop the disinterment. You were right."

"Of course I was right," she snaps.

Then she pulls me against her, hugging me tight.

My poor sister. I hate to think of her losing Darius and me both. The protesters are close now. Soon, I'll have to make a decision: to walk with them or walk alone—back to Heathwood.

"People are gonna die at this protest, Charlie. Can you ask Darius to stay home? Stop him, somehow? He loves you. He'll listen."

She slumps. "I'm not about to talk him out of being a man. Anyway, it's too late. Can't you hear them?"

I can. Their voices rumble like thunder, and their feet judder the earth.

"Will you walk with us?"

"I want to, Charlie, but—I don't think I can. I'm worn slap out. And the spirits have made their opinions clear, haven't they?" My voice runs bitter as saw grass tea. "I don't belong in Colored Town."

"Come inside. We'll get some water in you at least—"

"I've got Old Roland's grave dirt in my pocket." I swallow. "I may not be able to stay in Colored Town, but I deserve to understand why."

This is grave dirt, twice blessed, Old Roland said. Blow it onto glass. It will show you the moment the curse took hold. Like a sapling, taking root.

"Old Roland's a fake," Charlie says.

The protesters coming down the road are getting closer. Beyond the fence, torchlight flickers. Every man and woman in Colored Town has turned out tonight, chanting: *"Respect our dead! Let them lie!"*

"Respect our dead! Let them lie!"

Thunder cracks, and the sky opens up. Rain falls in a steady patter.

"If Roland's lying, it won't take but a minute to find out. Please, Charlie. Let's visit Mama's mirror again."

Moving past the kitchen, I try not to think that this is the last time I shall ever visit Freedom House.

In Mama's room, we stand in front of the obsidian mirror like we did before. The glass reflects my sister, the whorling, wild shadows—but not me.

I reach into my pocket for the vial of grave dirt. I open it, then spill rough dirt into my palm.

"Magnolia, I don't know if this is such a good idea—"

I blow out, hard, like blowing out a birthday candle.

Instantly, the glass begins to twist and change.

The lightbulbs flicker. The air sizzles with magic.

Charlie and I stand shoulder to shoulder, watching as two women, one white and one colored, shiver into being. They are ghostly at first, then more lifelike. Their faces are tight, arguing.

They argue over a cradle. Their voices, watery and ethereal, as if they're speaking inside a bell—or from underwater.

Watching, Charlie grips my hand so hard, my bones ache.

It is beyond strange, seeing our grandmothers together.

"You have no right, Jeannette!" Grandmother cries. *"The light child is the only thing left of my Dean! Can't you see I'm grievin'? I need this baby. I deserve this child!"*

"It ain't right, separatin' twins," Nana says. *"I'm sorry for what you've lost, but money won't make up for the hurt you'll cause—"*

"What hurt, when the children will never know? We'll swear secrecy, here, tonight. And the light-skinned child will be raised with every comfort." To my shock, Grandmother kneels at the feet of the colored woman. *"Sweet Jeannette, you've been through so much. I saw Marie's body, you know. And in her weddin' dress, too."*

I recognize that tone—that manipulative cajoling. Nana moans like Grandmother struck her. I know from experience: What Grandmother's fixin' to do is worse.

"Stop it, Mrs. Heathwood. Please, no more—"

"But your girl's free of all that now! Why, she's up in heaven watchin' over all of us, the sweet, pretty thing! Wouldn't she want the best for both her children? A white-looking child's safer with me than you. Just think of what happened to Don Bell. And what's more, I'll love her like she's my own! Don't you know I lost a child, too? I lost my Dean." The tears come, streaming. *"My poor, sweet son."*

Grandmother cries her crocodile tears, bawling her bad heart out. Nana doesn't know it isn't real; she reaches, trembling, for the white woman. She lays a hand on her shoulder.

They make an affecting tableau: the white woman weeping on her knees, while the colored woman rocks the cradle, holding all the power of absolution.

Oh, but my heart is hard as glass, because I know what Nana doesn't, or at least doesn't want to admit: *It's an act. Every inch.*

Ever so slowly, Nana reaches into the cradle to fish the light-skinned baby out. A small hand reaches back, but Nana catches it.

The baby wails.

"There, there," Nana says. *"Everything will turn out right."*

Watching, I want to scream, *No! No, it won't!*

Grandmother accepts the child like it's a tremendous blessing.

And then she drops the act.

"Here, gal." She flips open her alligator-skin wallet. *"Be sure you're outta town tomorrow, or I'll set the law on you."*

Charlie gasps as Nana cries out, but I saw it coming. I set my teeth and look away, though I can feel it all in my body, the ripping, tearing pain. The grandmother I never knew—Nana—has discarded me. She's given me up and broken the bonds of sisterhood. She's begun the curse that might kill me yet.

The glass goes dark once more.

Outside, the protesters bellow, *"Respect our dead! Let them lie!"*

Meanwhile, my chest feels as hollow as a cave. I have witnessed the moment that fractured my sister from me, and seen the primal horror of our separation.

It is too much. Far too much. We can't ever fix what's been broken. Old Roland was right: The curse is rooted too deep.

Charlie knows it, too. I see the knowledge in the mirror image of her eyes.

"Oh, Magnolia—I'm so sorry—"

"If you want me at the protest, I'll be there."

Tears course down her face. "Don't die for me. You have to live. Even if it means passing for white."

There's so much I want to say, but my words dry up.

"I love you," Charlie says. "I'll always, always love you."

I feel sundered, split down the middle along Eureka's color line, sharp and vicious as barbed wire. To live, I must lose my sister. Let her go.

Charlie follows me onto the porch.

The march has finally reached Freedom House.

A river of protesters streams down the road, headed toward the cemetery. Mothers with babies strapped to their chests. Old folks leaning hard into their canes.

My heart aches to join them. I want to be part of this movement, this wave of unbreakable hope. But beneath Eureka's stars, my fate is sealed. The spirits have not accepted me; I cannot be colored.

"Look out for Darius, won't you?"

Over the cacophony, Charlie has to raise her voice to be heard. "Where will you go?"

"Back to Heathwood. Don't worry. I'll be fine."

"Magnolia—"

I have always hated goodbyes.

I hike up my skirt and run, darting across the protest line and toward the road that will take me back to Heathwood.

Charlie doesn't follow, and that's fine. After all, she knows now what I do: We are too badly broken to ever be a family.

"Respect our dead! Let them lie!"

Dog-tired, I stumble down the pitted lane—headed back to the life Grandmother always wished me to have. I am sobbing, but I reckon it's somehow fitting.

As the saying goes, nothing ever changes in Eureka, and nothing ever dies.

26

Charlie

've marched in many protests in my life, but never one like this. There's a different energy to a southern march. Danger, like the reek off the swamp, haunts the air.

The river of protesters carries me to the cemetery. Walking, I try not to think of what Old Roland said about losing Darius. I can't control what happens to him—or to me. In an action, you can only control your response to white aggression. Nothing more.

In the cemetery, all Colored Town takes orders from Darius and his father.

"Stand beside the headstones of your loved ones," the preacher shouts. "Whatever comes, we must keep them in the ground."

I find my mother's grave. Her headstone, covered in foxglove.

MARIE ANN YATES, BELOVED MOTHER, DAUGHTER, WIFE.

With Nana's cane in my hands, I swear I won't let her rest be disturbed.

On my right, the Bell family spreads a blanket near their plots. Their youngest girl is yellow-toned. I stare long and hard at her, thinking of Magnolia. What she could've been like if she'd been raised colored instead of white. If that evil Heathwood woman hadn't snatched her from Nana's arms.

The vision we saw in the obsidian mirror will haunt me for the rest of my life.

Darius and his father march from family to family, keeping up spirits, clasping hands. Darius looks handsome. Noble.

On my right, Joe sits cross-legged on a grave. He looks like he might throw up.

"Hey, Joe," I call. "You all right?"

He smiles wanly. "Just scared, I guess. I don't want to die tonight."

"You won't. Really," I say, though I don't know. On an electric night like this, anything could happen. "Worst we'll get is the fire hose, so just roll onto your belly when it comes. Okay?"

"Thanks, Charlie," Joe says—though he doesn't look much better.

In a wooden etching, I watched Heathwood's slaves revolt—and die. But it's not the 1800s anymore. It's 1953.

White Eureka wouldn't massacre women and children—would they?

The colored cemetery's positioned at the bottom of a steep hill—not good. A few of the larger men form a line in front of the graves, shielding us with their bodies. I'm horrified when Darius stands with them—exposed to whatever white Eureka has in store. As the rain mists our skin, he blazes with fight.

Of course, no one really plans to fight—not physically. Nonviolent protest is the only way we can hope to survive.

Our only goal: to make white Eureka see us as *human*.

"No weapons, right?" Preacher Lucien looks hard at the faces of the colored men. "No guns, no pitchforks, no knives..."

The whine of police sirens, the harsh blare of a fire truck. White Eureka's already on its way.

I watch the horizon, waiting for men to appear at the top of the hill.

Waiting. Barely breathing.

Darius breaks away from the front line, headed straight toward me. Even on a night like this, the sight of him makes my heart race.

"Charlie. Where's your sister?"

"Long story." My throat feels thick. "You scared?"

He lifts an eyebrow. "Would I tell you if I were? Come on, now."

What about Charlie? Is she cursed? Magnolia asked, and Old

Roland cocked his head. *Spirits say yes, but she won't lose so much as you.*

Only her blue-eyed African prince.

I want to give him something. But all I have is Nana's cane.

"Will you take this? It's a snake. Supposed to protect colored folks."

"Looks too much like a weapon. Might get me shot."

"Keep it on the ground, then."

"Never figured you for the superstitious type, Miss New York."

"Well." I smile sadly. "Eureka's funny like that. What happened to your white ally—Finch Waylon? Is he here?"

Darius frowns. "Apparently he had some kind of domestic issue to take care of. We weren't so important to him after all."

I tense, hoping Magnolia isn't the "domestic issue" Finch Waylon needs to handle.

At the top of the hill, cars and trucks roar into view, headlights splashing. White men begin setting up construction floodlights. Under the moon, shovels glint like knives.

"Hold your ground, Charlie," Darius says.

"You too," I whisper—and then he's gone. Back to the front line.

Hands up, Preacher Lucien treks slowly uphill, gone to parley with white men.

My breath rasps.

Keep on swinging. Be brave.

The floodlights switch on and the night turns unnaturally bright, like day. I wonder what those white men see, looking at me, Joe, the Bell family. Do they see people, who love and lose just like them? Or do they see animals and criminals? It never ceases to haunt me—the unpredictable ways colored folk are reflected in a white eye.

At first, the white leaders talk with the preacher—and all seems fine.

The little light-skinned girl plays a clapping game with her mother, happy to be up past her bedtime. Joe settles down. I feel somehow naked without Nana's cane.

Scraps of conversation carry on the wind.

Preacher Lucien says, "We can't allow you to unbury our dead...move them to that swamp...not right...won't stand for it."

"All signed and dated," a white voice answers. "The proper procedures...fair warning...uppity, is what you are...Police are already on their way..."

With that single word, *police*, my breath comes faster, harder.

Preacher Lucien and the white man begin to shout.

And then all hell breaks loose.

Police park on the hilltop. At a disgusted word from the white leader, they come streaming toward us in a blue-black wave.

No, oh no.

The back of my neck prickles. I turn to see Old Roland, watching me from a grove of cypress trees. He lifts a hand. Waves.

"Women, get your children," Preacher Lucien shouts. "Take the high road. *Run.*"

I look at Joe, and Joe looks back at me. Neither of us moves.

But I'm relieved when the Bell family makes a break for the trees. The little ones are leaving now. Hopefully, they'll be safe.

Police carry billy clubs; other men brandish shovels. Our men, though unarmed, are ready. Hands balled into fists, bodies braced. When those policemen clash with the front line, it sounds like the universe tearing itself in half.

It's a brawl. A bad one. The protesters who aren't on the line stick beside their graves. Even as we watch man after man cuffed or tossed roughly aside, we don't move.

This is the moment we prove how much we care. With our ability to suffer, we'll put Eureka's white community to shame. My toes curl inside my shoes, gripping.

Finally, they turn on the fire hose.

Water blasts from my left, strong and stinging bright. Feels like my body's being belted, endlessly beaten.

Joe screams.

"On your belly!" I shout. "Drop down!"

Below me, my mother's grave turns to mud. I slip, my feet washed out from under me. Though I scrabble and scratch, trying to hold on, I'm sliding away. The water's blasting so hard I can't see Joe anymore. Can't see anything.

As muddy water fills my mouth, it's not Nana's name I scream. Not Mama's or Daddy's, either.

"Magnolia! *Magnolia!*"

After that, there's no more air for shouting.

Only Eureka's water, drowning me.

27

Charlie

n a watery ditch, I lose consciousness.

And I dream.

I see my great-grandfather Charles Freedom—that little boy who hid on the riverside during the slave revolt. His eyes a deep, spiraled brown. His mouth, moving.

"Change," he says. *"Even Eureka can change."*

My eyes snap open.

I'm soaking wet, hidden in a ditch just below the colored cemetery. Whip-poor-wills scream, and after-rain mist rises up from the ground like the spirits of the dead. I have no idea what time it is. I'd give anything right now to be safe back home in Harlem.

I elbow myself up to standing. My hands, scraped and muddied.

The cemetery's empty. The paddy wagons, the flood-lights, and the fire truck are long gone. Before I passed out, police arrested men on the front lines for the crime of standing up for our dead, and the fire hose took care of the rest.

I'll never unhear the sound of water blasting. Never unlive this night. Colored Town tried its best, but we couldn't stand up to Eureka.

Slowly, on cold, sore legs, I trudge back toward the cemetery. What I see breaks my heart.

Every colored grave has been dug up, hastily and unceremoniously. Our side is pocked full of holes—the earth, bleeding raw.

Keep on swinging, Nana said. But when you hurt this much—how?

And Darius—*where is he?*

I tramp through mud and soil, skirting empty graves. Those plots yawn like open mouths. The offerings colored folk left have all been washed away.

I find Mama's grave, the turned-over dirt still fresh. The headstone flopped onto its side. Water fills her burial plot. Soon the earth will suck that up, sprouting mushrooms in her place. I stare into those depths, stunned. Mama didn't deserve this. No one does.

Miserable, I moan into my hands.

"Charlie?"

Darius.

Sticking out of a nearby grave, Nana's cane glimmers. Darius climbs out of the ground, his hands grasping a tree root. I trip, then scramble up. Running even though I can't see him yet. Mere feet away he catches me, arm solid as a tree branch around my waist. He holds me close, swaying. Like dancing.

Only he's not dancing; he's weeping.

He didn't let the fire hose move him—somehow, he hung on—and he must've stayed fighting even as white men dug up these graves. Now Darius Lucien's wearing bloody rags. His face is swollen, his right eye shut. They hit him with something. A baton, or—

"Butt of a rifle." Darius spits blood. "Knocked me cold."

"Why didn't they arrest you like the others?"

"Don't know. I woke in Uncle Otto's grave—must've rolled in when they struck me. In all the chaos, nobody bothered to look." He's quiet. "Even after I failed him, my uncle protected me."

"You tried your best."

"Wasn't good enough."

"What happened to your daddy?"

Darius laughs bitterly. "I heard the foreman and the police arguing over what to do with him. Foreman wanted him jailed, of course—but the police said he should go home for the sake of community peace. They sent him back to Colored Town. I think he would've rather been arrested, like most of his flock. Must be killing him."

"Let me take you home. Bet he's worried about you."

Darius spits again; this time, a tooth rolls onto dirt. "No. Mama will fuss, and I know Daddy's heartbroken. I can't take it, Charlie."

"Okay."

"It's all my fault. I convinced my father to march, and what did it get us? Nothing."

"At least no one was killed."

"They've got Nat and Joe down at the jail," Darius says. "They're not safe."

I chew my lip, thinking of the black flag raised outside NAACP headquarters after a death down South: A MAN WAS LYNCHED TODAY.

All too often, those men were dragged out of some rural county jail.

"My father said, 'Eureka's not like those cities you hear about on the radio. Nothing's gonna change here, and you're a fool to try.' He was right."

Darius wipes his bloodied nose with the back of his hand. "I'm a damned fool."

Darius lies on the bed where Nana died, body curved around a pillow. I lay a damp cloth over his back, hoping to ease his pain.

I've cleaned his wounds, but they need disinfecting.

When I try to treat the cut on his face, he pushes my hand away.

I'm aching to help him, but his wounds are soul deep. I don't know what to do.

I'm relieved when Dr. Colt shows up at Freedom's front door.

"He's alive? Here?"

"Yes! He's here! Face smashed in—the fire hose tore skin off his back."

"Anything deep?"

"No, but he won't speak. Please come in. He'll need help getting home—"

Dr. Colt shakes his head. "Night riders may come yet—whole town knows who led this thing. Darius Lucien's safer here. Listen well, Charlie: Snuff the lamps out; don't light the stove. Don't play the radio, and keep your voice to a whisper. Understand?"

My hands tremble, realizing what Dr. Colt's saying. Ku Klux could visit my house tonight.

In New York, Ella Baker once gave a speech on southern conditions. How any colored person can die at any time. How whole communities hide behind darkened windows, living in fear of white hoods and long ropes.

Never expected I'd become one of those desperate people.

Dr. Colt presses ointment into my hand. "I'll get word to his parents. You just lie low."

In Freedom's entryway, I'm dizzy with fresh fear.

And I wish Magnolia were here.

I lock the door; check the stove. The lamps in this house like to misbehave, so I unscrew the bulbs. No accidents tonight. Before I draw the curtains, I beg the trees to keep us hidden. I think the woods hear me, because the dark seems to close around us like a protective shell.

Feels natural to crawl into bed with Darius. Natural to fit my own body around his larger one—gently, to spare his back, flayed but still so strong. He doesn't move, barely even breathes.

Nana always soothed me with stories. I try to soothe Darius, too.

"I never told you much about New York. Probably you know we all live in apartments—packed like sardines in a can. Where I'm from, it's not just Black and white. There're a million shades of brown, not to mention Asian folks, Irish, and Italian. You name it, we got it." I pause. Is he listening? "My favorite food's chicken lo mein from a street cart on One Hundred Fourth. Second favorite, Mr. Alfie's gelato. His prices run high, though; Nana and me only buy his desserts on special occasions."

Darius twitches. I hold my breath.

Finally, he drawls, "What's gelato?"

"Italian ice cream! But even better, because it's creamier— Mr. Alfie makes each batch with a dozen fresh eggs. It comes in every flavor under the sun, including mango and corn. My favorite's *stracciatella*."

Darius rolls over, bemused. "Say that again, Miss New York."

"*Straccia*—"

Mid-word, he kisses me. A burning, needful kiss. I press my body firmly against his chest, feeling his eyelashes on my cheek, his fingers grazing my hip. I want to drink him. Kiss him for years.

Then I change the angle of my face.

Darius winces. "Jaw's busted."

"I've got bandages. Hang on."

He grabs my wrist, pulling me down. "That's not the medicine I need."

I frown. "I shouldn't be kissing you with your lip cut."

"Lay with me awhile. Tell me more about New York."

I curl against him, awkward at first. But soon enough I feel snug and safe, even knowing Klan might be out there, hunting.

I tell him everything I remember about New York: the parks, the tree-lined boulevards, the underground trains. I tell him about the Macy's Thanksgiving Day Parade, the spectacle of St. Patrick's Day, and the Egyptian mummies at the Metropolitan. I tell him about every protest I've ever seen go right, and all the change we've made. Tell him, too, about all the change that's coming soon.

When my words dry up, Darius asks, "Think this magic city of yours would ever take in a country hick like me?"

I tighten in his arms. His eyes don't tease, like they usually do. He looks at me in such a wide-open way, I see straight through to the child he once was.

"New York'll take anyone. Hard work paying the bills, but if you don't mind going without—"

"I don't mind work. But I'm gonna need someone to show me the ropes." He touches my cheek. "Think that someone could be you?"

Unbidden, an image rises of Mama and Daddy, smiling over the book of *Love Sonnets*.

"Lots to learn about city living."

For the first time since the fire hose, Darius smiles. "I'm guessing you'll be a world-class teacher." His smile flickers out. "Would you go with me tomorrow? Or the day after?"

"You can't really be thinking of leaving? I know how much family means to you."

"What if I asked you to marry me?"

My pulse pounds. "Don't say that. I'm too young to get married."

"But would you think about it? Your sister could come, too."

Grief pricks my heart, sharp.

"I don't think she can," I say softly.

"Something wrong between y'all?"

"It's complicated."

How do I explain my sister's impossible choice—to pass for white, or die?

Darius frowns. "Your sister's in love with you, Charlie. She'd die for you."

I shake my head, trying not to cry.

"I mean it," Darius insists. "She'd pick you over a million bucks any day. I've seen it in her eyes. She's your family."

"Doesn't change things."

After Nana died, I felt sure I'd lost the only family I'd ever have in this world. Then I found Magnolia—and Darius. I have no choice but to lose my twin, but I can still save Darius. Take him home. Keep him safe.

"Let's go to New York, Darius Lucien. Catch the next train."

He pulls me against him. Wrapping me tight.

And I'm relieved, because I'm finally, *finally* going home.

Though, for a while there, *Magnolia* felt like home.

The last thing I feel, before sleep takes over, is the brush of Darius's lips on my hair. The last thing I hear is this beautiful, unbeatable man, slowly sounding out the name of my favorite dessert—*stracciatella*.

I force myself not to think of my sister.

Darius and me—we're going to be all right.

If the creek don't rise.

28
Magnolia

n the morning, I do not bother getting up.

My curse squeezes my temples like a vice, and I doubt I will ever see another tomorrow. I am a fly trapped at the center of an inescapable web. A lonely soul lost in the veil.

Go back to your life, Magnolia Heathwood, Old Roland said. *Pass for white. Choose the other side—and live.*

But I can hardly lift my head from my feather pillow. I fear I have changed course too late.

Aunt Hilda knocks, and then lets herself in. "Oh, Magnolia."

"*Oh, Magnolia* what? I had nowhere else to go."

"Lemme guess. You fought with your sister."

"Not exactly."

I can't tell her about the curse. She simply would not believe it.

Aunt Hilda rests a hand on my calf—beneath the covers, my legs are still muddy from trekking through the swamp.

At this hour, Aunt Hilda doesn't normally look so great herself. Only today her eyes aren't bloodshot. Her cheeks aren't florid, either.

I sit up. "Aunt Hilda, did you quit drinking?"

"Bourbon and I are taking a little break. I only have twenty-some days left to stay in this house. With you gone, I needed a clear head."

She smiles, but I cannot muster one.

Overcome, I burrow my face into my pillow.

Aunt Hilda sighs. "I have some experience with sisters, you know. I can tell you, it is never easy. Blanche never did like me, even when we were children. Once, in the dead of night, she cut off all my hair. Always sneaky, that Blanche. Mother's favorite."

My aunt strokes her long braid, shot through with white. I always knew Aunt Hilda was frightened of Grandmother, but we never talked about it. Grandmother's grip on our lives was too terribly strong.

"I tried to leave once, too, you know. Tried to escape."

"You did?"

"Mm-hmm. But you know what this house is like. None of us can ever really leave. Even if we move . . . I do believe Heathwood'll call us back before we die."

Horrid thought. "Aunt Hilda—"

"Sugarpie, when I was your age, I ran off with a boyfriend. Well, my parents had the police bring me straight home. But I think Blanche had a hand in what happened next. Yes, the more I think on it . . . Blanche is to blame."

My voice falls to a whisper. "For what, Aunt Hilda?"

"They sent me to Dearing Hospital. Half a year."

"No, they didn't!"

"Oh, yes. Six months for hysteria. What a terrible place that was, Magnolia. Smelled of filth, human waste. The colored ward was even worse—hell on earth, really. I heard screaming all night. I still hear it, in my dreams."

"Auntie, I had no idea."

"I try not to recall. But I do regret never telling anyone about how horrid Dearing was." She freezes, remembering. "Then again, who'd have listened to little ol' me?"

I reach for my aunt. Tenderly, she embraces me. The world is a lonely, dreadful place. And my dying without Charlie—or worse, *living* and passing for white without her— well, that seems the loneliest thing of all.

"Why didn't you tell me before?"

She strokes my hair. "No use. Past is past."

She's wrong. The past is always with us, poisoning everything.

"I'm telling you now because you've got some cards in your hand yet, Sugarpie. I know you don't love him, but

Finch Waylon's fixin' to propose today. He called to tell me himself."

My jaw drops. "You can't be serious. Wasn't Annamae gonna tell him I'm colored?"

"I reckon she already did, but Finch ain't like Annamae. Listen to what he has to say, Sugarpie. He might surprise you. After all, you're not *really* colored—and the Waylons and the Heathwoods have been destined for each other for centuries. His family's rich enough to protect you from any kind of slander—"

"Aunt Hilda, it's not slander if it's *true*—"

"And, as you know, women who don't conform suffer terrible consequences in Eureka. You don't want to travel my road, Sugarpie. Please. Say yes to him. Live the life you were born for."

"But I only want—"

Charlie.

"I know who you want. But you can start over, with Finch. Eventually, you'll have children of your own." She pinches my cheek. "You know, it was around the time you were born that I finally stopped craving Blanche's approval."

"Not completely," I whisper.

Her smile dims. "No. Never completely."

I am certain, now, that there's no other way out. Accepting Finch Waylon's proposal is the wisest, safest course—and it might could break my curse.

"Thank you, Auntie. For loving me."

"Oh, Sugarpie, don't thank me. You were always going to get your happily ever after. Blanche made sure of it."

My blood turns to ice. The truth is, the Heathwood family is powerful enough to *purchase whiteness*. Turn me white, whether I like it or not. It is surely despicable. But it is also how Eureka's always operated—through duplicity and lies. Skin color, the color line—it's all an elaborate illusion, an endless hall of mirrors. In the end, power's the only thing that matters.

Aunt Hilda leaves, gently suggesting I pretty myself up.

I do not have any mirrors to help me apply my makeup, but I do have a closet full of dresses. Taffetas and silks in every color of the rainbow.

We Heathwoods could never afford much, but fine clothing is an investment in a young lady's future. Or so Grandmother always said.

My hand stops on an emerald silk dress, as green as the plantation in spring. As for shoes, I choose a pair of black heels, high enough to help me meet Finch's eyes.

Whatever happens next, I shall have that dignity, at least.

29
Charlie

C ome morning, I slip into my brown traveling dress, which is also my goodbye dress.

Dr. Colt drops by early to let us know that the protesters made it out of jail. They're roughed up, but all right. He says Darius can probably return home. But Darius won't be going home again.

We're leaving for New York City today, though we're not riding the train. His uncle's Cadillac will ferry us across America's highways.

I study myself in the bathroom mirror, running my hands down my waist. The traveling dress is plain but clean. I worry what Darius's mother will think—we'll stop by Colored Town, to say goodbye—but this will have to do.

I wonder what Magnolia Heathwood's wearing today. Then I remember: I have to train myself not to think of her, or my heart will keep breaking, over and over again.

"Ready?" Darius stands over the kitchen sink, slicking back his hair. Overnight, his bruises have darkened into thunderheads. I can't wait to get him out of here.

He meets my gaze in the over-sink mirror. Winks with his one good eye.

Foreboding flows over me, like I'm forgetting something. But the air smells of rain. Sun peeks through clouds. For once, the mosquitoes aren't biting.

It's a perfect day to travel—isn't it?

I'm almost ready. Before we leave, I return, one last time, to Mama's black mirror. She's not there, of course. I approach anyway and press my cheek to its cold surface. My sorrowful breath fogging the glass.

"Goodbye, Mama," I whisper.

Then I leave her, to linger in the room where Nana died. For a moment, I sit quietly on the bed. A breeze sweeps in the scent of flowers. I miss her so much; it feels like a piece of my heart has been sliced out. I can't imagine the wound will ever fully heal.

Fingers tickle my scalp, moving deftly through my hair, separating its strands. I hold very still. Someone whispers in my ear, but I can't make out the words. Sounds like the voice comes from far away. Heaven, maybe.

It's Nana, saying goodbye.

I clap my hand over my mouth, my grief blazing like a fever.

Nana rings the braid around my forehead. Dazed, I stumble into the kitchen, pour myself a glass of water.

Darius pulls a double take. "Wow. You look beautiful."

I swallow, remembering the feel of those familiar fingers. "I'm ready now."

Darius holds out his hand. I clutch it like a lifeline.

"Think your parents will yell?" I ask.

"Sure, a little. But we'll write them, soon as we get to New York."

His excitement brings a smile to my lips. Darius Lucien can't wait to see what the world has in store for him. Up North, Darius can protest and struggle with only police to fear. No Jim Crow. No southern-fried evil.

Together we stroll into the new day. He carries my luggage; I carry Nana's cane.

"It's a long drive from here to New York," Darius warns. "I'm worried this old Cadillac won't make it. We should get an oil change in Tennessee."

"Sounds fine."

"Sure you don't want to say goodbye to your sister?"

I stop walking, picturing Magnolia's face. The grief in her eyes last night.

Fix what's been broken, Mama said.

But I couldn't. I failed.

"Please don't mention my sister to me now. I'll explain it all one day, I promise—but not today."

He adjusts his hat. "Okay, New York. If you're sure."

I don't want to leave Magnolia behind, but Eureka's spirits have left us no choice.

Time to go.

Soon as we reach the unpaved main road, I realize what I've forgotten. What I've missed.

Freedom House occupies slightly higher ground than the rest of the city; Colored Town is level with the swamp.

When the rainstorm blew in, it flooded the roads. Overnight, red dust turned to mud. People stand outside their houses, tossing buckets of water into the streets. They've put all their meager furniture, their rugs and blankets, out to dry. One house collapsed. Two men hammer at its rooftop, banging fast and loud. The youngest children, like little birds, watch from high branches.

"Oh God," Darius groans. "Not again."

"Why are the babies in the trees?"

"Last time the river flooded, two children died of cholera. And that was before—"

I see the knowledge strike him.

Darius grabs my hand, forcing me into a run. My shoes splash—muddy water leaks into my socks, freezing.

"Darius, man, better get home!" someone shouts. "Your daddy needs you!"

Darius drops my hand, sprinting ahead. I follow as best I can.

"No," I say when I see them. "Oh, no."

Preacher Lucien's in the road, kneeling in six inches of water. His wife's beside him, her hand on his back. At first, I think the preacher cradles a drowned man.

Only, it's not a man in his arms.

It's a casket.

Immediately, Darius joins his broken-hearted family.

Joe appears at my elbow, unshaven and bruised. I remember how scared he was last night, standing guard over his grave. I'm so relieved to see him, I throw my arms around his neck. He rocks me back and forth, then lets me go.

"D's uncle washed up," Joe says. "None of the other caskets did, because it didn't rain that hard. But Otto Lucien's casket floated, see."

"Because it's empty," I murmur. Since the war, Otto Lucien's body is still overseas.

"This morning, that coffin floated down the street like it knew right where it was going. Hand to God, it did."

From the circle of her family, Mrs. Lucien flicks a look at me. I see in the way her lips press together that she knows exactly what her son and I had planned. She beckons me closer, anyway.

"You were right, son," Preacher Lucien mutters. "We had no choice but to fight. No choice but to keep on fighting, either. Look what they've done to us."

"Daddy, don't cry."

"Brother Otto traveled muddy roads to tell me you were right. They can beat us down, but we'll stand up again. We'll do as much as it takes, for as long as it takes."

He sounds just like Nana: *Keep on swinging*.

Darius turns to me, pain raw in his good eye.

He mouths: *I'm sorry*.

He means: *Goodbye*.

I kneel beside Darius, holding his hand under the dirty water. He squeezes my hand once. Twice. Telling me that this isn't my hopeless fight. That I've got to get home, back to the place where the future is brighter. And I'm grateful for that. I don't know what I'd do, if Darius asked me to stay.

For the first time since I've known this preacher's son, he bows his head, to pray.

In that moment, Darius's life unfolds before me. He'll return here, after attending seminary in Baltimore. When his father passes, he'll take over the church. He'll become a protest preacher, marching in Eureka, Savannah, maybe even Atlanta. He's going to be magnificent.

I pray, too. *Please, Nana. Watch over Darius*.

The Luciens are still kneeling when I rise, my hem stained a rusty red. I walk away quickly, feeling too much.

Darius is a good man, choosing to stay. I'll miss him powerfully. But it's time I got back to where I belong. Away from this cursed, unchangeable town.

Halfway down the road, it strikes me that Old Roland's prophecy has come true.

What about Charlie? Is she cursed? Magnolia asked.

Spirits say yes, but she won't lose so much as you. Only her blue-eyed African prince.

I stifle a sob, thinking how inevitable it all was.

How every colored girl on earth knows what it feels like to keep on swinging—and still to lose, and lose, and lose.

30

Magnolia

By late afternoon, Finch Waylon does indeed come to propose. He's dressed finely in a white pinstriped suit, but tellingly, he has not brought flowers.

"Afternoon, Magnolia."

My mind is awfully clouded. I cannot stop thinking of Charlie. I picture her on Freedom's porch, smiling at me. Her hands wrapped around her grandmother's cobra-head cane.

"Magnolia." Finch snaps his fingers in front of my face. "Did you hear me?"

I blink. "No."

"I said, I'm willing to sweep it all under the rug."

"So Annamae told you."

He spits on the veranda, laughing darkly. "Sure did. Reckon I didn't believe her at first, but then I got to thinking. People still tell stories about your daddy, you know. About the kind of women he—"

Finch cuts himself off. Adjusts his tie.

I am numb from head to toe—as unfeeling as a statue.

He gentles his tone. "My apologies. But you must understand it's a shock."

I squint at my old boyfriend, backlit by the sun. "Then why are you here?"

"You know Annamae's been cryin' every night since the Gravediggers' Potluck?"

A pinch of surprise. "Annamae, cryin' for me?"

"You're her best friend. Or did you forget, running around town with that girl, that—Christie?"

Oh, I wish I had not mentioned my sister to Annamae.

"*Charlie*," I say heatedly. "Her name's Charlie, and she's not just *some girl*."

"You won't be able to see her again, once we're married. Not ever. That's my only rule."

I do not let my anger show. A southern lady never does.

It's plain to see that I disgust Finch Waylon now. So why is he here? His dalliance with civil rights doesn't signify. After all, he made it quite clear in the rowboat, days ago, that he prefers his women to remain lily white.

"I don't understand why you'd consent to marry a Negro, Finch Waylon."

Finch looks past me toward the cotton fields.

"My father raised me to see coloreds a certain way. But I am trying to see things differently now. The world—it's changing. I've been trying to change, too, ever since the protests at Georgia State."

He looks into my eyes—searching for something. Approval?

It's my own fault. When Grandmother was alive, I showered Finch Waylon with adoration, even when he did not deserve it. But at least he's here because he wants to be—or thinks he does.

"Certainly, your race is not ideal, but there's no trace of it. And our families are stronger united.

"With Heathwood land to my name, I could run for Senate one day. We'll plant cotton here again. And in the wider world—we'll make real change."

I wince, hearing him say *change*, because he does not mean it the way Charlie does. What use could Finch Waylon possibly have for a revolution?

"I've never met anyone like you, Magnolia. When we're married, I won't think of you as colored, I swear. I'll pay you the respect you deserve."

"But it will be an arrangement. Won't it? A secret in exchange for my land."

Gingerly, he takes my hand. "It was always meant to be an arrangement between us. My father does not know about your—background—but he sent me here, you understand? He said if I want to keep goin' to university, I've got to do right by our families first." He pauses. "Then Annamae told me your secret, and I knew you needed my help."

"What help do you think I need?"

A smirk flits across his face, quick as a breeze. "You must know that secrets like yours don't keep. You'll never have another suitor, Magnolia. But marry me and you'll always be above reproach. I'll see to it."

Finch Waylon never could resist a damsel in distress.

Chivalrous, he kneels. While he fishes in his pocket, I study the familiar part in his pale hair.

And that's when I see it.

My reflection above him, in the parlor window.

I stop breathing, terrified that if I move, it'll disappear. For the first time in over a week I see my own face, and I hear Grandmother's dying words: *Your place is here.*

Marrying Finch will break the curse; I know it for truth now.

If I marry this man, I won't be caught in between any longer. Won't die decades before my time. 'Course, Odessa will never speak to me again, and, one day, some Heathwood ghost might trip me on a stair. But I might could chance all that, to live.

Finch holds up a glittering ring—a burdensome diamond. My salvation, if I choose.

You've got to make a choice, Odessa said when my reflection first fled.

"Magnolia Heathwood, will you marry me?"

I am still watching my reflection.

That girl in the mirror—*is she me?*

Suddenly—and devilishly, for my face does not move—my reflection *grins*. The hair on the back of my neck bristles.

"Magnolia?"

"Finch." My voice squeaks out, a terrified whisper. "There are some things you can't sweep under the rug."

He frowns. "Like what?"

"A baby. If her skin's dark."

He's so stricken he fumbles the ring. "Well, that can be handled. Discreetly. If it happens." He hesitates. "We can always try again, after."

I tear my eyes from my reflection. "What would you do with the child?"

"Well, we'd have to send it away. To an adoptive family, or an institution. Somewhere safe," he hurries to say.

It's a crushing blow: Finch Waylon might accept *me*, for a time, but he'd never own a colored son or daughter. He'd send the child away—to another family, if the child's lucky; to a place like Dearing Hospital, if they were not.

And Eureka would remain forever and always frozen in time—never really changing. The cycle of suffering would go on. Ghostly and unending.

I won't look at the girl reflected in the parlor's window again. She is a stranger—not me at all. And so, doomed whichever road I walk, I make my choice.

"I cannot marry you, Finch Waylon."

He stands clumsily, his face as red as a beet. "I don't understand."

I say nothing.

"Magnolia, you'll never get a better offer."

"Maybe not."

"But—how will you live? Without protection—"

I turn away. "Reckon I'll manage somehow."

"You're making a mistake. Can't you see that?"

In a flash, I'm full of gumption. Like Charlie: "Maybe so. But it's my mistake to make."

In the parlor window, Finch's image shivers. My own reflection winks out like a cruel star.

All at once, I feel very, very tired. That feeling is death, dragging at my bones.

I gesture toward the road. "Please send my regards to Annamae."

His hands ball into fists. "Remember that I tried to give you a good life. You threw it in my face—like the ungrateful mule you are."

His words put the lie to his earlier promise—that he'd never hold my race against me. Married, it might've taken some time, but his hate, rooted deep, would've shown itself eventually. Like Grandmother, he'd have found reasons to despise me. Maybe he'd even insist on my straightening my hair.

"You'd best leave now."

He spits again. "If this is some kinda courtin' game..."

"It's not. We're done, Finch."

He jabs a finger at me. "That's Mr. Waylon to you."

I can't help it—I flinch.

As he leaves, heavy boots tramping down the cobblestone drive, I blink back tears. I have failed utterly to return to my white life. It is time to face facts head-on, like Charlie would: I, Magnolia Rose Heathwood, am gonna die.

For a time, I sit alone in my rocking chair, gazing over our fields. Aunt Hilda joins me but doesn't hector. Doesn't speak.

She reeks of bourbon.

"Aunt Hilda, I'm—"

"Don't apologize, Sugarpie. I'll lay off the drink tomorrow, I swear. There's a women's home in Savannah. We'll start over." She sighs. "We're Heathwoods. I'm sure we'll land on our feet."

The clock chimes five.

Rocking in her porch chair, dear, sweet Aunt Hilda falls fast asleep.

I kiss her papery cheek, then head inside. My silk rustles, shushing, on my way upstairs.

Exhaustion rolls over me in a powerful wave. When it passes, I lean against the railing, catching my breath. But another wave follows.

Then another. And another.

I imagine this is what contractions are like for women in labor. Only I'm not making life, but losing it.

My eyelids feel enormously heavy. My body, a great burden. In my bedroom, I lay it down.

Lying back against my pillow, death is a constant pressure on my chest. Thinking my last thoughts, I strive to picture something good: Charlie and me in Freedom House's kitchen. In my mind, I'm once again teaching her how to light a log stove.

Oh, but I loved Charlie so. Love her still. It is a grief unlike any I've ever known, that our bond could not be repaired.

Try though we did, we could not fix our broken sisterhood. Grandmother saw to it: From the start we were shattered, like a fallen mirror, into a thousand irreparable shards.

31
Charlie

Eureka's train station is swathed in after-rain fog. Mist layers upon mist, reminding me of Freedom's shadows. All those dark corners. Hidden secrets.

Nana.

Darius.

Magnolia.

I've weathered so much sadness here. Now I'm finally going home to New York.

I parcel out five dollars to the ticket master—the same redheaded white boy from before. I had to ask Odessa for a loan. Told her things between Magnolia and me didn't work out. She wept hard, but I can't fix anything in this broken town. Maybe I'll write Magnolia from Harlem. Then again, maybe that would just be too painful.

"You again," the ticket master mutters from his box. "You're the girlfriend of that troublemakin' boy. Ain't you?"

I fix furious eyes on my shoes. "I'm nobody's girlfriend, mister."

"Somethin' happen to him?"

My head snaps up. "Who wants to know?"

He shrugs, licking his index finger to count my dollars. "You just look real—different, that's all. Sadder."

I've lost Nana, Mama, and Darius, too. I've seen a protest turned bloody. Seen a casket float all the way to Colored Town and break a preacher's heart.

Worst of all, I've failed my sister. I swore I'd fix us—but I couldn't.

I can't fight the current any longer. In front of the white ticket master, I cry so hard it feels like the fire hose is blasting me again. Feels like I'm drowning.

"Hey, now." The ticket master steps out from behind his kiosk.

I recoil, but he holds his hands up.

"I hate to see a woman cry, that's all."

The young man's words hold no threat. I take in his blemish-scarred face, the curly red hair that does him no favors. Beside the bench for whites only, we share one of those moments that can happen even here, in the most racist place on earth: We see each other as human.

"I'm okay now. I'll just stand over there—"

"Sit," he commands. "This here's a colored bench today."

Bewildered, I sit. "Thank you?"

"You're welcome." He tips his hat. "Train'll be along shortly."

My throat aches. I feel like Eureka broke me.

No—*Blanche Heathwood* broke me. Years and years ago, when she tricked Nana into giving up my sister. Because of her, it was always too late for us—the miracle twins, one light, and one dark.

In New York, I'll start fresh. Forget Eureka so hard it'll practically cease to exist.

The train whistles into the station, bright headlights parting fog. I glance back at the ticket master, but the mist's a soup. I can't see him. The train judders to a stop. My heels click, carrying me to the train car door. I struggle to pull it open, but the door's stuck fast.

So's the next one.

I race from car to car. Why aren't the doors opening? Where's the conductor?

At last, metal doors part.

I slump, winded, into the nearest seat.

"All aboard!"

Strangely, the mist's followed me inside the train, swirling over burgundy carpet. And there's something wrong with the other passengers.

Is this car full of soldiers? Everyone's wounded. Hurt. But

it's worse than that. Across the aisle, there's a woman missing a chunk of jaw. Gristle hanging where the bone ends. And the man in front of her's got trouble with his neck: It's twisted at an impossible angle.

Almost like—

No. I shut the thought down before it has a chance to take root. There are children on this train—I hear them laughing, whispering—but I can't see them. Seated, the mist chills my legs.

"Want to play hide-and-seek?" a boy-child whispers.

A bubble of terror blocks my throat.

I can't see this child. Only hear him.

"Suit yourself," he says—then rustles away.

Finally, the conductor marches down the aisle, but he's not the stern white man I expected. He's black as coal. Punching tickets. Making small talk. Soon he'll come for my ticket. Fear churns in my belly.

"Hello, baby," whispers the woman beside me.

Nana.

The train lurches forward—I want to stand, shout that there's been some mistake. This is a ghost train, but I'm not *dead*.

Am I?

"Don't worry, Charlene. You're only visiting."

I turn to see her: Nana, who died the day we arrived in Eureka. I gasp, because she's beautiful. Glowing, smiling. Free of pain.

"Charlene." A crown of azaleas graces her silver head. "How I've missed you."

I reach out to hug her, but Nana shakes her head. "Never touch the dead. Only look."

Afraid, I wrap my arms about myself.

"Things haven't been easy for you, I know. But I raised you to outwit all the evils of Eureka. To keep on swinging."

"Nana, I couldn't help Magnolia. I—"

"Hush. Let's not talk about her just yet." Nana tilts her head back. "What do you think of my new look?"

Every other passenger aboard is broken in some way. Throats slashed, backs a mess of blood and gore. Behind us, a lady's face is riddled with buckshot. Yet Nana's never looked more alive.

"Why aren't you like the others?"

"This train's home to all Eureka's haunts." Nana twirls her finger in a circle. "Most don't have a connecting ticket. They're still stewing over what happened to them. Hurting, blaming, grieving. Jessie over there—" Nana points to the man with the twisted neck. "He's been riding in circles for almost two hundred years. Can you believe that?" She shakes her head, scandalized. "But my ticket's punched and ready. Soon as I make my amends, I'm headed to my reward."

Amends?

I'm dreaming. Must be. I fell asleep on the bench at the train station, that's all.

"Tickets, please."

I startle at the conductor's voice. Hand outstretched for my fare, his rolled-back eyes show purest white.

Silently, I hold out my one-way to Penn Station.

The conductor punches it. "When I call your stop, you best hurry. Trust me when I say: You don't want to miss it."

Behind me, a man whispers, "Amen."

Stiff with horror, I turn. He's another like Nana, dead-but-alive. He wears an olive-green flight suit covered in military honors.

"Name's Otto Lucien. Maybe you've seen me around."

"*Seen you?* You're dead! Darius said—"

"My boy D's why I'm still riding circles. Promised the Lord I'd always look out for him. And I do." He frowns. "Try, anyhow."

"It's hard to get through to the living," Nana says. "For instance—Charlene." Anger hums below her words. "Did I not tell you, *just today*, that you can't leave yet? That your sister needs you? While I braided your hair, what did I say?"

I touch the braid ringing my head. "I couldn't hear. I thought you were wishing me well. Me and Darius."

She snorts. "I didn't braid your hair for *Darius*. It's Magnolia you've got to be presentable for. Without you, she's going to die."

I tense. "No. Magnolia went home. She decided to pass for white—to live."

"No, she didn't, fool girl! She chose to die."

Furious, I leap to my feet, even as the train's motion threatens to knock me down. "She did *what*?"

"She turned down Finch Waylon's proposal today. The girl's made her stand—she'd rather die than pass for white, and who could blame her? That's a loveless life, spent passing. What's wrong with you, that you thought she'd choose different?"

"How could I know anything about how she'd choose? About curses or Eureka, either? You separated us. You gave Magnolia away—we saw it! How could you?"

Nana's face falls. "I made a mistake. A bad one. But I'm trying to fix it, baby. Why do you think I'm riding this ghost train?"

"I've got to get to Magnolia." She seemed so faint last night. Barely there. "Somebody, let me off!"

"Wait for your stop," Otto says. "If you get off in between, there's no telling what might happen. You'll be lost in the veil."

"My sister's lost in the veil!" I snap. Then force myself to sit, pulse pounding. "Nana, tell me what to do."

"Listen to me, Charlene: Magnolia's badly cursed, but Eureka's spirits will give her another chance. Trouble is, Blanche Heathwood will try to stop her."

I shudder at the name. "Blanche Heathwood's dead."

Nana's face pinches. "Didn't I tell you? Nothing ever changes in Eureka—and nothing ever dies.

"Blanche Heathwood's powerful on plantation land, but most of her tricks are smoke and mirrors. White power's always smoke and mirrors, when you get down to it. Now, what's the only thing stronger than white magic?"

The answer bubbles up from somewhere deep inside me. "Our magic."

"That's right. Our love's stronger even than their hate. Love your sister, Charlie. That's all you ever have to do."

I cast around. "I have to get off this train."

"Yes, you do," Otto says. "Your stop's coming soon."

"Stable Station, two minutes! Stable Station, next!"

For the first time since I boarded this train, Nana looks afraid. "Grab your luggage, baby, quick."

I grip my valise, the cobra-head cane.

Nana rises, taller than I remember. "Please save my grandbaby."

Blanche Heathwood will try to stop her.

"Nana, I'm scared."

"Fix what's been broken. Whatever happens, keep on swinging."

"But no happily ever after," I whisper.

My grandmother winces. "Maybe not. But you got to try."

"Stable Station!"

The train lurches to a stop.

"Run."

My feet pound the burgundy floor.

"Tell D I said hey!" Otto Lucien hollers.

I'm not fast enough. The doors are already sliding shut.

"GO!" Nana shrieks.

I nearly crash into the conductor's chest.

"Please—my sister needs me—"

The conductor gazes down at me with porcelain eyes. Just as the doors are about to meet, he shoots the knife-edge of his hand between them.

"Didn't you hear me calling?" he says calmly. "You almost didn't make it."

I glance back, looking for Nana and Otto. The train's filled up with that mist. I can't see them anymore.

"Where are we, exactly?"

"Stable Station, inside Heathwood Plantation. Just one of this train's many local stops." The conductor's voice grinds like locomotive gears. "River's another. City Hall. Auction Block. And Jailhouse, that's a big one."

Involuntarily, I shudder. These are all places colored folk die, from slave times to the present.

I'm itching to get off, but the conductor's not done with me.

"I love all my stops, but Stable has a special place in my heart. I died here myself." A smile swoops over his face. "Not to boast, but I *was* the first African to die in Georgia."

"I—I'm sorry."

"Don't be," he laughs, booming. "They strung me up before I'd learned a lick of English, but I had some power yet." He gestures to the mist-cloaked walls. "I built this train for the lost and hurting. To shelter them, until they were ready to move on. In time, all Georgia's slaves'd heard tell of me. Called me the *Conductor*."

Mind your manners down South.

I swallow. "It's a pleasure to meet you, Mr. Conductor."

He bows regally, from the waist. "And you, Miss Charlene. Good luck."

A dead man holding the door, I step into the pure white mist.

32
Magnolia

I do not expect to wake again, but someone's whispering in my ear, *"It's time."*

"Charlie?"

It's the child who haunts me. At my bedside, he's silvery as a reflection in an obsidian mirror. Up close, I notice that he has Charlie's brow. *My* brow.

And I think—is that not the very shape of my own eyes?

I sit up, quick. "Who are you? What relation of mine?"

The boy purses his lips and then turns smartly on his heel. From Heathwood's hall, he beckons with a bony arm.

I scramble out of bed, knowing this is it. The moment I live or die.

"Wait. You're taking me to the chest below the stables. Is that right?"

The ghost watches me, wary.

"Well, let me find the key, okay? I bet I know where it is."

Now the ghost child follows me. Walking, I am light-headed, shivery cold. Slowly disappearing.

Unless the spirits change their minds.

Oh, please, let them change their minds.

The little boy does not follow me inside Grandmother's bedroom, where the darkness is sharp as a knife, glinting with too many obsidian mirrors. I have not been inside this bedroom since my grandmother died. The walls still reek of Blanche Heathwood's demise. Of her decaying skin, sickly sweet.

My vision swims, and I am plunged back into my childhood, when I was always lonely and afraid.

I think to myself, *Charlie.*

Emerald silk trailing, I tiptoe to Grandmother's nightstand. Her master keys are still there, inside a dusty drawer. I lift the heavy ring, its keys a mix of iron and brass. One of these toothy things must open the locked chest.

My scalp prickles, warning me that I am not alone.

I spin around like a child caught sneaking.

Grandmother's here. Her image echoing in glass after glass. Her skull shows through her skin, bony and white. And her hair—it has overgrown the bonnet she wore to her final rest, white strands tangling around her shoulders like yarn. She wears the black gown in which we buried her.

I should run, but I am frozen. Roadkill.

Inside every mirror, Grandmother opens her mouth. It stretches too wide, her jaw unhinging. Clutching the iron ring, I gaze helplessly down the dark tunnel of her throat.

And then Grandmother screams.

The piercing sound shatters first one glass and then another. They explode in waves, flinging shards like shrapnel. Only when the mirror beside me breaks do I finally find the strength to run.

Oh, that scream—it goes on and on.

An obsidian shard slashes my cheek, but I do not stop. I fix my eyes on the door. When I hear the heavy slap of feet stepping out of the glass—Grandmother, bestirring herself to chase me—I absolutely do not look back.

"Magnolia Heathwood, come back and get what's comin' to you!"

I slide into the marble hall, where the little spirit waits for me.

"Magnolia! You listen to me, now!" Grandmother screams.

Against all good judgment, I turn.

The bony apparition's seven feet tall if she's an inch. Her white lips pull into a rictus grin. Her ivory teeth, far too long, flash like fangs, and black cloth shifts around her like so many vipers.

In death, Grandmother has become what she always was in life: a monster.

She snarls. "Magnolia Heathwood! You're a traitor to your race!"

Hard as I can, I slam the door in her ghastly face.

Then, the little boy's ghostly hand in mine, we run.

In the dark room beneath the abandoned stables, I kneel beside the wooden chest. I try key after key on Grandmother's heavy ring—to no avail.

Beside me, the little ghost shifts from one foot to another, eyeing the staircase. Like me, he is waiting for Blanche Heathwood's ghost to appear.

"It's got to be one of these," I mutter—then drop the ring. "Oh, foot!"

I am certain now that this place was once a slave pen—a room to punish rebellious slaves. With those shackles bolted to the wall, what else could it be? All my life, this evil place has existed—along with slavery's every other sign—but I never looked too close. I simply did not want to see.

In the damp, my skin pinches into gooseflesh. My heart is a hammer, breaking soft, internal things.

Above, the door creaks open.

Grandmother.

Though my hands tremble, I focus on the keys. Whatever

Eureka's spirits want from this chest—from me—I know I won't get another chance.

I try one key after another while footsteps tramp downstairs at a leisurely pace. Grandmother's heavy dress drags against wood.

Finally, a key fits perfectly into the chest's lock, opening it with a heavy *click*.

Triumphant, I lift the lid wide.

And I gasp.

Inside are thousands of slips of paper yellowed by time. They rustle just as if they were little birds, alive. Carefully, I pick the first paper from the pile. It reads: *Charles Heathwood, Child, P'rchased in the Year 1855, 123c.* It's a bill of sale, reflecting the worth of a little boy's soul.

I look at young Charles Heathwood—who would become Charles Freedom. His ghost stares straight back at me.

Inside the chest, the papers flutter and then, incredibly, begin to lift—born on an invisible wind. Even in death, these souls would be free.

Grandmother moves faster, hurrying. "Magnolia, you little fool! *Get away from that chest!*"

The lid slams, hard, on my fingers. I shout.

Grandmother blows into the room like a black taffeta wind. She's enormous, all moon-white skin stretched over bone. She leans over me, a dark cloud smelling of rot. Now we're nose-to-nose.

"I said, *Get away from there.*"

I whimper, slipping my hands from under the chest's heavy lid.

"You have failed miserably, Magnolia, but it is not too late. Give me those keys. Give them here, now."

"No," I whisper—my eyes seeking the little spirit. My great-grandfather.

To my dismay, he's nowhere to be seen. Like Charlie, he has abandoned me.

Grandmother blows out a foul breath, turning away. I exhale in relief, then shudder at a dreadful sound: the scrape of shackles, pulled across the floor. Impossibly quickly, my grandmother claps the shackles around my ankle. The metal against my skin, ice cold.

"No! You can't do this!"

Grandmother's lips curl upward—and that's when I smell the telltale scent of the hair iron, heating up. Grandmother pulls it from somewhere inside her billowing black gown. It is already smoking.

Shackled, I cannot run.

With cruel fingers, Grandmother parts my hair.

The fight goes out of me in a *whoosh*. With Charlie gone, and the little spirit fled, what's the use of keeping on? In the end, Heathwood always wins. Eureka's spirits wanted something from me, but it's too late now. I couldn't help them in time.

Grandmother brings the smoking iron near, and I flinch. A hank of my hair falls to the stable floor, blackened. Instinctively, I throw myself back, away from that blazing bar of metal. Then everything is pain—blinding white. A terrible noise scratches and claws its way out of my throat.

Below the abandoned stable, I scream.

33
Charlie

Stepping off the ghost train, I tumble into a pile of old hay. As promised, the Conductor's dropped me inside Heathwood's stable.

There's no sign of a train. Only a spot of ground where light doesn't fall, and a patch of cold so icy my teeth ache.

I can't help glancing up at the rafters.

Yes, you could swing a rope over them. Yes, you could hang a man. And, long ago, Magnolia's ancestors—*my* ancestors—did indeed murder a man who didn't even speak the language of his killers.

Magnolia. I've got to find Magnolia.

Already, my memory of the ghost train's fading, dissolving. Like dreams, it's not the type of memory you get to keep.

Fix what's been broken.

I should never, ever have let Magnolia go. She's my twin sister. My mirror girl. For the first time since that fire hose blasted me, my head's clear with purpose.

From somewhere nearby, my sister lets loose a bloodcurdling scream.

Save my grandbaby.

I struggle upright, leaning into Nana's cane. But I don't know where to go.

Silently, a cold hand slips into mine. A little boy's holding on to me, but not just any little boy. My great-grandfather's ghost.

He looks just the same as he did in Freedom House's wooden etching, hiding from the deadly slave revolt. His forehead broad like mine and Magnolia's. His eyes, heavy lashed and unspeakably sad.

He leads me between two horse stalls to a hidden hatch in the floor. Magnolia screams again. I rip that hatch open, then throw myself down the stairs that tumble out below.

Blanche Heathwood bends over my sister. Magnolia looks broken, sitting in a pile of her own blackened hair. Blood pounds in my temples like a war drum, but something tells me to wait.

"Charles, what's in the chest?"

He mouths, *"Change."*

"Magnolia!" I shout.

Blanche Heathwood's head whips around, nostrils flaring. Monstrously tall, the ghost flies to the foot of the stairs.

She snarls, meaning to scare me off, but I hold my ground.

White power's always smoke and mirrors, when you get down to it.

Nana was talking about Blanche Heathwood's ghost, but she could've been talking about segregation itself. Jim Crow's just one evil magic trick, trying to convince colored folks that we're worthless. All Eureka rests on the swampy foundation of one rotten lie.

But I don't believe it.

"Disgusting child. Begone from here!"

I drop Charles Freedom's icy wind of a hand, wielding Nana's cane like a baseball bat.

"Leave her alone."

"Magnolia's mine. *She belongs to Heathwood.*"

I swing Nana's cane, pouring all my strength into the blow. But it passes right through ghostly Blanche. I stumble. Her laugh scrapes the air like nails on porcelain.

"Puh-lease," Blanche Heathwood drawls. "Who are you to hurt me? Just another Negro. A worthless, ugly descendant of slaves. I said begone, now. Git!"

Blanche Heathwood commands me like I'm a mangy dog. My eyes seek Magnolia's. Hair wild, eyes bloodshot, she looks really hurt.

"Why would you hurt Magnolia? You *raised* her."

Blanche points. "Magnolia's a TRAITOR TO HER RACE! A TRAITOR! Just like her FATHER! Now git!"

I recoil from a rotten gust of wind. "You're just a reflection. Not real."

Magnolia's head snaps up. "Charlie, she *burned* me—"

"It's smoke and mirrors. You let her get into your head, Magnolia, that's all."

Blanche Heathwood shoots me a scornful glance, but I think, burnt hair aside, it's true.

Nana said, *Our love's stronger even than their hate.*

Eyes squeezed tight, I step right through Blanche Heathwood. In fact, she's nothing but memory. A nightmare.

On the other side, I'm breathing like I've plunged into cold water—but I'm okay.

Smoke and mirrors, Nana said.

"Stop right there, gal, I'm not finished with you!"

Striding toward my sister, I ignore her.

"Surely you must know by now that I arranged to have your bitch of a mother killed—and my traitor son, too."

I freeze.

Magnolia gasps. "What're you talkin' about, Grandmother?"

"She's trying to scare us. She wouldn't kill our father— she needed an heir for Heathwood."

Blanche Heathwood growls. "I needed *Magnolia* to have an heir. By the time she was born, Dean had already abandoned me. My son never appreciated our way of life. He had to be handled."

With a long, white finger, Blanche Heathwood points to the brick wall. In a flash, the brick turns glassy.

It's a mirror.

I shouldn't look, but I can't help myself. The promise of seeing Mama and Daddy calls to me like a siren's song.

Out of the corner of my eye, Blanche Heathwood smiles.

In the glass, a red car drives along a lonely southern road. A street sign reads SAVANNAH, 10 MILES. There's a couple inside the car. A beautiful woman in a white veil and a handsome white man driving her. My stomach twists, knowing what's next.

Another car turns onto the road. On its roof, red lights flash.

Magnolia moans.

"I hired two men from Alabama. Cost me two thousand dollars to have your parents killed."

Don't pull over, Daddy, I'm thinking—but of course, he does.

It happens fast. The white men flank the car, weapons already in hand. They fire off twin flashes of light, hot and bright.

I close my eyes, tears flooding, but it doesn't matter. I've already seen.

Blanche Heathwood hired the men who shot Mama and Daddy. She hated race mixing so much she killed her own son.

Now the black-clad ghost straightens, pulling herself up to her full and dreadful height. She towers over me, grinning cruelly. She expects me to flee in fear. She's miscalculated.

293

I'm not scared at all anymore. My rage, strengthened by years of struggle, is a powerful beast rattling my rib cage. Ready to be unleashed.

"I let you live once, Charlene," Blanche purrs, swirling closer. "I'll let you live again. But you must leave this plantation. *Now*."

I spear Blanche Heathwood with my hardest, meanest stare. The one that says: *Do your worst.*

Magnolia and I are separated by only a foot of cold ground. If I cross it, we'll be together again. Together, we're too strong for Blanche Heathwood.

"I'm not going anywhere, *Grandmother*. Maybe you haven't noticed, but it's 1953. Eureka *will* change—the whole country, soon."

The ghost dives for my sister, but I'm faster. I grasp Magnolia, sitting in her mess of hair. I wrap my arms around her, holding tight. And I press my nose along the length of hers, inhaling my first memory: the smell of her breath, both tangy and sweet.

Like she's hit a wall, Blanche Heathwood stumbles back.

Our love, stronger than her hate.

But Magnolia, sunk deep in misery, hasn't noticed yet. "You should go, Charlie. Run."

"But don't you see? We're stronger than her. We've already won."

Tears slip down my sister's exhausted face—she doesn't

believe me. I fish in my purse for my drugstore clamshell and snap it open. Hoping I'm right.

"Look. *Your reflection.* The spirits gave it back."

"What are you doing?" Blanche Heathwood snaps. "What are you looking at?"

At the sight of her own image, Magnolia's eyes widen. "Why?"

I nod to the chest. "You know why. You fought for them. For us. For *change.* You didn't have to win. You just had to fight."

There's no sight on earth more beautiful than my twin sister's smile, breaking across her tired face.

"No guilt, remember?" I whisper. "Get mad instead."

Shackled, Magnolia stumbles to her feet. With hell's own fury, she glares at her evil grandmother.

My shoulders relax, because Magnolia Heathwood, fiery southern lady, has come back to me.

Save my grandbaby, Nana said.

But I've got a pretty good feeling that Magnolia's about to save herself.

34

Magnolia

Charlie hasn't abandoned me.

She could just as well have gone back to New York, but instead she's come here, to Heathwood's decrepit heart.

With my sister near, I am no longer broken, but whole.

I stare down Blanche Heathwood, who's helpless to approach Charlie and me. Our love, like a circle of strong light.

Hanging tight to Charlie's hand, I stumble toward the chest, the chain snaking behind me. For unlocking that chest, Heathwood's spirits returned my reflection. Now it's time to finish what I've started: open that box wide and force it to spill its secrets. Let Heathwood's bad legacy face the light—and burn.

Grandmother slithers between the moldering box and me. "Don't forget, Magnolia, you belong to me—to Heathwood!"

She uses her most terrible voice, but I am not the same person I was on the day she died. I am no longer a weak little fluff of nothing.

After all, didn't I reject my inheritance? Didn't I finally stand up to Annamae? And didn't I, against all odds, forge a bond with the sister who was stolen from me?

All my life, I have always believed that what matters is what others see when they look at me. But that's not right at all. What matters is what I see.

"I am not afraid of you, Grandmother. You're nothing but a ghost—and ugly, to boot. I think it's *you* who belong to Heathwood. *You* who will never be free."

Wild-eyed, Grandmother throws herself at the chest, long white hands outstretched. Her pale mouth twists.

I ignore her, flipping the lid wide.

Wraithlike now—*only smoke and mirrors*—Grandmother swirls and thunders, but can't stop me. Like a wounded animal, she howls.

The papers stir, fluttering. Then those bills of sale lift into the air. Thousands sweep together, winging high. They surround Grandmother, beating madly. Inside their tornado, the air roars.

Charlie snatches me backward. Together, we huddle against the wall that showed us how our parents died. It's plain brick once more.

"Magnolia, help me!"

Hanging on to my sister, I don't answer.

Swarmed, Grandmother disappears as if into a cloud of wasps. Blanche Heathwood screams, coming apart. Her long, smoky tendrils unwinding. In the force of the gale, her white fingers flash like ivory—and then, she's gone. Vanished.

The papers begin to settle, falling like snow. My burned scalp beats along with my pounding heart. Charlie lets go of me, reaching for the bills of sale.

"So many people," she says sadly. "So many names."

One I already know.

According to his slave paper, my great-grandfather was purchased by the Heathwood family as a child—and saddled with the Heathwood name. But he would reinvent himself on Emancipation Day as Charles Freedom. He'd have a daughter, Jeannette. He would become, too, the great-grandfather of a namesake—*Charlene*.

Even at Heathwood, my great-grandfather watched out for me. He helped me find my way here, to the truth at Heathwood's core.

"Magnolia, *look*."

As the paper settles, people appear. Heathwood's ghostly slaves encircle us. They are as silver and insubstantial as moonlight—or mist. When the light falls in the right way, they are solid as Charlie or me. In another heartbeat, they fade. I examine their faces, scarred or aged beyond their years. Tired, hungry, and full of timeless grief. They are men, women, children. Ghosts.

Charles Freedom steps out of the crowd, smiling like a little boy ought to smile. He tips his head back, mouthing a single word. My skin tingles, and then, in a flash of foxfire green light, Charles Freedom disappears.

"What happened to him? Is he finally ...?"

"Free," Charlie whispers.

The sacred, long-fought word seems to rumble up from Eureka's belly, its shallow, colored graves.

Charlie and I turn to the shackles around my ankle, bolting me to the brick wall. Scalp blazing with remembered agony, I grasp the long, cold length of chain. Charlie mirrors me, her brown hands cupping mine.

Tears crowd my eyes, feeling the cold touch of spirit hands, ghost hands. Hundreds—a thousand.

Charlie sucks in a breath. "Oh, Magnolia."

Standing with us are all the colored spirits of Heathwood, who died in rivers and cotton fields and dreadful bondage. Despite the years I spent living in willful ignorance, Eureka's ghosts have embraced me. They lend their strength now.

I will not forget it. Not as long as I live.

Like the leader she will someday be, Charlie shouts, "One—two—*three!*"

Together, we tear those iron shackles free.

35

Charlie

"Two tickets to Penn Station, please," I tell Eureka's one and only ticket master—or so it seems to me.

"Two tickets? Now, that's new," he jokes. "Normally, you only ask for one."

"This is my sister," I explain.

He squints at light-skinned Magnolia. "Really?"

"Yes, really. She's coming home with me. And we're actually leaving this time."

He shuffles our money around, not bothering to hold it up to the light. When he looks at me again, his gaze is soft.

"I'm glad you're getting outta here. The whole state's about to boil over with this race business. Whole country, maybe."

I nod. "I know."

"Boyfriend followin' after you?"

Blinking into the southern sun, déjà vu nearly blinds me. "No, sir. He's not."

"That's a shame." He sounds like he means it.

"Well," Magnolia says, a smile in her voice. "Maybe one day."

I give her the eye, but say nothing. It helps to think I might see Darius again someday. Somewhere on the protest line, maybe, in the years to come.

I've brought my valise and Nana's cane; Magnolia's stuffed her calf-leather duffels full of bright-patterned dresses. It'll be a real blow when Magnolia realizes pansy prints aren't fashionable in New York. She's already smarting about her hair, which we had to cut into a pixie after all her curls burned away.

Above us is a pure blue sky, southern and bright. I tip my head back, taking one last, long look at it.

The train shrieks into the station, an explosion of dust and noise.

The white conductor hollers, "All aboard!"

We find seats in the colored car, settling in for a two-day ride. The car's empty now, but won't be for long. Eureka's but one small stop in this vast and varied country. I can't wait for Magnolia to see how much world there is—even for girls like us.

A smile plays on my lips, because my sister's already

pressing her palms against the window glass. She's gazing, rapt.

"What's so interesting?" I tease.

"Why, my reflection, of course. I really am quite beautiful."

I snort. "Humble, too."

One manicured fingernail taps the train's window. "It's a precious thing to see yourself for who you are, and not who others want you to be."

"You see a colored girl in the mirror now?"

"Yes. And a mixed girl, a twin sister. More."

I lean over Magnolia's lap, bringing our reflections together. My face beside Magnolia's, brown where hers is light, is a true miracle now.

Fix what's been broken, Mama said—and we did.

Sadness tugs at my heart, realizing I'll never see Mama again—or Nana's ghost, either. Ghosts aren't quite so real in a place like New York. Part of me worries I might forget Mama. Forget everything I've witnessed.

"We won't forget," Magnolia says, startling me.

In the last few days, that light-skinned girl has learned to read my mind in the same way Nana used to.

"Well, some memories we might lose over time. But what it all *meant* will always be with us. Don't you think?"

"Wow, Magnolia. You almost sound wise."

She settles herself in her seat, crossing her ankles. "You think Darius and the church will come up with the money for those mausoleums?"

In places like New Orleans, bodies aren't buried in the ground but in aboveground stone. Segregated to the swamp, Darius and his father came up with the idea to entomb our dead. They told me all about their plan on the morning I finally buried Nana in the marshy ground. A day I will never forget.

Old Roland attended my grandmother's funeral—and, to everyone's surprise, so did Aunt Hilda. She didn't speak to me, but during Preacher Lucien's sermon, she dabbed her eyes with an old lace handkerchief. Now, the poor old white lady's off to live with distant relations in Savannah. Magnolia's promised to write her from time to time—but I don't believe they'll ever meet again.

"If Preacher Lucien can't raise the money, we'll write the NAACP. Do whatever it takes."

"Think we'll ever travel down South again?"

"Not me. I've had enough." I peer at Magnolia. "What about you?"

She rests her chin in her hand. "I've been thinking a lot about that light-skinned man—that Walter White. How he went undercover in the Deep South, investigating hate crimes."

I'm appalled. "Magnolia! What happened to marrying rich and sitting pretty?"

"Why, bless your heart, that's a funny story! I *was* plannin' on doing exactly that, when this northern girl showed up, fillin' my head with wild ideas...."

The train pulls away from the station, churning beneath us like a powerful river. Magnolia leans her head against my shoulder, and I take her hand, holding tight. For the foreseeable future, neither of us is planning on letting go.

In my head, I hear again the song those old men were singing after Nana and I crossed the Mason-Dixon Line.

This train is bound for glory, this train.
This train is bound for glory, this train.
This train is bound for glory,
Ridin' with the righteous, the righteous and the holy.
This is bound for glory, this train . . .

Magnolia shakes me. *"Charlie.* Do you see them? *Do you?"*

On the swiftly disappearing station platform, Mama and Daddy are dancing. Waltzing to some song only they can hear.

Mama glows in her white-silk wedding dress, whole and clear, and Daddy's smiling wide. They whirl and turn, beaming happiness.

Magnolia and I race down the aisle, trying to keep them in sight. Mama's pretty, her hair neatly plaited. Daddy's dressed sharply in a three-piece suit—and he's thrilled just to have her in his arms.

"Do you think they'll be there forever, just dancing?"

"No. They'll move on soon. Find rest."

"Together, I hope," Magnolia whispers. "They deserve it, after all they've been through."

I'm heartbroken when Mama and Daddy fall behind us—the train whisking us toward the future. Even when we can't see our parents anymore, my sister and I are slow to return to our seats.

"Will they live happily ever after, do you think?"

For colored girls, there's no such thing as happily ever after, Nana used to say. But wise as she was, my grandmother was wrong.

For Magnolia and me, happily ever after won't come easy—or on time. That's sure. When it finally arrives, it'll be because we've broken the mirror's enchantments, those wicked spells that try to trap us from the moment we're born. Magnolia and I have shattered our mirror curses, but the journey's not over. The world's still riddled with hateful gazes, trick mirrors, and stories that would make us feel lesser. Ugly. Small.

"It's too late for Mama and Daddy to live happily ever after," I tell Magnolia—whose eyes shine. "But you'd better believe we will."

"You think so?"

"I know so. Even if we have to change the whole world first."

That's the thing about colored girls: When we finally see ourselves for who we truly are, we can't help but realize we deserve happily ever after, too.

Keep on swinging. Keep on.

ACKNOWLEDGMENTS

Some events in this story truly occurred—and some of the people truly lived. Caleb Hill lost his life to a lynch mob in Georgia on May 30, 1949. Walter White served as the executive secretary of the NAACP from 1931 until 1955. In 1952, Ella Baker became the first woman president of the NAACP's New York City branch.

For research, I depended heavily on Jerrold M. Packer's *American Nightmare*, Clarence Taylor's *Civil Rights in New York City*, Laura Wexler's *Fire in a Canebrake: The Last Mass Lynching in America*, and Isabel Wilkerson's *The Warmth of Other Suns*. This book would not have been possible without the oral histories recorded in *Remembering Jim Crow: African Americans Tell About Life in the Segregated South*, edited by William H. Chafe, Raymond Gavins, and Robert Korstad as well as *Remembering Jim Crow: African American Women and Memories of the Segregated South*, edited by Anne Valk and Leslie Brown. When Charlie says "life for me ain't been no crystal stair," she is quoting "Mother to Son" by Langston Hughes.

Many thanks to my editors, Alvina Ling and Ruqayyah Daud, for their tremendous help bringing this vision to life. Thanks also to Annie McDonnell and the entire team at Little, Brown Books for Young Readers.

To my agent, Michael Bourret, I owe thanks for the steady confidence, and for resurrecting me several times.

I'm deeply indebted to the brilliant Kim Johnson for her insightful early reading and research guidance. It's a true friend who reads an early draft! Thanks to Kayla Dunigan of Writing Diversely, for her helpful sensitivity read.

Namina Forna, thank you, thank you!

I'm ever grateful to Christina Hammonds Reed, who gave this project a much-needed winter boost with her friendship and writerly camaraderie.

Jodi Meadows, as always, pushed me to believe in myself and discover the book *inside* my book. I am eternally grateful for her mentorship.

Finally, thanks to my mother, Jewell Parker Rhodes, for her critical eye and comprehensive knowledge of craft; thanks to Jack Mullen for his expertise on historical trains; and thanks to my partner, Bill Mullen, for literally everything.

DISCUSSION GUIDE

1. Why do the spirits refuse to accept Magnolia after she decides to quit passing for white? What do they want her to do before she can claim her true heritage?

2. At the start of the book, Magnolia falls under a dreadful mirror curse. What might it mean that she literally loses her reflection the night she learns the truth about her heritage? How do mirrors work as a metaphor throughout the story?

3. Jim Crow is a powerful force throughout the book—and throughout the real-life 1950s. Because Charlie grew up in the North, she has a lot to learn about segregation. What shocked her most about the apartheid society? What lessons did Darius try to impart to her?

4. The title of the book refers to the long-separated twin sisters, who are in some way mirror images of each other.

What do they have in common, and what sets them apart? Despite their vastly different upbringings, what did they find in each other that they couldn't live without?

5. Race is an important theme in the book, but so too is femininity and its constructions. What did the story have to say about girlhood—and especially about Southern womanhood? How does the society portrayed in the book try to control women, both white and Black?

6. Why were Magnolia and Charlie's parents such a threat to segregated Eureka? Why did loving each other put them into such grave danger? What did you feel for them and their love story as Charlie and her sister uncovered the truth?

7. A passage in the book reads: *"White power's always smoke and mirrors, when you get down to it.* Nana was talking about Blanche Heathwood's ghost, but she could've been talking about segregation itself. Jim Crow's just one evil magic trick, trying to convince colored folks that we're worthless. All Eureka rests on the swampy foundation of one rotten lie." What does this passage imply about oppressive societies and how they operate?

8. What did you make of the ghost train? What does it have to say about hauntings, ghosts, and the past?

9. Magnolia has a choice to make in the book—to continue to pass for white, or to join the Black community. What dangers does each option present? What is she most afraid of?

10. Why does Darius stay in Eureka, when he clearly has no love for life in the South? What influenced his choice, and how did you feel about it?

Turn the page for a sneak preview of

AVAILABLE MAY 2023

CHAPTER 1

LET'S START BY getting one thing straight: I do *not* live on a plantation. Not the kind you mean.

Once upon a time, enslaved people did work sugarcane in Westwood's fields, but years ago, Mom, Dad, and I restored it into an enslaved people's museum—and that's a totally different thing.

Of course, there *is* a Big House at Westwood, white with columns like thick marble teeth, poised to devour everything in sight...but we don't sleep there. Dad and I live in a new home in the woods, because we're not about to be the Black family in the horror movie that doesn't leave the haunted house.

I've been a Westwood tour guide since my fifteenth birthday, when Dad gave me an ID card and his blessing to teach the hard truths we learned while restoring this place. I love what I do, but guiding tours can really take it out of you. It's the proximity to suffering, to a history that should feel ancient, but doesn't. In the long grasses, amidst the orchards and bare-floor cabins and whispering live oak trees, time collapses like a wormhole. Yesterday is today and tomorrow feels impossible. You know what I mean, especially if you're Black or Indigenous or otherwise marginalized. You don't even have to live on a plantation museum to breathe air soaked with history you can't escape.

At the end of today's long shift, I'm sitting slumped at my desk in the Welcome Center, vaguely staring at our exhibit on the Middle Passage. My last tourists have finished buying their books and postcards, the parking lot's emptying out, and I'm stuck here manning the phones, wishing to God that we'd invested in central air. Southern summers don't mess around.

But my biggest problem right now is a jackhammer.

Last year, a mystery woman purchased the plantation next door: a neglected cane farm called Belle Grove. All summer, they've been doing endless construction. It feels like I can hear every hammer striking every nail.

If I know anything about River Road, which is plantation central on this stretch of the Mississippi, there's zero chance that Belle Grove's being transformed, like Westwood, into a memorial. More likely than not, it's about to be some awful bed-and-breakfast—and I'd bet my right thumb the proceeds will benefit somebody white.

And *the jackhammering*. It goes on and on. I've never been so ready to clock out, get home, and fall into a Netflix-shaped hole.

With two minutes until closing, I slip a sweaty lanyard off my neck. The ID tag reads HARRIET DOUGLASS, VOLUNTEER GUIDE. Outside, a high voice spirals out of control, and that's when a bad feeling sinks its claws into me, familiar to anyone who's ever held a customer-service position. You get a kind of premonition that some bull's about to go down—especially when it's bound to make you late.

In my case, the premonition takes the form of a stout white woman—one of my four o'clock tourists—making her way across the grounds, a surly preteen in tow.

Please don't come in here, lady. I am not in the mood.

A silver bell rings, and she's arrived. Her hand's wrapped around her phone like a claw, and her kid, maybe twelve or thirteen, looks utterly resigned. Like he knows his mom's about to make a scene. I don't want to stereotype, but her Ritz-Carlton visor totally screams Vacation Karen.

Behind the desk, my spine snaps straight. *Customer-facing systems engaged.*

Meanwhile, I rack my brains, trying to remember if she looked this pissed on tour. But honestly, I didn't pay her much mind. I was too focused on Mr. Goodman, a Black retired janitor who came to our museum looking for his ancestors.

Long ago, he'd heard a rumor that one of his kinsfolk passed through Westwood. He wore an old-fashioned camera slung hopefully around his neck, and every time I looked at it, I felt like the red heart emoji, cracked in half. The group held their breath while he examined our memorial wall, inscribed with the name of every enslaved person who worked this land. The green-black marble shone, shivering like water…and there it was, his family name. Mr. Goodman let out a surprised huff, and then broke down in big, gulping sobs. Black men, tough all year long, often weep at Westwood, but I never get used to it. The sweet older white couple from Florida started crying right along with him, snuffling into their matching flamingo shirts.

But this lady I'm facing now? She looked straight-up inconvenienced—and she didn't shop like the other tourists. I bet she's been sitting in her rental car this whole time, just stewing.

"Excuse me, young lady! Where is your manager?"

I hate this part. "Ma'am, what seems to be the problem?"

She jabs a finger at me. "*You* are the problem. This isn't a plantation tour. It's an ambush."

Between my ribs, a critter I call the rage monster wakes up, flexing sharp claws. Ever since Mom died, I suck at controlling my temper.

"I mean, the *nerve* of trying to make us feel guilty for something that's not even our fault!"

"We never intended—"

"And what about the Westwood family, hmm? They built this country, but you don't have a kind word for them. Don't you *know* slavery used to be *normal*? There were good owners, too."

That phrase, *good owners*, explodes behind my eyes like a firework.

It's a tale as old as time: A white woman who's read one too many historical southern romances takes a vacation to Louisiana, then shows up at Westwood expecting to see the plantation from *Gone with the Wind*. She wants nothing more than to visit rooms full of antique furniture, maybe buy a cute parasol from the gift shop and call it a day.

But what we do here isn't like that at all. Westwood is more like the Holocaust Museum—or the 9/11 Memorial. Some ex-plantations will sell you a fairy tale, but here, we tell it like it is.

Why can't this lady see that?

Dr. Maples says that when I feel overwhelmed, I should look around. Remind myself what's real.

Outside the window, a willow sways in the swampy breeze, and the chickens nap in their coop. Dad's scared of chickens—I know, right?—but Mom always wanted fresh eggs in the morning. Now that she's gone, I take care of the flock.

I turn back to my angry tourist.

"At Westwood, we focus on the perspectives of enslaved people. I'm sorry you feel guilty, but that wasn't our intent."

The woman throws her son in front of her like a shield. "Look at my Brayden. Just *look at him*. He's traumatized."

Brayden slouches, obviously wishing he were anywhere but here.

Like I've been dunked in freezing water, I suddenly miss Mom.

As a museum operator, she never blamed white folks for the feelings they brought to our tours. She'd know exactly how to reach out to Brayden—how to calm his mother, too.

My mouth opens and closes, but nothing comes out. I just don't have my mother's irresistible calm. Don't have anything of hers, really, unless you count the tiny upturn of my nose.

"I know it's *cool* these days to be the victim, but this was a bit much. Those creepy statues of African children. This is not what we signed up for *at all*."

Though my smile stays stitched in place, fury mounts behind it.

Unlike Brayden, the enslaved children memorialized in statues throughout Westwood were *actually* traumatized—their childhoods stolen forever. One of the Lost Girls stands outside the office, overlooking the chicken coop. She's dressed in sackcloth, and her eyes are open, iron-forged sores.

Her name is Louisa.

In a snap, I tumble off script. "What exactly were you expecting from a plantation tour, ma'am?"

She's thrown. "You know—Civil War heroes and the antebellum lifestyle. The *real* history."

"Our mission, as clearly stated in our brochure, is to fight present-day racism with historical education. If we don't study the past, we're doomed to repeat it. There's no reason to be ashamed by what you don't know about this country's racial—"

"Are you calling me racist? My *best friend* is *Black*, young lady!"

Karen takes a threatening step toward me, smelling of sweat and sunscreen.

"Where's your manager?" She cranes to see behind me, then starts banging on the call bell. "Hello? Is anybody there?"

My "manager" is my dad, and he's a historian with a doctorate from Stanford. Right now, he's busy working on his new book. I'm not about to bother him for this Real Housewife of Wherever.

I snatch the bell away. "It's just me today."

"Well, I don't accept that."

"You're welcome to put your complaint in the comment box."

Her eyes drop to the old shoebox we keep as a decoy for aggressive guests. She snatches up a piece of paper and scribbles intently, sweat clinging to the hairs on her upper lip. Past her shoulder, the sailcloth of the Middle Passage exhibit shudders in the breeze, beckoning to those who care.

Brayden rolls his eyes upward, examining our ceiling—and my heart goes out to him. His mother's a lost cause, but Westwood might be a formative experience for this kid. He could use what he's learned to grow up differently from his mom. It's a slim chance, but not impossible. And it's one of the reasons Westwood exists.

While far-off construction workers holler, I try to catch his eye.

What would Mom say to him?

She always found grace under pressure. Even for racists. *Especially* for them.

Just then, my very favorite chicken, Rosemary, pecks the back door. *Tippity tap.* She's notorious for flying the coop.

"There." Red-faced, Karen punctuates her letter. "Don't be surprised if you find yourself out of a job. It's completely inappropriate to discuss whippings and—" She lowers her voice to a stage whisper. "And *sex* around children."

I blink. "What?"

She scowls. "That *woman*."

Face heating, I rear back. We don't talk about sex on the tour, obviously, but we do tell the truth about the women Westwood purchased specifically for the purpose of bearing children.

I think it's Anna's history that she objects to.

Poor freaking Anna.

I always save her story for the end, as I'm leading the group across the Freedom Bridge. According to Dad's findings, Anna was a teenaged girl who bore five children in five years—all of them sold away from her. Just think about that: She birthed her babies, held them, nursed them, and then handed them over to a stranger who would never, ever love them.

Anna ran from slavery three times. Louisiana plantations followed a very specific protocol for those who tried to escape. As punishment, she suffered ear cropping, whipping, and branding with the fleur-de-lis. But she never stopped running. Eventually, Westwood's enslavers sold her to a plantation in Barbados as a "breeder." They wrote her up like cattle, in scratchy, evil penmanship: *Anna, strong-willed, but an excellent breeder.*

Dad doesn't know what happened to Anna in Barbados. The historical trail went cold. Today, her sculpture stands proudly on museum land, her gold-brown back sprouting a pair of gigantic angel's wings.

"That *woman* was a human being," I grind out. "I only told her story."

"That's a fine way to spend your time, telling unsuspecting people nasty stories like that. What must your mother think?"

At the back of my throat, I taste blood. "Keep my mother out of your mouth."

"Are you *threatening* me?"

Deadass we're threatening you, lady! the rage monster crows. *You are everything that's wrong with this country! NOW SIT DOWN. BE HUMBLE.*

Self-preservation holds me back. Some women actually do find me physically threatening. Never mind that I'm only five foot four. Sometimes, I feel like white people live inside a video game.

"I want the price of our tickets returned. Right now."

"No refunds."

Rosemary pecks louder, clucking for corn.

"Well, make an exception."

I hesitate. "Hang on."

Karen smiles triumphantly, but I'm not about to return her money. I open the back door and let Rosemary in. She nips grumpily at my ankles. *That's my girl.* I pick her up—her white feathers velvety against my cheek—and carry her to the desk.

Brayden makes a sound in the back of his throat.

I think hard at Rosemary: *Do it for Anna.*

Like a good attack chicken, she spreads her wings and launches herself at my disgruntled tourist.

Vacation Karen stumbles back, hollering, "What is *wrong* with you people!"

And there it is: plain-as-day racism.

For the first time, Brayden looks directly at me.

"Come on, Mom," he whines. "I want to go back to the hotel."

On impulse, I reach for one of Dad's books—*Oral Histories of the Transatlantic Slave Trade*—and offer it to Brayden, whose preppy-ass name is not his fault. My heart's pounding. All that anger transformed into need. The rage monster rolls over, whimpering and showing her belly. After all, we don't run this museum for our health. We have a mission. *Mom's* mission.

"Take the book. Free of charge."

Brayden's mother is running from the now-grounded chicken, clutching her purse like the bird might steal it.

"Don't you speak to him! Brayden, *come here*."

In the end, Brayden doesn't take the book. Sadness pinches my heart, watching him follow his mother out the door. Behind them, glass slams, shuddering.

I groan, regretting setting Rosemary on my unhappy tourists. Wishing I were more like Mom. After a while I glance out the window, making sure Vacation Karen's really gone.

Then I pull her letter out of the stupid comment box.

> Our tour guide should be FIRED for the way she
> spoke to me, and I WILL be leaving a Yelp review!!!
> Westwood Plantation doesn't deserve one more tourist.
> What a WASTE of an afternoon.

Poisoned by the toxic fumes of this white lady's rage, I sink helplessly back into my chair. A negative Yelp review would be trash, because we need tourists now more than ever. Restoring a plantation's not cheap— my parents took out over two million dollars in loans. We could lose money we don't even have.

At this rate, I'll never be out of therapy.

I don't know why I keep letting the rage monster win—except, I guess, that anger feels better than the sadness that yawns beneath. Sadness for

Brayden, for his mom's closed-mindedness. And sadness for me, because Vacation Karen's whole attitude means that I failed to make her understand the meaning of this place.

Outside, a sunray glances off Louisa's bronze, sculpted cheek. I wonder if it's weird that I feel more strongly about a little girl who died over three hundred years ago than I do about most living people. If there's maybe even something a little bit wrong with me.

Then again, what did Mom and Dad expect, raising a Black girl on a plantation turned slavery museum?

The jackhammer drones on, endlessly puncturing my sanity. I lift my best chicken, nuzzling her soft feathers.

She stinks, of course. Most chickens do.

I consider giving Rosemary a bath. But I'm just putting off the moment when I'll have to tell Dad about impending Yelp doom.

Kelly McWilliams

is the Golden Kite Award–nominated author of *Agnes at
the End of the World*, *Mirror Girls*, and *Your Plantation Prom Is
Not Okay*. She's also written for outlets such as *Time* and
Publishers Weekly. *Mirror Girls* was a Junior Library Guild
Gold Standard Selection and Target Book Club Pick.
She lives in Seattle with her family.